FRONTIER:
POWDER RIVER

This Large Print Book carries the
Seal of Approval of N.A.V.H.

FRONTIER: POWDER RIVER

S. K. SALZER

THORNDIKE PRESS
A part of Gale, Cengage Learning

GALE
CENGAGE Learning·

Farmington Hills, Mich • San Francisco • New York • Waterville, Maine
Meriden, Conn • Mason, Ohio • Chicago

GALE
CENGAGE Learning®

LIBRARY OF CONGRESS CATALOGING-IN-PUBLICATION DATA

Names: Salzer, Susan K., author.
Title: Frontier : powder river / by S. K. Salzer.
Other titles: Powder river
Description: Large print edition. | Waterville, Maine : Thorndike Press, 2016. |
  Series: Thorndike Press large print western
Identifiers: LCCN 2016019333 | ISBN 9781410490803 (hardcover) | ISBN 1410490807
  (hardcover)
Subjects: LCSH: Large type books. | GSAFD: Western stories.
Classification: LCC PS3619.A444 F7635 2016 | DDC 813/.6—dc23
LC record available at https://lccn.loc.gov/2016019333

Published in 2016 by arrangement with Pinnacle Books, an imprint of
Kensington Books Corp.

Printed in the United States of America
1 2 3 4 5 6 7 20 19 18 17 16

For Karen King Silvoso,
sister and best friend

ROSE

April 1870, Paradise Valley, Montana Territory
Her last morning began like any other. Rose woke before dawn but remained in bed, eyes closed, listening to the familiar, comfortable sounds. She heard baby Harry's rhythmic breathing from his crib, the dog's soft, wet snore from his nest of blankets on the floor, the cheerful chirrup of spring peepers by the creek. A cool breeze, smelling of damp earth, stirred the curtains made of fabric she intended for a dress but repurposed when she realized the color no longer suited her complexion. Yellow used to flatter her, but no more. Her skin was darker and her auburn hair several shades lighter than it had been back in Missouri. She smiled to wonder, as she had many times before, if the home folks would know her if she passed them today on the streets of St. Louis.

She rolled onto her side, her face to the

window, and wished the peaceful interval could last. Rose was tired all the time; she woke up tired. This was understandable, she told herself, given her condition, but her fatigue seemed different, more crushing and unlike the last time. She cherished these few minutes of quiet she had all to herself before the day's work bore down on her.

But now it was over. Rose threw back the gray wool army blanket she and Daniel still used, with U.S. stamped in black, blocky letters in the center, even though her husband's time as an army surgeon was years behind them. The spring morning was cold, and she wrapped her wool shawl around her shoulders as she tiptoed to the kitchen to light a fire in the new, cast iron cook stove squatting malevolently in the corner. Rose hated the thing. Two weeks before, she and Daniel had had one of their rare arguments when he and Billy Sun carted the stove home from Bozeman in the spring wagon. Dan had wanted to surprise her, and he did.

"It has a separate 'auxiliary air chamber' just for baking bread," he said, proudly pointing to said feature. "It's the newest model. Nick Stono says all the women back East have one. You'll be the first in Montana Territory."

"Nick Stono says that, does he?" Rose

said, folding her arms across her chest. The fast-talking merchant was famous for convincing people to buy items they didn't want or need, and her husband, she suspected, had fallen victim. "Really, Dan, I wish you'd asked me first. I don't want this. I'm happy with my old Reliance." It had taken Rose a long time to make friends with the quirky little cooker she had used since she first went to housekeeping four years before at Fort Phil Kearny. It had involved much trial and error, many cakes and biscuits had been reduced to blackened lumps of charcoal, but now she and it understood each other. Rose was not keen to start all over.

"Return it and get our money back," she said. "I want you to."

Daniel's face fell so dramatically Rose almost laughed. "Now, Rose, honey," he said, "don't be like that. It took Billy and me the whole day to get it here." He and the Indian boy exchanged a look that spoke of shared misery. "You can't imagine how heavy that thing is. Just give it a try, will you, love? Just try it?"

In the end Rose relented, for she could never deny Daniel anything he asked of her, but she was annoyed. Learning a new stove added a good deal of work at a time when she already had plenty. It also galled her to think of how much Dan must have paid when there were so many other things she would have rather had, what with the new baby coming. They could have added a new room on to their two-room cabin. The space would be desperately needed, with two young children in the house. And they desperately needed furniture. Dan didn't know it, but she longed for a proper dresser with a marble top and a mirror large enough to show more than only her head and shoulders when she dressed for the day.

With a sigh, she opened the oven door and tossed wood from the box onto the glowing embers. At least the thing threw good heat. Bob was waiting at the door to go out and Rose obliged him, then ladled water from the barrel into a kettle and put it on the stovetop to boil. She did not put a match to the coal oil lamp, preferring instead the ambient light from the window. The sun was rising behind the snow-covered Absarokas, coloring the sky in glowing bands of pink and gold. It was a sight she never tired of, and the setting of the sun behind the Gallatin Range was equally glorious. How lucky she and Daniel had been to find a home in this beautiful valley, a place the Indians named Valley of the Flowers. Yes, they'd been fortunate in this as in so many things, and so far this spring, they'd been lucky in the weather, too. Not as much rain as usual and warmer days as well. Rose hoped the warmth would continue today for she had piles of clothes, whites and darks, in need of washing.

Bob was scratching at the door. After letting him in, she poured steaming water into a pan over the roasted coffee beans she'd ground the night before, stirred the mixture with a fork, and let it steep for three minutes — no more, no less. When the grounds were fully settled she poured the aromatic brew through a fine mesh strainer and into her blue tin mug. Daniel liked his with cream and sugar, but Rose took her coffee strong and black.

As she walked to the table, she felt a tightening sensation across her abdomen. She'd been having mild contractions for weeks, but this one, though not painful, was stronger than the others. She sat and sipped her coffee, fighting down faint stirrings of fear. She'd had similar sensations during her pregnancy with Harry, but not this soon. The new baby's time was at least seven or eight weeks distant. She had not mentioned the contractions to Daniel, but he seemed a bit worried when they parted the day before.

"Are you sure it's all right for me to go?" He placed his hand, palm down, on her rounded stomach. "Those horses will probably still be there next month when Mrs. MacGill comes. Burgess knows I want them; he wouldn't let anyone else have the pair. Or I could send Billy — he never turns down a chance to go to town."

Billy Sun was their hired man, the lanky, green-eyed son of a Crow woman and a French fur trader. The Frenchman had been killed by a grizzly one week after his son's birth, fourteen years before. The woman's brothers tracked the bear and killed it, making a necklace of the giant animal's claws. Billy wore it every day.

"No," Rose said, shaking her head, "you should go. It's not only the horses, there will be patients waiting for you in Bozeman, people who've come a long way. Don't worry about Harry and me, we'll be fine. Besides, it's only two days."

Harry was beginning to stir in his crib. When she stood to go to him, the tightening came again, this time so strongly it took her breath. Rose closed her eyes and breathed deeply, exhaled, then inhaled again. Unable to walk, she sank onto the chair and wrapped her fingers around the hot mug. She hoped the warmth would relax her, but the contraction grew in intensity. Clenching her jaw, she prayed for the pain to pass. When at last it did, she raised the mug to her lips with a shaking hand. Usually her first cup of coffee brought her pleasure, but today it was bitter as bile.

Bob came to her, his nails clicking on the puncheon floor, and laid his blocky brown head in her lap. "We might be in trouble, Bob," she said, stroking his velvety ears. His eyes never left her face.

Harry wailed from his crib, and Rose realized she had not started his breakfast. Well, she thought, he'll have to make do with a cup of warm milk and leftover biscuit. She hurried to fetch the fat baby from his bed, hoping he wouldn't try to climb down. The crib, a gift from Nelson Story and his wife, stood well above the floor, and a fall could break a bone. She'd meant to ask Daniel to lower it before he left.

"There's my baby man." She took Harry in her arms and nuzzled his warm neck, breathing in his sweet, milky smell. With a happy gurgle, Harry settled into her arms. As she did every morning, Rose crossed to Daniel's shaving mirror and stood so Harry could see himself. "There," she said, kissing him on his downy head. "See what a good boy looks like?"

At that moment Rose was gripped by a pain so searing she almost dropped him. She fought her way across the room to the bed and collapsed, with Harry still in her arms. He gave her a smile, thinking they were having a game.

Beads of sweat popped out on her forehead and upper lip, though the morning air was cool. Yes, she thought, this was definitely unlike her experience with Harry. Then, things had started slowly, with contractions that were painless for the first four or five hours of her labor. Although Harry was her first child, she had not been frightened but confident, arrogant even. After all, she thought, countless women have done this since the beginning of time, how hard could it be? Things went on longer than she expected, but still, Rose was unafraid. She had the calming knowledge that her physician husband was pacing in the other room, ready at any moment to lend his medical expertise, should it be necessary. Most reassuring of all, Helen MacGill, tall, white-haired, and confident, had been at her side, comforting her and telling her what to expect. The pain had been tolerable until the end, and then it was immediately forgotten when she held her howling, healthy eight-pound son in her arms. Although the

14

birth had been uncomplicated, the experience had left her with a new respect for her gender.

Now everything was different. She knew the pain that was coming, and she was alone. Helen MacGill was not there to help and neither was Daniel. Could she bring this child into the world unassisted? Though her confinement was nearly two months away, she was already bigger than she had been with Harry at term. What would she do if the child were nine pounds or even ten? Rose felt a sick sense of dread. Every woman knew all too well what would happen to her and her baby if she could not deliver it. The unborn child was very active now, and Rose suspected he or she was responding to her fear and the racing of her heart. She had to take control, for both their sakes.

Harry was beginning to fuss and wriggle in her arms. He was adventurous these days, forever tottering around on stout, dimpled legs, and required constant watching for there were many ways a child could die in this rough country. Just a month before, Daniel had witnessed the death of a neighbor's ten-year-old daughter when she, in passing, playfully slapped the leg of her father's draft horse with her bonnet. A stockinged foot flashed out and the girl dropped like a stone, dead before Daniel and her father could reach her side.

Rose pulled Harry close and sang to him, hoping he would sleep again though she knew this was not likely. Her only hope was that Billy Sun would arrive soon. When he went to the barn and saw Suzy had not been milked and other morning tasks were undone, he would know something was wrong. Billy would come to the house and she could hand Harry over to him. But even as she imagined this she felt another pain building, growing power like an ocean wave. She told herself to be calm, to ride it out, but Harry would not cooperate. He struggled from her arms and climbed down from the bed. Rose watched him toddle around the room and then toward the kitchen where the hot, wicked stove was waiting.

"Harry," she called, trying to make her voice sound normal, "Harry, come to Momma." When he didn't respond she spoke to the dog, seated by her bed, his eyes on her face. "Bob," she said, "bring Harry." At once, the dog sprang to his feet and herded the baby back into her room. Gradually the contraction faded.

Gingerly, knowing she did not have much time before the next pain grabbed her, Rose got out of bed and opened the cedar chest at the foot. She smelled the clean scent of cedar and the green leaves of rosemary she packed with the clothes and blankets to keep them fresh, and recalled a happier time. The tiny linen garments Harry had worn and the cotton flannel blankets she had bundled him in were on top. She traced the decorative stitchery along the blankets' borders with her finger, remembering the anticipation and joy she felt doing the needlework on those cold winter nights as she and Daniel sat by the fire. Those had been peaceful evenings, warm and happy, and infused with a golden glow. How different the world seemed now.

She put the baby's things on a chair by her bed, then changed Harry's napkin and dressed him in warm clothing, with sturdy shoes, and carried him into the kitchen where she sat him in his high chair. She put a pan of water on to boil, knowing she would need it later. By now the sun was fully risen; Rose thought it must be seven o'clock or later. Where was Billy?

She took a biscuit from the tin and gave it to Harry who ate it hungrily. Next he would need his milk, which she kept in a cooler by the well. For this Rose would have to go outside. She took her shawl from the peg

17

and wrapped it tightly around her shoulders. The dog followed her to the door, but she stopped him.

"Stay, Bob. Stay with Harry." Reluctantly, he turned back to his charge. Rose stepped out in the morning sun, shielding her eyes as she looked to the barn, hoping to see Sugarfoot, Billy Sun's buckskin gelding, drinking from the trough. She was disappointed. Billy was never late — why did he choose this day, of all days, to be delinquent?

The pain came again as she started to remove the well cover. She grabbed the planks, her knuckles whitening with the ferocity of her grip, and held her breath as the pain grew in intensity until reaching a searing crescendo and sensation of tearing that brought her to her knees in the dirt. Rose rolled onto her side, tucking her chin and drawing her knees upward as far as her belly would allow, until at last the muscles began to relax. She exhaled with a gasp.

"God in heaven," she said to the child inside, her voice sounding small and tinny to her own ears. "What are we going to do?" Somehow she would have to save them both. As she lay on the ground she heard Harry's wails from the kitchen. He was still in his chair and she had to get to him before he fell.

Rose put her hands on the ground and pushed herself to a seated position. Her hair, still unbound from the night's sleep, fell about her face like a curtain so she did not see Billy riding up the graveled lane. When he saw Rose on the ground he put the spurs to his horse and came on at a gallop.

"Mrs. Dixon!" He jumped from the saddle and ran to her, kneeling at her side. "What happened?"

"Billy," she said, grabbing his arm. "Thank God you're here. Get me inside. The baby is coming."

The blood drained from the young half-breed's face until he was pale as a white man. "Oh, Mrs.," he said. "Where is the doctor?"

"Gone to town. He won't be back till tomorrow night. Please, help me inside."

He put his hands under her arms and lifted her to her feet. When she faltered after the first step, he picked her up as if she weighed no more than a box of groceries, carried her to the door, opening it with one hand, and into the bedroom where he put her gently on the rope bed. Harry, still in his chair and red faced with rage, was so surprised to see Billy carrying his mother he stopped his wailing.

19

"I'll go to the village for a woman," Billy Sun said. "I'll be back in two hours, no more."

Rose shook her head and gripped his hand. "No. I don't have even one hour." She clenched her teeth; the pains were coming quicker now, and each was stronger than the one before. Things were happening much faster than they had with Harry. "Please, Billy, it's happening now. You must stay and help me."

Billy saw the truth of her words with wide-eyed horror and muttered something under his breath in his Crow language.

"There's hot water on the stove," Rose said. "Bring it in here with clean rags from the cupboard. You know where I keep them. Bring scissors also." The Indian boy swallowed hard and nodded. "Then take Harry from his chair and tie him to a leg of the table, and tie him securely. We won't be able to watch him when it starts."

Billy looked at Harry, then back at Rose. "Tie him to the table? He'll holler."

"Don't argue — just do it!" Rose immediately regretted yelling at her savior. "I'm sorry, Billy. Yes, he'll complain but there's nothing for it. You might give him a cup of milk first, and another biscuit."

Billy nodded and left the room, returning

a minute later with rags and a basin of steaming water, which he set on the floor beside Rose's bed. She soaked a rag in the hot water and laid it across her stomach, feeling her muscles relax as the heat soaked in. The child inside her grew less restless, less sharp elbows and knees. "Let's have a bit of rest first, shall we?" Rose whispered.

She heard Billy go outside to take the coil of rope from his saddle, then Harry's wails as Billy Sun bound him to the table leg. "I'm sorry," the Indian said. "Mother's orders."

Soon the contractions were so close together they were almost constant. Rose fought to contain her fear. Billy sat beside her, holding her hand and occasionally wiping her sweaty forehead with a warm cloth.

Harry's cries grew weaker and weaker and finally stopped altogether. Rose was in too much pain to notice, but Billy discovered the boy had merely cried himself to sleep.

Time passed and it seemed Rose was no closer to birthing the child. Billy could see she was tiring; sometimes she appeared not to know where she was, or who was with her. She called out for her husband and for her mother. Once she spoke to a woman named Margaret.

Billy contemplated riding to his village for one of the grandmothers. He was not the right person for this; he should not be here. But he was all Rose had. He would not leave her.

"Mrs.," he said during one of Rose's moments of clarity, "when the women in my village do this, they do it differently. Maybe you should try another way."

Rose looked at him with sunken eyes. Her lips were pale and bloodless. "How do your women do it, Billy?" she said. "Tell me."

Childbirth was a sacred event in Billy's village, secret to the women, but one he had surreptitiously viewed as a young boy. "First she drinks tea made with the powder of a snake's rattles," he said. "When things start to happen she does this." He walked to the wall and dropped to his knees, leaning his arms against the chinked logs for support. "At the same time a grandmother stands behind her, pressing so." He put his hands on his lower back and moved them in a downward motion. "This brings the baby quick."

Rose doubted she had the strength to get out of bed, but she knew she had to do something. To remain as she was would mean death, not only hers but the baby's. "Help me," she said, raising her arms.

Billy took the gray wool blanket from Rose's bed and spread it on the floor by the wall. When he came for her she again marveled at the boy's strength, unexpected in one so slight. Bob watched from across the room, silent with his animal way of knowing.

"They start on their hands and knees," Billy said after he lowered her to the ground. "Can you do that?"

She did as he suggested, letting her belly hang. Instantly, she felt a profound relief. Her aching back muscles released and at last she could fully breathe. She rocked side to side, front and back.

"Now, rise up and put your hands so." Billy Sun demonstrated and Rose did as instructed. He began to massage her back as he had seen the grandmothers do, starting with the strong muscles beneath her shoulder blades, then moving to her spine, working with his thumbs on each vertebrae, separating one from the other, creating space, then working on the knotted muscles of her lower back, stroking and rubbing until he could feel them loosen.

The child, freed from its muscular prison, finally began to descend. Within a few minutes, a boy, tiny and blue in color, with the umbilicus wrapped around his neck, lay upon the blanket. Billy picked him up, unwound the bloody cord, and gave the babe a sound slap on the back. The baby gasped and released a small mewling cry, no louder than that of a kitten.

"Is he all right?" Rose said, still on her knees, leaning against the wall for support. "Is he breathing?"

"Yes, he is breathing." Billy wrapped the baby in a fresh blanket. "Here, see for yourself." He offered the child to Rose, who made no move to take him.

"Something is happening," she said, and now everything made sense. Another baby was coming. Rose bore down and the child, a girl, emerged. After a moment of stunned silence, she unleashed an indignant howl. She was bigger by several pounds than her brother and a healthy pink in color. Billy Sun wrapped the babies in soft cotton blankets and laid them on the bed, then turned his attention to their mother.

Rose had collapsed, hot blood flowing from her, surging with each beat of her heart and spreading over the blanket and onto the floor. Though only semiconscious, she understood something was wrong, that there had been some kind of rupture, and one look at Billy's face confirmed her fears. One of her body's life-giving rivers had been breached. Maybe Daniel could have saved her, but she thought not. She had come to the end of herself, and sooner than she expected.

Rose was no longer in pain, and for this at least she was grateful. She was not afraid but felt a deep disappointment and a profound sadness for the people, Harry and these two tiny infants, should they survive, whom she would leave behind. She would be missed, she knew that. Daniel should marry again — she wanted him to — but only to a good woman who would be kind to her children. If only she had thought to tell him so . . .

As Billy carried her to the bed she experienced a strange heightening of her senses. She saw each fiber of his red and black plaid shirt, smelled the earthy but pleasant scent of his skin, heard her blood dripping onto the puncheon floor. He put Rose on the bed and placed the swaddled twins beside her, one on each side. Harry, still bound to the table leg like a sailor tied to the mast, was awake now and was calling for her.

Rose, too weak to speak, looked at Billy who understood she wanted to see her firstborn one last time. He hurried to the front room and freed the squalling boy, but

by the time they returned, his mother was
gone.

BIWI

Daniel Dixon returned at sundown with two horses tied to the rear of his wagon. All day he'd been looking forward to showing Rose the fine, matched pair, but his excitement evaporated when he saw Nelson Story's buggy tied to the rail. The busy cattleman wouldn't come unannounced unless something was wrong. Dixon waited until Story and his wife came out of the house, holding hands. Dixon could see the news on Story's somber face and in Ellen's red, swollen eyes. Rose was dead. When he climbed down from the bench, Dixon's legs buckled and he fell to his knees in the dirt.

Later, he stood before his wife's body lying on the bed they had shared. Her skin was white, and when he touched her face it was cold. Could this lifeless apparition really be Rose? he thought, his beautiful, laughing Rose? Dixon did not speak to her, and he did not cry. He felt nothing at all, other than a mild, unformed curiosity about the distant sound of infants crying.

Story entered the dark room and stood at Dixon's side. "I'm sorry, Daniel," he said. "Rose was a fine woman. None better. When Billy came for us, I couldn't hardly believe it. Didn't want to believe it." He folded his thick arms across his chest. "Yes, it's a hard thing, and I grieve for you, but you got three little children counting on you now. Those twins, they aren't strong, especially the boy. He don't weigh much as a five-pound bag of coffee. The girl's bigger, but they're going to need care. You got to think about that."

Dixon gave no sign of hearing. He was trying to understand what he had done to bring this curse down on the women who were unfortunate enough to love him. For the second time in his thirty years, he found himself a widower. He had killed his first wife, Laura, and their daughter, Mary, by afflicting them with a disease he brought home from the war. Their deaths could have been avoided — he was a physician, he knew what to do — but he was too selfish and in too much of a hurry to take the proper precautions. Now Rose was gone, and her death, too, he should have prevented.

"I suspected she might be carrying two," he said, more to himself than to Story. "She was too big, I saw that, and twins most always come early. I shouldn't have left her alone, but I wanted those horses."

"Don't blame yourself, man," Story said. "There's no call for —"

Dixon did not let him finish. "Get those horses out of my sight or I'll kill them, I swear it. Take them back to Burgess tonight."

"I will, Dan, I will." Story reached out and touched his friend's arm, unnerved by his strangeness and talk of killing. "Just calm down, for God's sake."

All through the night Dixon sat by the bed, holding Rose's hand, showing no interest in the twins or even Harry. For two days he remained at her side, not eating and not sleeping. At the funeral he was stone faced and dry eyed. Ellen Story stayed on at the ranch for the next week to care for the children and keep house, but even her kind ministrations and attempts to reach him failed. Dixon sank deeper into his solitary darkness.

"I'm not sure he even knows I'm here," Ellen told her husband and Billy Sun. The three stood beside Rose's enemy stove, speaking in lowered voices. "He never says a word. And those poor, poor babies, why, the boy especially is just barely hanging on. The doctor can't even care for himself, let alone those children. What are we going to do about this, Nelson?" To her sorrow, Ellen Story had no children of her own at home, having endured the death of an infant daughter the previous winter. "I can't stay here forever."

"Hell if I know." Story pulled on his beard. "He won't talk to me, either. What do you think, Billy? How do the Crow handle such matters?"

Billy said, "My uncle's wife bore a dead child four days ago. Her breasts are full with no child to take from them. I know her well, and she would be pleased to mother these children. She is a good woman."

Story and his wife exchanged glances. The idea of a white child nursing at the breast of an Indian woman was troubling, but what choice did they have?

"The girl might make it on the cow's milk I've been giving them," Ellen said, "but the boy is failing. Nelson, we must try this."

Story continued to pull on his chin whiskers. "Maybe so, but I won't send those babies off to the Crow village. No disrespect to you or your people, Billy, but your uncle's wife must come here. Ellen and I will take

30

Harry home with us, and the dog, too. Old Bob's been looking peaky since Rose passed over."

Billy put on his coat and black felt hat. "I'll bring her this evening."

And so the Crow woman Biiwihitche came to live in the Dixon home. The stillbirth of her own child pained her deeply, beyond what was deemed normal by her kinsmen, and Billy Sun's uncle had grown impatient with her. He was pleased when his nephew appeared with his offer, which Biiwihitche was quick to accept.

When Billy and Biiwihitche returned to the ranch, Story's wagon was gone. Inside the silent house, Dixon sat at the table, his head in his hands. He was unshaven, and his unwashed hair hung into his eyes. Alarmed by the quiet, Billy went to Harry's crib, where he had left the twins some hours before, and found them awake, looking up at him. Billy thought they were like Indian babies, who learned early on that silence often meant survival. The girl, he noticed, had covered her brother's tiny hand with her own.

Billy looked around the room. Ellen had removed the blood-soaked mattress from the rope bed and replaced it with a fresh one. She had also sanded the stained floor clean, or clean as it would ever be. The house seemed profoundly empty. Billy had always understood that Rose was the heart and soul of this family; he felt her vitality and had been more than a little in love with her. He grieved for himself but even more for these lost white people whose center part was now gone.

"What are their names?" Biiwihitche stood behind him. He had not heard her enter the room. Though a solid, stocky woman, she moved on cat's paws.

"They do not have names," he said. They spoke in the Crow language.

"Then I will call them Curtain Boy and Spring Girl." These twins from Crow folklore were ripped from their mother's womb by an evil relative and grew to have magical powers. Without another word, Biiwihitche took them up, one baby in each arm, and carried them across the room to sit on the floor by the window, facing the wall. In less than a minute, Billy heard the wet, snorty sounds of babies feeding.

Maybe it was this that finally stirred Dixon from his torpor. He rose from his chair and walked toward the bedroom, stopping in the doorway. Only when he saw him standing did Billy realize how reduced the doctor was. His eyes were like two burned holes in a blanket, and there were shadows below his cheekbones.

"Who is that?" he said, gesturing toward the Indian woman on the floor. These were the first words he had spoken in days, and his voice was hoarse.

"She is from my village. Her name is Bii-wihitche, which in our language means Woman who Swims Good. We call her Biwi. She has come to care for your children."

Two spots of color appeared on Dixon's ashen cheeks. Without disturbing the babies, Biwi turned to look at him. There was no mistaking the anger and disgust on Dixon's face and Billy, alarmed, placed himself between them. The doctor was not himself.

"Biwi's baby was born dead," he said, "and your children are in need. They are very small, especially the boy. Even with her help, they may not live."

Dixon stepped forward until he and Billy were inches apart. Dixon was a head taller and, even in his emaciated condition, fifty pounds heavier, but the Indian boy did not flinch. Whatever came, he would do anything he had to do to protect Biwi.

The sounds of feeding had slowly subsided. Dixon looked over Billy's shoulder to see Biwi raise the girl to her shoulder to coax forth a burp. After doing the same to the boy, she carried the drowsing babies to Harry's crib and placed them on their backs, side by side, covered by the same blanket.

"Do Nelson and Ellen Story know of this?" Dixon said.

Billy nodded. "Yes."

Dixon lowered his head and covered his eyes with his hands. After a few moments of silence he said, "She can sleep in here with the babies. I'll stay in the barn." He took a blanket from the cedar chest and left the cabin, closing the door firmly behind him.

LORNA AND CALEB

Paradise Valley, 1882

Dixon eventually engaged Mrs. MacGill, the Scottish widow woman who delivered Harry, to help with his three children, but the twins were coming up wild and everyone said so. Lorna and Caleb were difficult to manage and truly happy only when Billy Sun took them for visits to the Mountain Crow village, which he often did so their father could have some peace. They were more comfortable on the back of an Indian pony than on foot, and sometimes, mostly to annoy their older brother and Mrs. MacGill, spoke a patois of English, Mountain Crow, and wholly invented words, a language they called Bird Talk, intelligible only to them. They grew sturdy and brown as nuts, though they would never be mistaken for natural children of the Mountain Crows, for the Dixon twins had eyes that were pale blue in color and hair white as

35

the flowers of the wild clematis that grew along the river.

The doctor was devoted to his work and often called away, especially after Fort McKinney was established to the south, in Powder River country, on the fertile benchlands of Wyoming Territory. The post was named in honor of young Lieutenant John A. McKinney, killed by the Cheyenne warriors of chief Dull Knife in the winter following the Custer fight. McKinney gained a sad kind of posthumous fame as one of the last bluecoat soldiers to give his life in the U.S. Army's campaign to eradicate the Indians from the northern plains. Dixon was frequently summoned to the post as soldiers billeted there were forever ill or injured and needing medical attention beyond what the regimental surgeon could provide.

Because of this, Dixon decided to pull up stakes and move his family south to Wyoming Territory, to the new town of Buffalo, on the Clear Fork of Powder River, some six miles downstream from the military reservation. His children did not welcome their father's decision. Fourteen-year-old Harry had grown up in Nelson Story's Bozeman home and loved his three sons (Ellen's much-loved and long-awaited babies) like brothers. All four boys wept like girls when it came time to say good-bye.

The day before they were to leave, Cal and Lorna mounted double on their pinto pony and rode away to join Biwi and Billy Sun in the mountains. The Indian woman embraced the twins warmly, for she loved them and had no child of her own, but she told Billy Sun he must take them back at once.

"Curtain Boy and Spring Girl, your place is with your father," she said, speaking in the Crow language. "He is not a warm man, but maybe he will change. His heart is cold because he is sad. He is not happy with himself. Be good to him and to your brother and to each other. Keep your heart open to the world around you and be kind. Above all, be kind." Here, she took each child by the hand and lowered her head so her face was just inches from theirs. "When the other voice speaks to you — the one we've talked about — do not listen. That one will bring the wolf to your door."

Billy followed their pony back to the valley where Dr. Dixon was preparing to come after them. When he woke to find them absent, he knew at once where they had gone.

"Thank you," Dixon said, offering Billy

his hand. Behind him workers for a German-owned freighting company were loading the family's furnishings, including Rose's stove, into heavy wagons. "Thank you for all you've done, for me and my family. The children will miss you."

"I'll miss them, too," Billy said as they shook hands. The two were not close, though they had developed a respect for one another. Dixon was a skillful physician, one area settlers traveled long distances to see when a loved one was afflicted. Billy Sun recognized that, but at the same time he could not forget the disgust on Dixon's face the night he saw Biwi with his children the first time. For his part, Billy had built a reputation as one of the region's best horsemen. Ranchers sought him out when they had a green animal no one could ride. Within a day, Billy could turn one thousand pounds of angry bone and iron muscle into a docile palfrey, suitable for even the most delicate of lady riders. There was no mustang Billy Sun could not gentle, and he never had to stoop to cruelty to do it.

An awkward silence followed the handshake. Billy sensed Dixon had something to say.

"I want to thank you for everything you did for Rose that day." Dixon's voice went thick with feeling, but he did not look away from Billy's green eyes. "I haven't said this to you before, Billy, and I should have. No one could have done more for her — I could not have done more. I was angry when she died, but not with you. If I've ever been unkind to you, or a member of your family, please accept my apology."

Billy nodded. Like Dixon, he chose not to look back on that bloody day. For the rest of his life, he would regret he had been there, not because of the pain it caused him, but because he wanted to keep Rose in his heart as she had been. Billy wanted to remember her healthy and full of life, with freckles across the bridge of her nose and a right ear that stuck out just a bit, sometimes peeking out through the veil of her auburn hair. Their last hours together had robbed him of that memory.

"Thank you, Doctor," he said. "This is good to hear."

"Best of luck to you, Billy. I hope our paths cross again."

Late that evening, when Billy returned to the village, he found Biwi in her lodge, sitting alone at her fire. He asked what she had meant when she warned the twins about "the other voice," the one that brings the wolf.

She shook her head, her eyes on the glowing embers. "The child understands," she said.

Dixon was happy to be returning to the green-skinned hills of Wyoming's Powder River country. His heart grew lighter with each passing mile, lighter than it had for years, and he felt an almost-forgotten sense of anticipation. This was true, even though his time at Fort Phil Kearny had been difficult. Besieged by Sioux and Cheyenne warriors led by Red Cloud and Crazy Horse, Dixon and Rose, along with others of Colonel Henry Carrington's 18th U.S. Infantry, had endured long months of bitter cold, hunger, and fear. The night of December 21, 1866, brought horror that would never leave him. The sights, sounds, and smells of Massacre Ridge — where Captain William Judd Fetterman and all of the eighty men who rode with him were slaughtered — had burrowed deep in Dixon's brain and would haunt his dreams forever. Fetterman's story was a tale of hubris, like

George Armstrong Custer's ten years later, but now those heady times were gone. Fort Phil Kearny itself was reduced to a charred ruin, abandoned by the army and burned to the ground by the Indians. The departing soldiers saw the smoke as they marched away. Red Cloud and his warriors had won a great victory, though their time in the sun would be short. The Sioux leader and his ferocious fighting men were confined to reservations and no longer posed a threat to anyone.

The Dixons' journey to Buffalo would take them close by the site of the abandoned fort. Daniel had often thought of someday taking his children there, telling them of the adventure and hardship he and their mother had endured together, but he would not stop now. The sadness of walking those grounds again, standing in the very places where he and Rose had stood together, was still too great.

He hoped his children would come to share his passion for Wyoming's Powder River country. Dixon had loved it from the moment he first saw its rolling green hills, clear sparkling streams, and lush valleys where the blue meadow grass grew tall enough to brush the belly of a man's horse. The land filled him with a sense of hope.

Perhaps in this lovely country he would come to know and love his younger ones as he loved Harry.

"What will Buffalo be like, Pa?" Harry said.

"It's a new town," Dixon said, "just getting started, but it's growing fast. Already there are two dry goods stores, a bank, a hotel, a dentist, and a school you children will attend. It's about time. We'll stay in the hotel until our house is finished."

Cal and Lorna, sitting in the rear of the wagon with Mrs. MacGill, looked at each other when their father said the word "school." "He can't make us," Cal said in Bird Talk.

Dixon turned his head toward the twins with a frown. "What did I say to you two about talking that gibberish? There'll be no more of that, you hear?"

"Yes, Pa," they said in unison. Lorna reached out and took her brother's hand.

They rode on in silence, the only sound the clop-clop of the horses' hooves on the rocky road. Late in the afternoon they made camp along a wooded creek. Harry unharnessed the horses, rubbed them down with empty feed sacks, and fed them nosebags of grain while Dixon pitched two tents, one for him and Harry and another for Mrs.

MacGill and the twins. The Scotswoman and her charges had no trouble finding dry wood, and soon a good fire was blazing.

"It's been a while since I slept out under the stars," she said as she peeled potatoes. "Not since me and my old man, Keddy, first come out here all them years ago. Eighteen and sixty-three, it was and, aye, things was diff'rent then. My hair was black as midnight when me and him set out and white as you see it now by the time we put in at Alder Gulch. It was those nights sleeping rough and fearin' the Indians and the wolves what did it." She rose and walked to the fire where she dumped the potatoes into a pot that already held salted meat, chopped onions, and carrots. Their meal would also include fried eggs and powder biscuits, now baking in a Dutch oven, with strawberry jam.

"Indians ain't nothing to fear, Auntie," Cal said. "Who would be afraid of Biwi or Billy Sun?"

Mrs. MacGill stirred the stew with a long wooden spoon. "Mebbe they ain't so fearsome now, but they was plenty diff'rent back then, I can tell you that. Jerusalem!" She batted at an ember that leaped from the fire and ate a hole in her apron. "And I'm not sure you can ever completely trust them. The Injuns, they remind me of the Selkie folk from back home, from the Orkney Isles. You think you know 'em, but you don't. To think different is to get your heart broke."

"Selkie folk?" Lorna said.

"I'll tell you and your brother about the Selkie after dinner, but only if you promise to be good and don't do nothin' to set off the doctor."

The twins were good as their word, and the meal passed without discord, with plenty of stew and biscuits for everyone. After, Dixon smoked his pipe as Mrs. MacGill and the twins cleaned the pots and dishes in a wash pan of hot soapy water and toweled them dry. The snapping logs turned from black to gray and the evening sky purpled as a chill wind blew down from the mountains.

Finally the work was done, and Lorna and Cal wrapped themselves in warm blankets, ready for the widow's story. Her yarns were almost as good as Biwi's.

Mrs. MacGill plumped her pillow and lowered the lamplight so they could barely make out her white hair and dark, shining eyes. "So," she said, "there once was a young man, a hunter of seals, who lived alone on the tiny island of Suleskerry. He was a proud young man, bonnie and strong, and he made good" — "guid" as she pronounced it — "money as well. There was no shortage of lassies on the mainland who had an eye out for him, but he would have none of 'em.

" 'What's wrong wi' ye then?' a friend asked of him, and the proud young man said he simply had no use for females.

" 'Wimmen was put on earth to try us men,' he said. 'Adam was an owld fool, who would be living in Paradise still today if he haddna been led astray by Eve.'

"Well, time went by and one day the Suleskerry seal hunter was workin' on the beach when he spied a group of bonnie young people sunning themselves on a rock by the sea, and they was nekkid as the day they was born."

"Naked?" Lorna said, her eyes widening. "Out in the wide open?"

"Aye," the widow said. "As the day they was born. One was a lovely woman with hair yellow as gold, kinda like yours, my loves, and skin white as the finest Italian marble with nary a bump nor blemish on it. Well, the proud young man had never seen a vision like that before, and he was smitten. He started toward her, but the folk saw him comin' and grabbed up the sealskins that

46

was lyin' beside them on the rock and dove into the sea. But the lovely woman's skin had fallen to the beach and the seal hunter got to it first. She fell to her knees, sobbin' most pitiful she was, and begged him to return it. 'Please, please, kind sir,' she said, 'I kinna live with my folk withoot it.' The man looked out to sea and saw a pack of selkie — seals is what you English call 'em — bobbing in the water, watchin' with sad, mournful eyes."

"The young people turned into seals when they put their skins back on?" Cal said.

"Aye, and the beautiful maiden wanted to be with 'em but couldna without her skin, which the hunter wouldna surrender. Instead, he made her go back to his hut with him and be his wife. She had no choice, for he hid the skin from her and she couldna find it, no matter how she tried.

"They lived together for many years, and the seal-maiden bore the hunter four bairns, three lads and one lassie. They were a bonnie family, but there was a stone in the seal-maiden's heart. She pretended to be happy, but niver did she stop searchin' for her skin. One day, the lassie asked her, 'Mam, watcha lookin' fur?' and the seal-maiden said, 'Oh, peedie, I'm lookin' for a pretty skin to make you slippers wit.' The girl said she had seen her father take a very pretty skin from the rafters in the barn.

"Well, that was all the seal-maiden needed. She ran to the barn, found the skin, and fled to the sea where she slipped it on and dove into the waves, aswimmin' out to her seal-man husband who had been waitin' for her all these years. The proud man and his children never saw her again, though for the rest of his long life the Suleskerry seal hunter walked along the beach, asearchin'. He died a sad and broken owld man."

Her story was met with shocked silence. Lorna spoke first. "But what about her children? Didn't she love them?"

"Aye, she loved them well enough, but she loved her seal-folk more."

"She was a bad woman," Cal said flatly.

"No," Mrs. MacGill said, shaking her head. "The Selkie maiden was not bad, she was just bein' true to her natural self. That's the way the world is. No matter how much you love a person, ye canna change him or her, no matter how you try. Sometimes you have to say your good-byes and move on, no matter how it pains ye. Otherwise, you'll end up like the Suleskerry seal hunter, walkin' alone up and down that beach for the rest of his days."

She expected more questions but none

came. Soon she heard rhythmic breathing and thought the children were asleep. She was drifting into sleep herself when Lorna's voice startled her.

"You told that story because of Billy Sun," she said. "You think me and him will never be together because of the difference in our ages and because he's Indian, but you're wrong. I love him and I am going to marry him someday. Just you wait and see."

"Has Billy ever given you cause to think this, child?" Mrs. MacGill said.

"No, he doesn't know yet. I know things other people don't. You'll see."

Buffalo did not look prosperous, but neither did the Dixon family by the time they finally rolled into town. The journey had taken two days longer than the doctor had expected, and there had been snow the second night out. When they woke in the morning, they found four fluffy white inches on the ground, though the day warmed and it melted quickly. Even so, it turned the road to a muddy gumbo that clung to the iron wheels and the horses' feet and slowed progress to a crawl. They arrived at noon, cold, dirty, and hungry.

Dixon stopped the wagon by the town's largest building, a structure of chinked log construction fronting the muddy main street. A hand-lettered sign saying OC-CIDENTAL HOTEL hung over the front door. Nearby were a freestanding kitchen and a livery stable. A number of hard-looking men lounged in chairs on the boardwalk, watch-

ing the Dixons' arrival with amused curiosity.

Dixon climbed down and handed the
reins to Harry. "Make sure the twins stay in
the wagon, and keep an eye on those dogs."
He nodded toward a pair of mangy-looking
hounds rounding the corner of the kitchen.
"Hold tight on the horses."

The mud was so deep Dixon sank almost
to his ankles as he made his way to the
boardwalk. He tipped his hat to the watching men and stopped to scrape his boots
before entering the lobby. The interior was
dark after the bright noontime sun, and it
took several seconds for his eyes to adjust.
On the far wall was a long counter, with a
pale, bespectacled clerk standing behind it.
A restaurant occupied one side of the
cavernous, barnlike interior and a saloon
the other. At the bar stood a tall man, with
one foot on the rail. He watched Dixon
cross the room and address the clerk.

"I'd like three rooms," Dixon said. "My
family and I need a place to stay until our
house is finished."

"Three rooms?" the clerk said. "Well, I
don't know if I can do that. I only got six
and four are occupied. I guess I can let you
have the two for a time. When will your
house be done?"

51

Dixon smiled. "I hired Jim Kidd and his boys about a month back, but I haven't heard from him for a while. I'll be going out there tomorrow. I'll let you know."

The tall man put his drink on the bar and crossed the room, his boots loud on the uncarpeted floor.

"So," he said, "I'm guessing you're the new doctor. Dixon, from Bozeman?"

"Yes, I'm Daniel Dixon. And you are . . . ?"

"Frank Canton." He offered his hand with a smile, studying Dixon with clear blue eyes. "Welcome to Buffalo, Doctor. You are most welcome. This town needs a good medical man; we have for a while now."

The clerk smiled for the first time. "So, you're the doctor we been hearing about? Well, you'll have plenty of business here, though maybe not so many bullet holes now that Frank, here, is sheriff. Things have calmed down considerable."

Canton ran a hand through his straw-colored hair. "Slow down, Milo, I'm not sheriff yet. Election ain't till November."

"Don't matter, Frank. You been the law around here for the past year and everybody knows it. Nat James and that deputy, Tom Ferrell, they're good at cowboying and not much else. You'll get elected, Frank. Ain't no doubt about that."

Canton gave Dixon a wink. "I do have an opponent."

"Ha! Ain't no way some granger's gonna beat out Frank Canton. Ain't no way."

"Thank you for your confidence, Milo, but I'm sure Dr. Dixon doesn't want to hear about this. As for your place, Doc, I was just out there the other day and Jim and the boys have been working hard, for them anyhow. Your place is nearly done and I think you'll be pleased with it too. I'll ride out there with you tomorrow, if you want. Maybe I can light a fire under Jim, get him to speed things up a little."

"Thank you. I'd appreciate that."

"My pleasure." Canton turned to Milo. "Four rooms occupied, you say?"

Milo nodded.

"Occupied with who?"

"Well," Milo said, clearly nervous. "There's Fred Jolly and two of Lord Faucett's associates, up from Denver. Then there's Hi Kinch, sleeping off a drunk."

Canton laughed. "Kinch? Why, there's your solution. Kick him out, clean it up, and give his room to the good doctor and his family. There's your three rooms."

"I don't know, Frank," Milo said. "Hi paid for it."

"So what? Kinch can stay at the jail if he wants. It's not like he ain't been there before." Canton turned back to Dixon. "I'll be by tomorrow around ten or so. We'll go see how Jim and the Kidd boys are getting along."

Dixon and Harry were having breakfast in the restaurant when Canton arrived the following morning.

"I thought my boy Harry might come along, too," Dixon said. "He's anxious to see his new house."

"Of course," Canton said. "Glad to have the lad." He clapped a warm hand on Harry's shoulder, causing him to drop the buttered biscuit he was lifting to his mouth. "When you folks are done here, come over to the livery. I'll have the horses ready." Canton had an unusual voice, Harry noticed, deep and resonant, as if coming from a vault. On the way out, Canton stopped to talk to three men having breakfast together, the restaurant's only other customers. They wore fine clothing and polished boots, and Harry thought he and his father looked shabby by comparison.

"Morning, Fred," Canton said. "Morning, gentlemen. Will you be heading out to The Manor this morning?"

"This afternoon." The man spoke with a British accent. "First I thought we'd tour the range some. Weather favors it."

The conversation continued, but Harry could discern only a few words: nesters . . . crowded . . . roundup . . .

"Finish your eggs, son," Dixon said. "We've got a big day."

Twenty minutes later, Harry, Dixon, and Canton were riding south out of Buffalo, three abreast on the Big Horn Road, toward the small ranch Dixon had purchased on Clear Creek, midway between the town and Fort McKinney.

"You found yourself a good spot, Doctor," Canton said, "and you were damn lucky to get it for the price you did." Dixon was surprised Canton knew what he paid, but in a place small as Buffalo secrets were probably hard to come by. "You plan on running any stock?"

"Maybe a few animals for our own use. Horses, a few head of beef cattle. My medical practice will be my livelihood — if things work out."

Canton nodded, apparently pleased with Dixon's answer.

"How long have you been in these parts, Mr. Canton?"

"Call me Frank, Doctor, everyone does. I

settled here a few years back."

"What made you leave Texas?"

Canton turned in the saddle, looking at Dixon with surprise. "What makes you think I'm from Texas?"

Dixon sensed he had trod on sensitive ground. "Only the way you talk. I thought I heard some Texas in it."

Canton smiled. "No. I was born in Virginia. From there we moved to Missouri, then on to Colorado in sixty-eight. Me and Pa raised stock outside of Denver, and after that I bounced around some. Montana, Cheyenne. Didn't put down roots till the stockmen here in Wyoming hired me on as stock detective. That's how I come to know Fred Jolly, that English fellow back at the hotel. His boss, Lord Richard Faucett, also from across the pond, owns Powder River Cattle Company, the biggest outfit in the territory. He's a man you'll want to know."

Harry, drowsing in the saddle, perked up. "You're a detective?" In his eyes, Canton seemed to sit a little taller in the saddle. He wore a gun holstered below his right hip, and his hands were not red and calloused, like those of a farmer, but elegant with long, slender fingers and clean, squared nails. The hands, Harry thought, of a gunfighter.

Canton winked at him. "Yes sir. It's good

work, fine way for a man to earn his living. When you get a little older, you might look into it, son. The cattlemen are always looking for a good man. If not for this sheriff business, I'd still be at it."

"What does a range detective do?" Harry said.

A light kindled in Canton's pale eyes. "He hunts down waddy scum who build their herds with a long rope and a running iron, and unfortunately there's plenty of those in this country. Thieves." He spat, as if the thought of them put a bad taste in his mouth. "A range detective keeps the country safe and secure for those it's meant for."

Dixon knew there was tension in the Powder River country between the large cattlemen, members of the Wyoming Stock Growers Association, and the smaller ranchers. Word of their struggle for the rangeland had drifted north to Bozeman, where it was often discussed in Nelson Story's household. Story sided with the WSGA, and the subject was a rare point of disagreement between him and Dixon. Clearly, Canton was one of those who believed the country was meant for the big augers alone. Dixon understood at once that he would remain in good odor with Canton and his wealthy employers as long as he kept to doctoring.

It occurred to him to ask what a range detective did with a "waddy scum" when he caught one. Dixon had heard stories of necktie parties, when the accused was hung by the neck from the nearest stout tree without benefit of trial. He did not put the question.

The men rode the rest of the way without much talking. The sun had been hiding behind the clouds all morning, but now it emerged in full, baking the ground and scenting the air with sage. Harry felt its warmth on his neck and shoulders and began again to relax in the saddle. Sensing this, his rented horse decided to take advantage, lowering her head and kicking out with her rear legs. Harry very nearly lost his seat and surely would have had Canton not grabbed the mare's bridle before she could finish the job. Harry thanked his rescuer with embarrassment.

They crested a rise to find themselves looking down on a lush valley that was beginning to take on its rich fall colors. The aspens lining the water were turning gold, the leaves of the wild plum bushes scarlet red, and the stems of the tall bunch-grass in the meadows bluish purple. Wild clematis dusted the creek banks, like bits of fine white lace. A nearly complete, two-story white frame house stood in the bend of the creek, with two men on its steeply pitched roof hammering shingles in place.

"What do you think, son?" Dixon said, turning to Harry with one of his rare smiles. "Maybe this wasn't such a bad idea after all?"

HARRY

Dixon sat upright in his bed, his heart racing. What was that? What woke him? He reached for the pistol on the nightstand and waited until the sound came again; someone was on the porch, pounding on the door. Dixon pulled on his pants and stepped into the hallway. Mrs. MacGill stood on the landing at the top of the stairs, a coal oil lamp in her hand. The night was cold and she wore a shawl around her shoulders. Her face paled when she saw the gun in Dixon's hand.

"Who could it be at this hour?" she said. "It's two o'clock." Harry and the twins appeared at her side, frightened faces in the yellow lamplight.

"Children, go back to your beds," Dixon said. "Mrs. MacGill, make sure they do as I say." The pounding started again. Dixon walked to the front room and looked out the window. A horse he did not recognize, old and swaybacked, was tied to the porch rail. He opened the door to find Carl Schmidt, a boy of about Harry's age, the son of a neighboring rancher. His eyes were wild with fear.

"Dr. Dixon, please come! It's Pa, he's hurt bad!"

"Come in, Carl, get out of the cold," Dixon stepped to one side so the boy could enter. "Now, tell me what happened. How was your father hurt?" Despite his instructions, the three children and Mrs. MacGill were watching from the top of the stairs.

Carl took a deep breath and struggled to compose himself. "Three men came to the house when Pa was out in the barn. I saw them go in, then I heard yelling and the sound of shots, two shots. After that the men came running out and rode off. When I went out to the barn I found Pa on the ground, bleeding bad. They shot him, here and here." The boy put one hand on his stomach and the other on his jaw. "Ma's with him but she can't make it stop, so she told me to come for you. Oh, we got to hurry, Doc!"

"All right," Dixon said. "I'll come straightaway. Mrs. MacGill, please make Carl a cup of tea while I dress and pack my supplies. I won't be long."

Harry followed his father to his room. "Let me come with you, Pa. I can help."

Dixon sat on the bed to pull on his boots. His face was worried and gaunt in the flickering lamplight, and, for the first time, Harry thought his father looked old.

"Thank you, Harry, but I need you here to look after the twins and Mrs. MacGill. I don't know how long I'll be gone; it may be a while. I noticed Carl's horse looks done in. Take him to the barn, will you? Rub him down and give him a nosebag. Then put Carl's saddle on one of ours, the bay. Carl can come back for his horse later." Dixon stood and put a hand on his son's shoulder. "Thank you, Harry. I depend on you."

Harry nodded, disappointed. He was tired of being treated like a child and eager to start his own life; he was tired of simply taking up space at the edge of his father's. Much as he loved Powder River country, Harry was beginning to sense if he didn't get away soon, he'd end up spending his best years taking care of his brother and sister and Mrs. MacGill. That was not what he had planned.

Glumly, he pulled on his hat and boots and started for the barn. On his way out, he passed the kitchen where Carl sat with his elbows on the table and his head in his

62

hands. He was crying; Harry could see that by the way his shoulders shook. Carl must know there was little his father could do for a man with such serious injuries. Harry felt bad for him, but at the same time he almost envied him. Carl could be his own man now, in charge of his own future. It was a hard world, no doubt, but Harry was burning to get out in it, all the same.

When Harry opened the door, a blast of winter wind grabbed it from his hands and blew it back on its hinges against the wall with a bang, loud as a pistol shot. It was beginning to snow.

DIXON

They rode against the wind. The snow took the form of sharp splinters of ice that stung the skin and eyes. Dixon wished he had thought to bring his sun goggles, not standard equipment for a winter journey in the dead of night. The trip took longer than Dixon anticipated. By the time they arrived at August Schmidt's small but tidy farmstead, the sky was beginning to lighten.

They went directly to the barn. Only one lamp was burning, and the interior was dark and cold as the grave. A woman sat on the floor in a circle of lamplight, a man's head in her lap. She was stroking his hair and speaking in a low voice.

Dixon walked to them and looked down on August Schmidt's lifeless face. His eyes were at half-mast and the front of his shirt was black with blood. The chest wound alone would have been fatal, Dixon saw that at once, but Schmidt had suffered a second

64

injury, a vicious blast to the side of his face that exposed broken, bloody teeth. With a groan, Carl dropped to his knees beside his father's body. His mother, stone faced and dry eyed, did not acknowledge him but continued smoothing her dead husband's hair.

"Who did this?" Dixon said. The woman did not respond.

"Mrs. Schmidt, who killed your husband?"

Finally, she raised her eyes to his. Her face was drawn and gray as Mrs. MacGill's oatmeal. Ordinarily, Doriselaine Schmidt was a good-looking woman, but she was not good to look at now.

"Faucett," she whispered. "The devil."

Dixon thought he misheard. Lord Richard Faucett was the wealthiest man in Johnson County, possibly in the whole of the Wyoming Territory. Why would a man with so much kill a hardworking German farmer who barely managed to keep his little farm a going concern? "Lord Faucett shot your husband?" he said.

She smiled grimly at the disbelief in his voice. "He didn't pull the trigger — he doesn't have to, he's got his killers to do that for him — but he's behind it, sure enough. I warned Gus, I told him to sell like Faucett wanted, but Gus was stubborn.

He wouldn't listen." She lowered her eyes to her husband's face. "Now, look at you."

The barn was bitterly cold, and Dixon was hungry and tired after his long ride. He wanted a cup of hot coffee but doubted he would get one anytime soon. The woman was distraught and, he suspected, unhinged. A long and difficult day lay ahead.

"We'll have to notify Sheriff Canton," he said. "I'm sorry about what's happened to your husband, Mrs. Schmidt, but I would be careful before making any accusations without solid proof. You don't want to make things harder for yourself and Carl."

She shook her head. "You're still fairly new around here, aren't you, Doctor? What, been here four or five months or so?" When she looked up at him he was startled by the contempt he saw on her face. "You've got a nice new house, your good work, you don't know how things are in Johnson County. You're not trying to make your living off the land like me and Gus. You don't know how Faucett and them claimed land that ain't theirs by rights and thumbed their nose at the rest of us." Her eyes filled with tears as she threw his words back at him. " 'Notify Sheriff Canton' you say! Ha! Fat lot of good that'll do. You've still got a lot to learn about how things work in Powder

River country, Dr. Dixon."

He could think of nothing to say. Although he had come to help, he sensed he had only added to the woman's distress. He wanted to comfort her, but he felt clumsy and useless.

"Carl," she said, "take the doctor into the house. Make a pot of coffee and give him some of last night's corn bread, then let Dr. Dixon get on home to his family. You and me can handle things here." She placed her husband's head gently on the barn's earthen floor and got to her feet, smoothing her blood-soaked apron. "Good-bye, Doctor. There's nothing for you to do here. I am sorry for your trouble."

FRANK CANTON

When he finally arrived home, Dixon was surprised to see Sheriff Canton's horse, Fred, tied to the porch rail. He'd had plenty of time to consider Doriselaine Schmidt's words of reproach on the long, lonely ride. Though his first impulse had been to dismiss her allegations as the rantings of a grief-stricken woman, her calm dismissal of him had altered that perception. Could Canton be one of Faucett's hired killers? She had not mentioned him by name, but still . . .

He entered his house to find the sheriff sitting at the table in the warm kitchen, a steaming cup of coffee in his hand and a plate of Mrs. MacGill's pancakes in front of him. Harry and the twins were at the table, too.

"Hello, Doctor," Canton said as Dixon took off his hat and brushed the snow off his shoulders. "Your boy Harry was telling me about some trouble over to the Schmidt place. Is that so?"

Dixon did not answer at once but crossed the room to hang his coat on a peg beside Canton's. The sheriff's demeanor was friendly, but Dixon felt a worm of unease. When he turned back to the table, Canton was watching him attentively.

"Harry," Dixon said, "see to the horses, will you?"

"But what happened at Carl's? Did you save his pa?"

"No, I did not. The man was dead when I got there. Now Harry, please see to the horses as I said. Cal and Lorna, give your brother a hand cleaning the tack."

Reluctantly, Harry and the twins obeyed. Dixon poured himself a cup of coffee and sat at the table, waiting until they were out of earshot before answering Canton's question.

"Someone murdered Gus Schmidt," Dixon said. "Shot him in the stomach and the face. He'd been dead for hours by the time I got there."

"Murder you say?" Canton's eyes locked on Dixon's, and there was no surprise in them. "Doriselaine or her boy have anything to say about who might've done it?"

Dixon hesitated. Something told him not

to repeat the woman's allegations. "No," he said. "If she has any ideas, she didn't share them with me."

Canton sipped his milky coffee, wetting his long mustache and cleaning it with his lower lip. Dixon found this habit disgusting.

"They didn't see anything?" Canton said. "Well, that does surprise me some. I don't know the boy, but Doriselaine is a sharp woman. She don't miss much." He maintained a cordial smile.

"No, not that she said. She was upset, of course. I didn't want to press her."

"I guess not." Canton finished his coffee in one long draught. "Reckon I better get on over there. You know my deputy, don't you? Jim Enochs? If he shows up here, send him along, over to the Schmidt place. Could be I'll run into him on the way."

Dixon watched Canton put on his hat and well-tailored wool overcoat, obviously new. Johnson County must pay its lawmen well, he thought.

"Oh, I almost forgot," Canton said, "the reason I came out here in the first place. Lord Faucett wants you to come to a dinner party at his house this Saturday night. He says it's time you met. You seen The Manor, Doc?"

"No, I haven't."

Canton smiled. "It's quite a place. You'll understand why folks around here call it that. Bring a bag, he wants you to come on Friday and stay over till Sunday. Lord Faucett won't have his guests traveling at night. It ain't safe, too many road agents and cutthroats around nowadays." Canton winked. "But that's about to change."

After he had gone, Mrs. MacGill turned from the sink where she had been washing breakfast dishes. "I wouldn't trust that man, Doctor," she said. "That one's a right devil, and no mistake."

ODALIE

Lord Richard Faucett's home was south of Buffalo, on a flat, grassy meadow near the place where the three forks of Powder River came together. The short, balding Englishman was on the piazza, smoking a cigar, when Dixon arrived. Despite the cold, Faucett wore only a long silk jacket, tied at the waist, trousers, and velvet smoking slippers. He bounded down the stairs to shake Dixon's hand.

"Lady Faucett cannot abide the smell of a cigar, even the fine ones I smoke. Takes a cruel woman, Dixon, to force a man out into this beastly Wyoming cold just to enjoy a smoke." He tossed the burning cylinder into a snow bank where it sank with a hiss. "It's almost enough to make a man swear off cigars! Come, let's get inside."

A waiting servant, a Chinese man, opened the heavy, oaken double doors, and Dixon stepped into a gleaming world of grandeur and richness beyond anything he had ever seen. They stood in a great hallway that ran the length of the house and was open to the two-story roof. Roaring fires burned in giant, stone fireplaces at each end of the hall, heating the vast space and lending it the look of a medieval palace. Indian artifacts, tanned buffalo robes, and the preserved heads of bison, elk, deer, and mountain cats hung on the walls. A curving staircase of solid walnut, highly polished, led to the rooms of the second floor. Just below it was a gallery level, furnished with potted plants and hanging vines. "That's where the musicians will be tomorrow night," Faucett said, pointing to the gallery. "I can fit a full orchestra up there. Works brilliantly. The acoustics are splendid and putting the musicians up there leaves more room for dancing. My idea. Brilliant, if I do say so myself."

They toured the ground floor, which included a dining room — large enough, Faucett said, to accommodate twenty diners — a library with all four walls lined in leather-bound volumes, a pantry, and a kitchen. Faucett's office was equipped with a telephone, a device Dixon had read about but never seen.

"The first in Wyoming Territory," Faucett said of the instrument with obvious pride, "hell, maybe the only one for all I know. It connects me to my store, supply depot, and post office twenty-four miles away. I tell you, Dixon, that gadget saves me all sorts of time and trouble. It's expensive to keep the lines up, man hours you know, especially in the winter, but it's damn well worth it."

In the summer and fall, Faucett said, he and his wife, Odalie, liked to keep the place full of relatives and guests from England. "I take them on hunting trips, fishing, that sort of thing. Only the best people — here, take a look." Faucett led Dixon to a guestbook in the great hall, standing open on a pedestal. Dutifully turning the pages, Dixon saw the signatures of lords and ladies, dukes and earls.

"Very impressive," Dixon said, wondering how a man so young — Faucett looked to be about thirty or thirty-five — had accumulated such a fortune. Dixon also was curious as to why Faucett had invited him and what he wanted. When he looked up from the guest book, he saw his host smiling, as if he read Dixon's thoughts.

"Come, Doctor," he said, "let's sit by the fire, have a drink and chat a bit before dinner, shall we? Chang, take Dr. Dixon's bag upstairs to the blue room."

They settled into comfortable leather

armchairs before a warm fire. Chang served them whiskey, a fine, single-malt, in cut-crystal glasses that sparkled like diamonds. They sipped their drinks in silence for a few minutes, then Faucett said, "So, what do you think of all this, Dixon?" He waved his hand about the room.

"As I said, it's most impressive. I admit, I am wondering what brought you here all the way from England. The people, the country, it must seem very primitive."

Faucett smiled into his drink. "It does, rather. It's ironic, I came for my health — weak lungs, you know — but in fact, the country almost killed us. By us, I mean my brother, Dick, and me. It was in seventy-eight, mid-November, and we'd been on a hunting trip. Started out from Fort Washakie. Make a long story short, we ended up crossing the Big Horns in the dead of winter. When we finally reached the headwaters of the Powder River, everything was buried in deep snow and no landmarks were recognizable. Our guides couldn't find the pass and brother Dick was gravely ill. Well, I thought we were finished when our chief guide, Jack Hargreaves, brilliant fellow, came up with a solution. He stampeded a herd of buffalo, knowing when they started running they would instinctively make for the pass, which is exactly what they did. Not only that, they pounded the snow down, making a hard, smooth road that we followed right to a place called Trabing. Perhaps you know it?"

Dixon nodded. Trabing was a rough ranch and way station on the Bozeman Road at the Crazy Woman Creek crossing. The spot had been notorious for Indian attacks in the 1860s, when Dixon and Rose first passed that way. He thought of her, and how she would have loved this palatial home. Rose had never had much herself, but that didn't stop her from appreciating, without jealousy, the fine things in life.

"Well," Faucett continued, "Trabing and his clientele were astonished when we staggered in. At first, they didn't believe our story, they thought we must be fugitives from the law or some such, but when Hargreaves and I went out the next day for poor Dick — we'd been forced to leave him behind in a deserted shack, you see — and brought him back on a travois, thin as a skeleton and barely alive, they finally believed us. We may be the only white men ever to have made that terrible journey in winter. Hargreaves believes it, and I rather suspect he's right."

Dixon nodded, remembering his own,

hellishly cold rescue ride from Fort Phil Kearny to Horseshoe Station in December of 1866. He and Portugee Phillips, a civilian employee of the post quartermaster, had left the night of the massacre, traveling at night and hiding in bushes and ravines during the day. The first sixty-fives miles to Fort Reno had been the worst. Many times Dixon thought the subzero temperatures would kill him if the Indians didn't. The army had paid each man three hundred dollars for his efforts.

"Did your brother recover?" he asked Faucett.

"Yes, matter of fact, he did. Old Dick was tougher than I thought. He chose to remain here in Wyoming when I returned to New York for the winter. When I came back in the spring, he'd already started building this place, already ordered furnishings and fittings from Chicago. That summer I bought my first herd, from a rancher on the Sweetwater. Now I have thirty-nine thousand animals, including horses, all bearing my brand. I don't mind telling you, Dixon, my range runs from the headwaters of the Powder River south to Teapot Rock divide. That's ninety miles north and south, and east thirty miles from the Big Horns. Soon, I'll have two more ranches, one on Crazy

Woman Creek and another on Tongue River. I'll need a good man on each to help run my outfit, an intelligent man, one who already knows something of the cattle business. You did some work for Nelson Story up north, didn't you, Dixon? How'd you like to come work for me?"

Faucett gestured to Chang, who refilled their glasses. Dixon had begun to suspect Faucett was working up to such an offer, though he had no intention of accepting. Story was a good man and a friend, and Dixon had been happy in Paradise Valley, but he'd had his fill of working for another man, of spending his time and energy looking after someone else's interests. He was ready to be his own boss. Beyond that, the isolation of ranch life was hard on children. The twins especially needed school and civilizing.

"Money is no object," Faucett said, misinterpreting Dixon's hesitation. "I need a man I can trust, and one who can start immediately. Name your price."

Before Dixon could answer, they were interrupted by a woman's voice from the curving stairway.

"Oh, do be quiet, Richard," she said. "Our guest isn't interested in becoming another one of your cow servants. Leave the poor

78

man alone."

The two men got to their feet as she entered the room. The woman was tall, taller than her husband, and striking, with pale hair worn in a gleaming chignon and skin that was white and unblemished. She wore a silk brocade dress, cut low in the European fashion, of an ivory color that accentuated her cool, bloodless beauty. Unlike her husband, Lady Faucett was not English. In her speech, Dixon heard the languorous lilt of the American South.

"My darling," Faucett said, "come meet our neighbor, Daniel Dixon, the physician. I've no intention of making him one of my cow servants, as you say. I want him to join me as a kind of partner. Dr. Dixon, may I introduce my wife, Odalie?"

When she offered her hand, Dixon, because of her exoticness, was not sure whether to clasp it or raise it to his lips. He chose the latter. As their eyes met, he felt a shock of recognition, a stirring he had not experienced in years. He knew these eyes; they were large and blue, rimmed with long dark lashes. What moved him most was not the beauty of those eyes but the delicate, dewy skin below them, faintly blue or maybe silver, that made them so remarkable. Rose's eyes.

"So nice to meet you at last, Doctor," she said. Dixon saw surprise and amusement on her lovely face, and he realized he was still holding her hand.

"The pleasure is mine, Lady Faucett," he said, finally releasing her hand.

The meal began with chicken gumbo soup, served with a crusty, French-style bread, followed by a broiled leg of lamb bathed in an oyster sauce made rich with sweet butter and cream. After this, a fricassee of veal, served with mashed potatoes and asparagus points, and, to finish, English plum pudding with brandy sauce. Chang served the food, cleared the plates, and kept the wine flowing throughout.

"Lady Faucett, I do believe that was the best meal I've ever had," Dixon said without exaggeration. As a young man growing up in Lexington, Kentucky, and later as a physician-in-training in Cincinnati, he had patronized the finest restaurants those sophisticated cities had to offer, but nothing to compare with this. "Where did you find such a cook?"

Odalie smiled happily, revealing dimples in both cheeks. "Arnaud — he is a treasure, isn't he? I discovered him last year on a journey home. I poached him from a Mississippi steamer. I'm worried though; I don't know how long I'll be able to keep him. We pay him handsomely, God knows, but one of those railroad tycoons in Denver will woo him away soon, I fear. It's already been attempted."

"I'm not surprised," Dixon said. "And where is home?"

"New Orleans. Do you know it?"

"Yes, though I haven't been there since before the war. I remember it as a lovely but strange city, like being in another country." In fact, though it would be impolite to say so, Dixon had been happy to leave the place. He and his traveling companion had made the mistake of visiting in summer, and his friend, a fellow medical student, had fallen ill with yellow fever and very nearly died. When Dixon thought of New Orleans, he saw jaundiced skin, yellow eyes, and pools of bloody vomit.

Odalie's smile faded at his mention of the war. "Yes, well, it's all quite different now," she said bitterly, "thanks to the Yankee beast Butler, a vile pig." Her eyes clouded as the specter of General Benjamin F. Butler entered the candlelit room.

Lord Faucett cleared his throat. "Yes, well . . ." He searched for a change of topic. "I am by no means expert in these matters, but I like to think I have a keen ear for language. Are you, Dr. Dixon, by any chance a child of Dixie, like my wife?"

Dixon smiled. "I grew up in Lexington, Kentucky, though I haven't been back to the Bluegrass Country for many years. I hope you won't hold it against me, Lady Faucett, but I fought with the Union during the late war. My family and I disagreed on the subject of slavery, and it caused a rupture that has yet to heal. Someday, I hope to change this, but so far, I have not found an opening."

Odalie sighed, abandoning her previous gaiety. "Yes, a story that's all-too-common, I'm afraid. No, Doctor, I don't fault you for your wartime allegiance. What's done is done, though I do hope you can heal the rift. Family is so important."

She smiled sadly at him and, again, Dixon felt a throb of powerful emotion. Other than the eerie similarity about the eyes, Odalie Faucett did not resemble Rose in any way. Still, in some strange way, Dixon felt his departed wife's presence in the room. He had almost forgotten how much he loved her, until this lovely woman reminded him.

BILLY SUN

When Dixon returned to his house on Sunday morning, Mrs. MacGill ran out to meet him, breathless and disheveled.

"They're gone," she said. "They've run off, Caleb and Lorna."

"Run off?" he said, sliding to the ground. "Why? When? How long have they been gone?"

"Oh, Doctor, I don't know," she said, twisting her apron in her work-roughened hands. "I haven't seen them since last night. They went out to do their chores, like always, but when I got up this morning they were gone. They took the pony and the blankets off their beds."

Dixon looked north, toward the snow-covered mountains. Though the February afternoon was uncharacteristically warm, the weather was preparing to turn. Dark clouds were moving toward them, like crouching bears. "Where's Harry?"

"In town," Mrs. MacGill said, "staying with the Donahues. Remember?"

Dixon nodded absently. He'd forgotten Harry was spending the week in town with a friend's family, and now he was sorry he'd agreed to it. He could use his help.

"I think I know where they're headed," Dixon said, "and I have to go after them now, before the snow comes. Is there anything else you can tell me? Did something happen to upset them?"

Mrs. MacGill put her hand to her white head; her topknot had loosened and was listing to one side. "Well, I scolded 'em, I did. I told them to muck out the horses' stalls, and when they were done there to fill the barrels in the kitchen and upstairs. Cal would've done it — and Lorna's share, too — but she commenced to complaining and so he started in. So I switched 'em, the both, on the backside. But I didn't expect the two to take off. I've switched 'em before."

Dixon frowned. He did not hit his children and did not want anyone else to strike them, either. "I thought we had an understanding about that," he said.

"Yes, Doctor, but they need discipline! Lorna won't make old bones without someone to take her in hand. She'll find trouble,

84

and sure enough. Save her and you'll save the boy, too, the way she owns him. Anyhow, like I said, I don't think 'twas the switchin' made 'em take off."

Dixon did not argue. What Mrs. MacGill said was true, the twelve-year-old twins were out of control and it was his fault. He hadn't given them a father's love or a father's attention. Sometimes he could barely even look at them. Even though he knew, in his rational, physician's mind, that Caleb and Lorna were not responsible for Rose's death, he had not been able to make his heart believe it, too.

"Please pack some food, Mrs. MacGill. I hope to be back with them tonight, but give us enough for two days, just in case."

Dixon left at two o'clock, riding his mare, Alice, a long-legged sorrel with a flax mane and tail, and leading a mule with the food and a tent. The day's sunny warmth held for the first few hours, and he had no trouble following the pony's tracks. As he suspected, Lorna and Caleb were going north, probably to the Crow village. Even now, more than a year after leaving Paradise Valley, the twins were more Indian than white. Unlike Harry, neither had any interest in schooling — it was all he could do to get them to wear shoes.

After about three hours, the wind acquired a sting and the first few flakes of the snow that had been threatening all day began to fall. Dixon turned up the collar of his sheepskin coat and hunched his shoulders, hoping he would not regret his decision to travel alone. Mrs. MacGill had tried to talk him into riding to Buffalo to enlist Sheriff Canton's help, but Dixon refused. "There's no time," he said, "not if I'm going to catch up with them tonight." Guilt and fear drove him to take speedy action, but now he was forced to admit another pair of eyes would have been useful, especially if they were in for a heavy snow.

The sky was going red, and the valleys ahead were bathed in violet shadow. The snow was coming faster and the pony's tracks were becoming harder to see. Dixon's mind drifted back, sixteen years, to the first time he'd traveled this stretch of the Bozeman Road. It was late summer, and he rode with the three-man team of Montgomery Van Valzah, the barrel-chested civilian who carried the locked mailbag between forts Laramie and Phil Kearny, with stops at Fort Reno and Bridger's Ferry. This was still Sioux country then, and the sixty-five-mile journey from Fort Reno to Phil Kearny was a perilous one, but all of Red Cloud's painted warriors could not have stopped him, for Rose was at Fort Phil Kearny and nothing would keep him away.

Even in the bright sunlight, the fort's blackened skeleton held the power to chill him. Now, as he neared it again, Dixon found himself growing uneasy about confronting the ruins in the winter moonlight. Would ghosts of the slaughtered soldiers stand sentry in the ruined block-houses? Would spectral voices echo through the gutted barracks and the quartermaster's yard? A shiver ran through him, and not only because of the cold wind that blew down his collar.

It was fully dark now and the snow was thick and blowing. Though he could no longer see the pony's tracks, Dixon had no choice but to press on. The twins would follow the old Bozeman Road, he was confident of that. With any luck, Jesse, the overburdened pony, would tire and the children would be forced to find a place to stop for the night. Had they brought bedrolls suitable for the weather? He thought so; Cal and Lorna were wild, but they weren't stupid. No one had ever said that of them. They would build a fire if they could, though it would be difficult in this weather even for a seasoned outdoorsman.

Dixon raised his eyes to the inky sky, trying to gauge the time. He reckoned it was getting on toward eight o'clock. The snow was letting up, but the wind was not. After one especially savage blast, Alice turned her head and gave him the side eye, as if to say, *Do you have any idea what you're doing?*

They crested a ridge and Dixon found himself looking down on the remains of Fort Phil Kearny. Though he'd been anticipating the sight, and the eerie stillness of the frozen Piney Creek Valley, his nerve endings tingled as Alice daintily picked her way down the steep trail, followed by the mule. Every part of Dixon's soul rebelled. He did not want to return to this haunted place. He sensed a malevolent presence waiting, yet he knew he had to press on. His children might be sheltering there.

The ice groaned under Alice's feet as they crossed the frozen Little Piney. They rode through the collapsed water gates and over the blackened ground that used to be the quartermaster's yard. Dixon looked to the right, at the remains of the stables and the teamsters' quarters. He saw the charred remnants of the slag pile, where young Private Rooney chopped off a thumb while splitting firewood, and the listing clothesline that held the bed sheets that comically entangled Colonel Carrington one windy day as he scolded a soldier for a minor uniform violation. Some cabins still stood along laundresses' row, though they were roofless. They would provide little protection from the elements, but a child might seek shelter there. Dixon dismounted and checked each one, without result.

He climbed the slope from the quartermaster's yard and into the fort proper, leading Alice and the mule along the red gravel path that ran between officers' row and the parade lawn. How many times had he and Rose trod these iron-red stones? He stopped before the hulk that once was her cabin, and then their cabin, the place where he first kissed her, where they first made love. His throat tightened, and he closed his eyes. They thought they had long lives ahead of them, a joyful future together, but this was a lie, just another of God's cruel jokes.

Alice nickered and nudged him with her nose. He turned to see a shadow moving toward him through the snow. He saw the dark shape only briefly before it vanished behind a blowing curtain of white. Dixon closed his eyes and looked again. Nothing . . . then, yes! It was closer now, bulky and slow moving. Alice saw the apparition also; she remained motionless, ears forward, tail blowing between her legs. Dixon was surprised by the horse's calmness; generally, she was quick to sense and react to the presence of an intruder. Gradually, above the keening of the wind, Dixon heard a voice calling. The words were not intelligible until the man — for it was a man and not a ghost — drew nearer.

"Doctor! I've got them, Cal and Lorna. They're safe."

Dixon peered into the snow, shielding his eyes with his hand. "Who is it? I can't see you."

"Billy Sun." He came closer until Dixon could make out his features. Years had passed since he'd last seen the half-breed, and he was virtually swallowed by the soldier's buffalo coat and red woolen scarf he wore, but there was no mistaking those pale green eyes. He turned and waved a wolf-hide mitten toward a crumbling structure Dixon recognized as the remains of the bakery, the post's only stone structure. "They're in there," he said. "I got a fire going."

Dixon felt a rush of relief and gratitude. "Thank God," he said. "Thank you, Billy. Thank you."

"They were in a bad way when I found

90

them," Billy said. "Cold and hungry but they're good now."

They started walking toward the bakery. "Where did you find them?" Dixon said.

"North of here, about half a mile, on the old Fort Smith Road. Their pony died and they were trying to make a shelter out of blankets and rocks. They weren't having luck, or with a fire, either, because of the wind. It was a good thing I came along when I did."

As they neared the stone walls, Dixon smelled a wood fire and saw its warm glow flickering through an open window. Before they arrived, he put out an arm to stop Billy. "Where were they going? Back to your village?"

Billy hesitated, looking at his feet. He wore tall moccasins, like his gloves, made of wolf skin with the fur on the inside. Dixon, whose own feet felt like blocks of blue ice inside his square-toed leather boots, would have given one hundred dollars for a pair like them. "Yes, they were going to the village," Billy said.

"The surgeon at Fort McKinney told me there is sickness there. Is it true?"

"Yes. Many of the people have died and many more are sick. Biwi fell ill."

"Do the children know of Biwi's illness?

Could that be why they were going there, to see her?"

Billy shook his head. "I don't know. They will have to tell you their reasons. I'm going for more firewood."

Dixon almost stopped him; he would have liked to have Billy with him when he reunited with his children, but the half-breed had already vanished into the darkness. Dixon went on alone, the dry, ankle-deep snow squeaking beneath his feet. It was bitterly cold; if Billy hadn't found them, Cal and Lorna would have frozen to death. If Rose was watching from above — and sometimes he felt she was — she would have been angry with Dixon for letting that happen.

The bakery door had burned away, but the charred frame was still in place. He stooped to enter and found the twins, huddled in their blankets, like a pair of towheaded Indians, before the fire. They raised their pale eyes to their father, but neither spoke.

"Well?" Dixon said. "What do you have to say for yourselves?"

They looked at each other, a pair of defeated conspirators. When Lorna finally spoke, her first words were for the pony. "Jesse kept going slower and slower. I could tell he was tired, so we got off to walk, but he fell over and couldn't get up." Tears ran from her eyes, and she brushed them away with the back of her hand. "Jesse made awful noises when he was dying, Pa. I've never heard anything like that before."

Dixon said, "I'm sorry. Jesse was a sweet pony." *You knew how old he was, how his wind had gone,* he thought. *You shouldn't have used him so hard.*

Lorna nodded miserably, the firelight gleaming red on her hair. Cal kept his eyes on the flames and said nothing.

"The two of you could have died with him," Dixon said. "Why did you do this foolish thing? I expect an answer."

Again, it was Lorna who spoke. "It was my idea. I needed to go to the Crow village and Cal wanted to come with me."

"Why did you need to go there?"

"I just did," she said.

Dixon shook his head in disbelief. "You didn't think about telling me, or Mrs. MacGill? You didn't think about the storm?"

"You wouldn't let us go," she said sullenly. "I didn't know about the storm."

"There's sickness in the village; many people have died. You could have gotten sick, too."

Lorna gestured toward a canvas bag lying

on the ground. "I had medicine."

Dixon picked up the bag and loosened the drawstring. Inside, a number of glass vials glistened green and blue in the firelight. He examined them: quinine and laudanum. Somehow, she had taken them from the medicine cabinet in his surgery without him noticing.

"I watch you," she said. "From that little upstairs room with the bed in it. Those two bottles were the ones you used on that old lady last fall, Mrs. Dillard, and she got better."

Dixon had never noticed Lorna hanging around the surgery. Why would she do that, and secretly? If she was interested in his work, as Harry was, he would be happy to instruct her. He looked at her and shook his head. Lorna was his child, but he saw nothing of himself in her and certainly nothing of her mother. He did not know his only daughter at all. Sometimes, her strangeness almost frightened him.

"Mrs. Dillard had dengue fever, Lorna, and yes, it's treated with quinine and laudanum. Those are dangerous drugs, the laudanum especially. We don't know what's making the Indians sick, and anyhow, stealing is wrong. You know that."

Do they? Have I taught them not to steal,

lie, cheat, take advantage of the less fortunate? Have I taught them to be kind? In truth, Dixon didn't remember imparting those or any other life lesson to these two. He assumed Mrs. MacGill was taking care of those things.

Billy Sun returned with his arms full of wood. Dixon noticed how Lorna's eyes brightened when he walked in, how they followed him as he tossed bits of the old stockade into the flames.

After a hot meal of cornmeal, water, and salt, boiled over the fire, along with coffee and canned milk, Billy and Dixon pitched the tent, a relic of Dixon's army days. Caleb and Lorna spread their blankets on the oilcloth floor and fell immediately into a deep, untroubled sleep. Despite the cold, Dixon and Billy lingered by the fire.

"Why were you on the road today, Billy, in this weather?" Dixon said.

Billy stirred the embers with a long stick and threw more wood on the fire. "I was coming for you," he said. "The sickness is spreading quickly, and it respects no one; the strong and healthy die just as fast as the old and frail. I had been away from the village, so I knew nothing of it until my cousin came for me." He prodded the flames. "The healers go without food and water for days, they hold the eagle fan and baaxpee bundle to the chests of the sick, but the people die anyway. Like I said, the sickness respects no one."

Dixon suspected the village had fallen on hard and hungry times, which weakened the people and left them vulnerable to illness. Even Billy showed signs of poverty. He was thin and his buffalo coat bedraggled and moth-eaten, something he or one of his relatives must have bought or taken from a soldier years before. Nowadays, because of the dwindling of the buffalo herds, such a coat in a new condition was hard to come by.

"How many are afflicted?" Dixon said.

"Half the village, maybe more."

"What are their symptoms?"

"Symptoms?"

"How does the sickness take them? Do they cough? How do they look?"

"They shake with cold though the skin burns, and their muscles tighten and bunch. At the end their skin goes blue and when they cough, there's a sound of water here." He touched his chest. "A man fights to breathe, like he's drowning."

Influenza, Dixon said to himself, *and death by pneumonia.* Such a contagion could wipe out an entire village, and the accumulation of unburied corpses could lead to other problems. He had heard of cases where the villagers fled in terror, leaving the dead to rot on the ground and in their lodges.

"What happens to the dead?" Dixon said.

Billy hesitated, surprised by the question. This seemed a strange time for discussion of such matters. "After a period of time, the spirit moves on, to the world behind this one."

"No," Dixon said. "I mean, what do your people do with the bodies?"

"Oh." Billy smiled, despite the grimness of the topic. "The dead person is wrapped in a blanket and removed by wagon to the burial ground. When I left this morning, there was a long line of wagons. Because they are so many, the people are talking of resting the bodies in the trees and burying the bones later."

Dixon and Billy joined the twins in the tent, settling in their bedrolls on the crowded floor. The two men took the outside of the circle, affording the children the warmth of the center. The four bodies generated some heat, but even so the breaths of the sleepers produced little white clouds of vapor.

Tired as Dixon was, sleep would not come. He lay on his back, staring at the sloping canvas ceiling. In his mind's eye, he saw the terrible line of death wagons Billy had described, and bodies rotting in the trees. His people did not deserve this. When the U.S. Infantry had first come to this country, the Crows had been kind to the bluecoat soldiers and their families, sometimes fighting shoulder to shoulder with them against their mutual enemy, the Sioux. The whites had rewarded their friendship by imprisoning them on reservations and shorting their rations. Now the Crows were suffering and dying in their villages while the white world turned a blind eye.

Dixon would go to them in their mountain village. Chances were there was little he could do, but it was his duty to try.

DIXON

The morning sky dawned clear, promising a sunny day and a warmer one. Dixon was impressed when Lorna, unasked, fried up a breakfast of the salty ham and eggs Mrs. MacGill had packed, while Cal toasted slabs of corn bread between a pair of green sticks. Billy struck the tent as Dixon made coffee. He was glad Mrs. MacGill had thought to include a can of condensed milk and packets of sugar. She teased him about the way he took his coffee — "white and sweet, just like a wee child" — but Dixon could not tolerate it any other way. He marveled at those who drank the stuff as it came, black and inky. Rose had taken hers that way, as did Billy Sun.

After breakfast he took Billy aside. "I want you to take the twins home. I'm going north to the village. If I can't do anything to help, at least I can triage the situation, see what's needed."

Billy said, "The people may be gone when you arrive. You might need me to help you find them."

"I need you to take Cal and Lorna back to Buffalo. If I don't return in three days, go to Fort McKinney and ask the post surgeon to come to the village with you. If he refuses," and he will, Dixon thought, "then come alone."

Dixon expected the twins to want to accompany him — after all, Biwi had been like a mother to them — but neither did. Cal kneeled by the fire toasting himself another piece of corn bread while Lorna helped Billy break camp. He fashioned a travois from tree branches, rope, and blankets, to pull the gear so the twins could ride double on Dixon's pack mule. Lorna was working industriously, Dixon noticed, something she never did at home. He threw the saddle over Alice's back and bent to tighten the cinch, wondering if Biwi was truly the reason Lorna took off for the village.

"I don't like Buffalo," Cal announced from the fireside. "I wish we'd never moved there."

Dixon straightened. "Why's that?"

Cal turned his toast. "Everybody's afraid."

"What are they afraid of?"

"The cattlemen, especially Lord Faucett

and his riders." Cal fixed his eyes on his father. "Don't you know that?"

"I've met Faucett; he seems all right," Dixon said. "What do people say?"

Cal settled back on his heels and popped a bit of toasted corn bread in his mouth. He chewed as he spoke, not looking at his father. "If they think you're stealing from them, they send one of those cowboys to hang you or shoot you."

Dixon said, "Are you talking about Gus Schmidt?"

Cal nodded. "Him and others. They hung a woman and her husband a while back. Left them swinging till their faces turned black and the birds were eating them." He took another bite of toast.

Dixon had heard about the hanging of a woman, though he didn't give the story much credence. No one seemed to know anything about her, or the man who died with her, or even if there was a man. Dixon did not want to believe he had put down stakes in corrupt soil, though the murder of Gus Schmidt did trouble him. The crime was still unsolved. There were rumors Lady Faucett had given Doriselaine a certain amount of money, how much no one knew. The widow didn't say and no one had the bad manners to ask. Last week, Dixon

101

learned Doriselaine and Carl were leaving the Territory.

"Just because people say things doesn't make them true, Cal." Dixon felt a sudden wave of sympathy for his pale, undersized son squatting by the fire. "Are you afraid?" he said. "Do you think someone might try to hurt you?"

Cal regarded his father with cool blue eyes. "I'm not afraid of anyone."

They broke camp at nine o'clock. The sun shone brightly and a fair day beckoned. As they rode away, Cal, behind Lorna on the mule, turned in the saddle to wave to his father. Dixon waved back. Maybe he and his strange son had made some kind of connection. He hoped so.

He watched until they disappeared over a rise, then turned Alice's head north, toward the great lonely mountains.

BILLY SUN

The sun and warmth held through the morning, though by early afternoon Billy and the twins were traveling under a low, gray sky. They passed through a foggy valley, where thick black smoke, the product of a burning coal seam deep below, rose from fissures in the ground and corrupted the air with the smell of sulfur. Billy took the lead and Cal and Lorna followed, they and the mule blending into a single, shapeless black shadow trailing through the mist. Like a blanket, the smoke and fog muffled all sound. Billy raised his face to the dull gleam that was the sun and reckoned it to be about three o'clock. They should be in Buffalo by dinner.

Billy Sun had not been fully honest with Dixon when he told him why he was on the road. The Crow village was racked by illness, that was true, and Billy did plan to bring the doctor back to help them, but after that he was done with his Indian life. He was done with Montana Territory altogether. Nelson Story's cattle operation was winding down; now the boss man spent all his time in Bozeman where he was starting up a new bank, the Gallatin Valley National. He also had a flour mill on Bridger Creek. Story asked Billy to work for him at the mill and offered a handsome wage, but Billy had no interest. Wyoming was the place for a young man with plans, and Billy Sun had plenty of those.

Story nodded when Billy said he was leaving. "I've been expecting this," Story said, motioning Billy toward an overstuffed leather armchair. "Sit a spell, son, let's talk this over. I don't want to see you make a big mistake." Billy started to speak, but Story raised a hand. "Just listen to what I got to say, that's all I ask. There's trouble brewing down there, Billy, big trouble, and I'm not saying this only because I don't want to lose you — which I don't."

Billy smiled. "There's trouble everywhere, Mr. Story. I ain't afraid of it."

"No, I know you're not, and that's one of the things I've always liked about you, Billy. You're a good man, but you're also a young one and there's things about the world you don't know. Now, hear me out. In Wyoming they got an outfit called the Wyoming Stock Growers Association. These are rich men who own all the cattle and the land, too — leastways they say they own it and they might as well. There's bad feeling between these fellows and the settlers and smaller ranchers, and that's especially true if a cowboy dreams of starting a ranch of his own. The cattlemen worry he'll turn to rustling to build up his herd. If he tries it, he's blackballed. He can't get work, he can't ride in the roundups. He's finished." Billy knew about the spring and fall roundups, when the free-ranging animals were collected and counted. These were the times when a cowboy made his big money, thirty-five to forty dollars for only six weeks' work.

"Up here in Montana, we talked about doing that too," Story continued, "but we decided against it. It won't stop the rustling, not like it's supposed to. In fact, letting a cowboy run his own stock will cut down on the stealing, because thataway he's invested. With his own ranch, he keeps a sharper eye out for the thievin', and hell, you fellas know more about what's happening on the range than we do.

"That ain't all. Down in Wyoming they're doing away with the Texas system of dealing with mavericks. Used to be, anyone who gets a rope on a unbranded calf owns it, but that's gonna change. Wyoming stockmen are fixing it so those motherless calves go to the man who owns the biggest herd on the range. I know for a fact the territorial legislature's gonna pass a law that does just that."

Story leaned back in his chair and tented his fingers before his mouth. "So, you see, Billy, Wyoming ain't the place for a man like you. You want a ranch of your own, I know you do, and you ain't gonna be able to have it down there. You'd be better off here, workin' for me till you got the money to set up for yourself. Hell, I won't lie to you, Billy, I'd be better off, too. I never met your equal when it comes to breaking horses. You work for me at the mill and finish my mustangs, I'll make it worth your time. You won't never be sorry."

Billy replayed this conversation in his mind as he and the twins rode toward Buffalo. Nelson Story was a good man who had always treated Billy well. His offer was generous, and he trusted Story to make good on it, but it didn't matter. Billy Sun had made up his mind to make his stake in Wyoming's Powder River country, Absaroka, the fabled land his mother used to tell him about when he was a boy, where buffalo, bear, elk, and antelope were plentiful, where wild strawberries and raspberries grew thick beside icy streams, where the air was cool and sweet and the people rich in pelts and furs. Those were fat and happy times, his mother said, when the people carried on a lively trade with the trappers, like his French father, and American frontiersmen. Those were the days of the great warrior Arapooish, whose words were passed down from mother to son for generations. He remembered them clearly, words his wife would one day teach his own son:

"The Crow country is good country. The Great Spirit put it in exactly the right place. While you are in it, you fare well. Whenever you are out of it, whichever way you travel, you fare worse. The Crow country is exactly in the right place. Everything good is to be found there."

All his life, Billy Sun had dreamed of finding his place in that vanished world. Someday, by owning his own ranch on the very lands his mother and her people once called home, he would find it.

Sugarfoot stopped and raised his head, ears forward. Billy turned and lifted his hand, halting the mule behind him. Then he heard it, too, a man's voice, and the sound of walking horses. Whoever they were, they were heading his way. He figured there were at least two riders, though only one was talking. He waited motionless until finally they emerged from the fog; two horsemen on big, fine horses. When they saw Billy they reined in. After a pause, they kicked their horses forward until they were no more than ten feet apart. If they had dismounted, courtesy would have required that Billy do the same, but the strangers remained in their saddles.

"Identify yourself, boy, and declare your business." The speaker was the smaller of the two. He looked to be in his late thirties and wore a well-made woolen overcoat, a brimless fur hat, and plaid muffler.

The word "boy" was an insult, and Billy did not answer. He heard a murmur from the twins behind him. They were still wrapped in the blankets they wore the night before, and the mule pulled the clumsily made travois.

"Well, chief?" the second man said. "Didn't you hear Sheriff Canton?" The second man was tall, well over six feet, with a powerful build, and he sat poker-straight in the saddle. His hair and mustache were dark and he wore range clothing, high-heeled boots, and a Mexican-style *sombrero*. "But maybe you only talk Injun." His red lips parted in a smile. "Too bad he ain't Apache, Frank. If he was, I could translate for you. Hold on, maybe the nits understand me." He craned his head to look beyond Billy at the twins. "Well, nits? You talk American?"

Lorna threw off the blanket, revealing her angry face and white-blond hair. "Me and Cal ain't Indians, mister," she said.

Canton's mouth dropped open. "Damn me, it's the Dixon twins. What are you doing out here with this Indian? Where's your father?"

"My name is Billy Sun." He spoke in a calm, measured voice. "The doctor asked me to take his children to Buffalo. He has gone to the Crow village because there is sickness. I am doing as he asked."

"Bill Sun?" Canton said. "Nelson Story's man? Yes, I've heard of you; they say you got a gift for busting horses. I heard about that bunch from Red Wall country couple years back. First-rate cow ponies, the lot."

Billy leaned forward to stroke Sugarfoot's neck. He called him that because of his sweet gait and disposition. "This buckskin was one of those. He can run all day, chase down a fast calf, and hold a nine-hundred-pound steer."

The tall man gave a short laugh. "He sure

109

don't look like much." His eyes were dark and not friendly. They looked older than the rest of him. "Hell, he won't stand twelve hands. Hard to believe a pony that small could hold a nine-hundred-pound steer." He spat on the ground, a tobacco-brown glob that just missed Sugarfoot's hoof. "But supposin' he could do those things, what's a Injun need with a pony like that anyhow? You think you're a cowboy, chief?" His eyes moved to the string of bear claws Billy wore around his neck.

"Shut up, Tom," Canton said. He smiled at Billy, shaking his head. "Don't mind him, he's been working down in Arizona Territory, where they put no premium on manners. So, there's sickness in the Crow village? What kind of sickness?"

"He's gone to find out. If he's not back in three days, I'm supposed to ride to Fort McKinney for the surgeon."

Canton smoothed his mustache with his thumb and forefinger. "Tell you what, Bill — you don't mind if I call you Bill, do you? Doesn't seem right to call a grown man Billy."

"I don't care what you call me."

Canton smiled. "So, how about this? Me and Tom, we'll take these two back to Buffalo. You can turn around, go back, and help Dr. Dixon with your people. Wouldn't you rather do that? Take care of your Indian people?"

Before Billy could answer, Lorna kicked the mule forward till he stood even with Sugarfoot. "No," she said. "Pa told Billy to take us. I heard him." She turned to Billy. "I don't want to go with them — especially him." She pointed to Tom, who tipped his hat with a grin.

"Now who ain't got good manners?" he said.

"No, she's right," Billy said. "I told the doctor I'd take his children to Buffalo, and I will."

Canton shrugged. "Suit yourself. I thought you'd want to be with your own kind, but maybe that don't matter to you."

"Me and Cal, we're Billy's people, too," Lorna said. "Ain't that so, Cal?"

Cal nodded. "That's so."

"And if Billy wants to work as a cowboy, he can. There's nothing wrong in it." She looked directly at Tom as she said this. "Ain't that so, Cal?"

"Yes, that's so."

Tom laughed. "That's so, that's so . . . you always say what she tells you, Cal?"

"Leave them alone," Canton said. "They're children."

111

"The boy is." Tom winked at Lorna. "Her, I'm not so sure about. How about it? You just a child, darlin'?"

"Shut up." Canton said. "All right, Bill, you go on ahead to Buffalo. I'll stop by your place tomorrow or the next day, make sure you and these young people make it all right."

"We'll make it," Billy said. "Don't trouble yourself."

"Oh, I think I will." Canton took up the reins that had gone slack in his gloved hands. "There's a low element about in these parts. Just yesterday a couple horse thieves made off with one of Lord Faucett's riding horses, the one Lady Odalie likes to ride, and we can't have that. No, sir. Lady Odalie, she is something special; she's got to be happy. Anyhow, I got a pretty good idea where that horse is. In fact, that's where me and Tom were headed when we run into you. You keep a sharp eye out, now Bill. Trash like that, there's no telling what they'll do."

Canton and Tom kicked their horses and were already past them when Lorna said, "And what'll you do if you find them, Sheriff? Necktie party?"

The two men reined in and turned in their saddles.

"Frank, ain't she just the sassiest little thing?" Tom said. "Sassy as she can be. Why, if I was your daddy, darlin', I would put you right across my knee and —"

Canton interrupted. "Why, I'll bring them to justice, Miss Lorna, unless they give me some reason to do different. But I wonder . . ." he paused, a smile on his lips but not in his eyes, "what does a young lady like you know of such things?"

Lorna's eyes cut to Billy, who shook his head.

"I'm sorry," she said, dropping her eyes. "I didn't mean nothing by it."

"I will accept your apology, Miss Dixon," Canton said, "but be careful. A young lady could get herself in trouble, running her mouth like that."

The two men rode on, Tom's laughter trailing behind them.

DIXON

He followed a narrow, winding path through a dark forest of pine, balsam, and hemlock. Years had passed since he last visited the Crow village, but Dixon recognized the trail. Nothing had changed. As Alice picked her way along the rocky path, Dixon remembered a summer day, long ago, when the Indians rode down the mountain with a friendship offering for the soldier fort. They brought painted bags full of sweet red berries, under a layer of damp cottonwood leaves to keep them cool and juicy. The men were handsome, with long, shining hair brushed up in showy pompadours, and the women confident and strong in their modest deerskin dresses. The government had treated these people shabbily, and his friend, Nelson Story, was complicit in this. Dixon should have called him out back in seventy-six when he first began to suspect Story was cheating the Crows on their rations. His clerks were counting the same bags of flour twice, filling meat barrels with viscera instead of edible pork, passing off underfed calves as mature cattle. Dixon discovered the truth of these allegations and, to his everlasting shame, did nothing. Eventually the army got wind of the fraud, but it did not bring charges or relieve Story of his contract. Dixon had no doubt money changed hands. Nelson Story always seemed to have plenty of that.

As Dixon continued up the mountainside, the trees thinned out and stars appeared in the ebony sky. Again he thought of years gone by, of magical nights when the fort's regimental band performed under the undulating Northern Lights. Rose was the wife of another man then, Mark Reynolds, an ambitious officer who put all things, even his marriage, second to his career. On those evenings, Dixon had watched her secretly, hungrily, hoping to catch her eye. They were dangerous times, and not only because of Red Cloud's Sioux warriors. Dixon had never hated a man the way he hated Reynolds, and he had indulged in dark thoughts the night Reynolds had to go under his surgeon's knife. How easy it would have been to let the knife slip, severing an artery, or to leave behind a tiny sliver of necrosed bone or bit of diseased tissue, something that would poison his rival slowly from within, so first the arm would rot and then the corpus entire. In the end, Dixon's knife did not slip, no pathogen was left behind, but it was a close thing.

Alice stumbled, so Dixon dismounted and led her the rest of the way. Despite the darkness he recognized landmarks, a mound of rocks to his left, to his right the music of a fast stream rushing over a bed of polished stone. Even on summer's hottest day it was cool by the water, in the shade of the towering lodgepole pines. He once spent a lazy fall afternoon by that spring, lying on the springy, pine-scented forest floor, watching fugitive beams of yellow sunlight pierce the canopy. No Indians had been seen for a time, so Dixon had decided to spend an afternoon alone, away from the fort. It was very nearly his last. A Sioux on horseback came upon him, startling them both. The two men simultaneously reached for their weapons as Dixon scrambled to his feet, but, in the end, there was no violence. Neither man had desire to harm the other. The Indian rode away, and Dixon returned to the fort and never spoke of it.

He was nearing the home of the Many Lodges People. During his previous visits, he had heard the village before he saw it. The sounds were those of children playing and women laughing; a host of barking dogs would run out to challenge him. Tonight all was silence. He stepped on something soft and, instinctively, recoiled, startling Alice who shied and pulled on the reins. Dixon stroked her neck to calm her, then struck a match to examine the object on the path. It was a large rat, freshly dead, its body intact and unbloodied. He kicked it off the trail and moved on.

He rounded the last curve and faced the clearing where the village stood. Only three lodges remained. The moonlight revealed dark, circular patches on the ground where other tepees had been, each with a cold, dark fire pit in its center. Dixon walked to the center of the clearing and turned a complete circle, searching for movement or any sign of life. There was nothing. He looked inside one of the standing lodges and found it empty, cleared of all belongings, as were the other two.

Dixon stood inside the final lodge, head back to the spangle of stars visible through the smoke hole. *What am I doing here?* he asked himself. *Why did I come?* Billy told him the village might be abandoned. *What do I do now — search the woods?* He exited the lodge, feeling like an idiot, with an inflated notion of his own importance. Rose used to tease him about his tendency toward self-righteousness, calling him the "Great White Healer."

Alice bumped him with her nose. "All right," he said, "I know what you want." He removed her saddle and blanket and she dropped to her knees, then rolled onto her back and wriggled in the dirt, waving her legs like a happy puppy.

Despite the wind, he got the tent up quickly and spread his bedroll over a mattress of green pine boughs. He got a fire going, but instead of cheering him it only made the tall, dark trees surrounding the abandoned village seem to close in. He sat before the flames, chewing elk jerky and, again, cursed himself for a fool. If he'd gone back to Buffalo with the twins and Billy, he could be sitting in his warm parlor right now, drinking a whiskey before enjoying a hot bath.

Alice stayed nearby, cropping grass where she could find it. There was little forage because the forest floor was covered with a thick carpet of brown pine needles. Occasionally she would stop, lift her head, and sniff the air. Her ears were rabbity, moving in all directions. Ordinarily, Dixon would hobble her with ankle ropes, but tonight he didn't think he'd have to. The mare, though perhaps a bit edgy, showed no signs of wanting to roam.

As he stood to enter the tent for the night, Alice's ears suddenly flattened and she raised a rear leg as if to kick. Like the horse, Dixon sniffed the air. There was an odd smell, a musty animal odor, combined with a corrupt sweetness, like rotting flowers.

He and Alice stood frozen, waiting for something to appear. There was no sound of approaching footsteps, human or animal, only the crackling of the fire and the wind whispering through the trees. Dixon felt a tingling in every nerve, as if he stood in the wind that runs before the storm.

But then, quickly as it came, the odor was gone and his sense of anticipation melted away. Alice lowered her head and went back to cropping grass, and Dixon, no longer sleepy, returned to his seat at the fire. Was something out there in the darkness, or had he let his imagination get the better of him? He shook his head, fished his fixings out of his kit, and rolled a cigarette. *I must be more tired than I thought.* He sat for another hour, smoked another cigarette, and crawled into the tent. When he stretched out on his blankets, the boughs beneath released a pleasant, piney scent. He fell at once into a dreamless sleep.

He woke with a pounding heart and the sound of blood roaring in his ears. It was still dark. What woke him? Had he been dreaming? He sat up in his blankets and took a deep breath to steady his nerves. There it was again, the musty smell of animals and dead flowers, stronger than before.

He crawled to the flap and threw it open. The fire was reduced to an orange mound of embers. Gradually, he became aware of a faint light on the far side of the camp, coming from inside one of the lodges. Dixon rubbed his eyes, mistrusting what they showed him. It must have been a firefly, he thought, or maybe a floating ember. But, no, it was not an illusion. Something glowed inside the tepee. The light flickered, like a campfire, and then grew stronger as he watched until the entire lodge was gleaming like a Japanese lantern.

Dixon stepped out of the tent and looked for Alice. She was close by, still as a statue, also eyeing the glowing lodge. This was a strange business. He had checked each one and found them all empty. Could someone have returned to the village while he was sleeping? There was no other explanation.

The night air was very cold. He returned to the tent for his gun and his coat, buttoning it as he walked toward the lodge. Dixon felt a sense of dread that grew stronger with each step. Who — or what — would he find in there? When he reached the door he paused. There was a sound within, a soft moaning, like a chant. It stopped.

"Come in, Dixon." It was a woman's voice, not identifiable but still somehow familiar. "I've been waiting for you."

He could think of but one woman who addressed him by his surname only. Dixon stooped to open the low flap and entered. An old Indian woman sat alone before a fire, wrapped in a red wool blanket. The animal smell was overpowering.

"Biwi?" he said. "My God, is that you? I looked in here earlier . . . well, I'm glad to see you. I saw Billy Sun on the road this morning and he told me you were ill. He said there was sickness in the village and you were among the afflicted. I've come to see if I can help."

She motioned to a spot beside the fire and Dixon sat cross-legged on the ground. He felt peculiar and cotton-headed. Was he dreaming? He remembered a broken button, made of bone, in his coat pocket and felt for it with his ungloved hand, pressing the sharp end into the fleshy part of his left thumb. He felt pain. He was not dreaming.

He studied the old woman's face through the fire's smoke. Her visage was not a happy one. It was Biwi, though her features were not quite as he remembered. The nose was longer and the mouth wider. The last time he saw her she had been a stout, powerful woman, but now her skin hung in loose folds, as if she had not eaten for a very long time. Well, he thought, perhaps she hadn't. The village had fallen on hard times. But there was no denying the strangeness of her eyes, which appeared sunken, not as he had often seen in patients with fatigue or dehydration, but the orbs themselves had settled within the lids. He had seen this, too, many times, but only in those who were dead or dying.

"I am glad you have come, Dixon," she said. "I'm glad you heard my call." Her voice was muffled, as if coming from a great distance.

"Your call?" he said. "I don't know what you mean. As I said, I saw Billy Sun on the Bozeman road. He said there was sickness, I thought maybe it was influenza, I thought I might be able to help. Where have the people gone?"

Biwi rocked from side to side, eyes closed.

She seemed not to be listening. "You and your family are in danger. Billy, too, Billy Sun most of all."

Dixon felt a cold wind on the back of his neck, as if someone had entered the tepee. He turned, but there was nothing. Once again he pressed the bone shard deep into his thumb.

"It's the child," she said, "one I fed from my own breast. I saw at once, I thought I could turn the angry spirit toward the light, but no. It hurts me to say it, for I loved the child. I loved them both, but I failed. You must take care. You must send the child away."

"What are you talking about?" Dixon said. "Lorna is headstrong, I grant you, but she's never done any harm, certainly not me or anyone in my family. She would never hurt Billy — I promise you that."

"You must do as I say, for your sake and the sake of your household. For Billy."

Dixon got to his feet. He was angry and impatient with this old woman and the strange smell was making him nauseous. He wished he had never come to this miserable place. "I won't listen to this nonsense," he said. "It's cruel. Lorna loved you like a mother and this is how you repay her affection? I don't understand any of this" — he waved his hand to include the lodge and abandoned village — "and I don't understand the ignorant, primitive superstition that makes you turn on her. In the morning we can talk about your people, where they've gone and whether there's anything I can do. But now, I'm going back to my tent to get some sleep. Good night!"

Biwi called after him. "Be careful, Dixon. The child's heart is black as the raven's wing."

With a shake of his head, Dixon walked to the door. Before leaving, he turned to the old Indian woman. She was huddled over with the blanket pulled over her head, obscuring her features. He threw open the flap and stepped out into the cold night, grateful to be breathing clean air again, and covered the ground with long, angry strides. Before entering his tent, he glanced at Biwi's lodge. It was dark.

When Dixon woke the sun was fully risen and shining brightly. He rarely slept past dawn. He sat up and rubbed his eyes. His head ached and he felt vaguely ill, as if he had drunk too much whiskey the night before. A few seconds passed before he recalled the glowing lodge and his interview with Biwi. He shook his head, trying to clear the fog. Had it really happened, or was it just the wandering of an overtired, perhaps fevered, mind?

He stepped outside the tent, shielding his eyes against the glare. When they adjusted, he could not believe what they showed him. There had been a storm, a violent wind, during the night, though he had heard nothing. Branches were strewn about the deserted camp and the tepee where he had met with Biwi was partially dismantled and listing to one side. Clearly, it was not inhabited.

He ran his hand through his hair, searching for a lump or some evidence of a blow to the head, perhaps from a falling branch. He found nothing to account for the weird memories — if that's what they were — or his confusion. Sniffing the air, he detected no trace of the strange scent he remembered. The air was sweet and fresh. *It must've been something I ate. Maybe the jerky.*

Anxious to be away, Dixon returned to his tent and started rolling his blankets. Only then did he notice the dried blood on his left hand. He stopped rolling and rocked back on his heels. There was a deep, fresh cut on the fleshy part of his thumb.

ODALIE

Billy Sun had no trouble finding work in Johnson County, thanks to a stroke of good fortune that came his way one warm spring afternoon, several weeks after his arrival. It was late afternoon and he was returning from town, on an errand for Mrs. MacGill. He was riding the high road above a wide green valley when he saw a buggy leaving a large, frame house on the bend of a pretty stream. The house, he knew, belonged to Moreton Dudley, the wealthy, British-born owner of the EK outfit. Billy watched the driver climb down to raise the crossbar blocking the lane. He led the team, two well-matched harness horses with glossy black coats and high, straight shoulders, through the gate and turned to replace the bar. As he did, the horses started forward at a walk. Disaster could have been averted had the passenger, a woman in a cream-colored dress and wide-brimmed hat, taken up the reins, but she made no attempt to do so. Billy heard the man shout for the pair to stop, but instead they quickened to a trot. The driver started running after the two-wheeled buggy, still yelling at the horses, who only went faster. When the woman screamed, they broke into a full-out run, with the buggy careening along behind.

Billy kicked Sugarfoot into a gallop, abandoning the road and heading straight down the steep, rocky hill toward the run-away buggy. The matched pair was fast, but Sugarfoot was faster, and he had nothing to pull. Billy gained ground quickly, but now the buggy was out of control, swinging from one side of the road to the other. Billy feared it would overturn and crush its occupant before he could reach her. The woman clung for dear life, losing her seat as the buggy bounced violently and tipped onto one wheel. Billy saw her cower on the floor, clutching the upholstered seat cushion, though her face brightened when she caught sight of him, riding hard to overtake the panicked team. Sugarfoot surged forward in response to Billy's urging, finally drawing even with the team. He leaned over and grabbed hold of the right horse's noseband, using all his strength to turn the animal's head as Sugarfoot planted his feet and dug in as he would when holding a steer. Luckily, the harness horses were exhausted and out of fight. They dragged Sugarfoot a short distance but then stopped, lathered and breathing hard, and lowered their heads.

Billy jumped out of the saddle and ran to the buggy to help the woman down. She was shaking and tearful.

"Oh, thank you," she said, holding him by the arm. "Thank you. I truly thought I was about to die, and well I might have if not for you. You saved my life and I am entirely, infinitely grateful. What is your name?"

She was tall and very pretty with a lovely shape, which her fitted dress made no attempt to disguise. She spoke in the Southern way that Billy recognized, because of Dr. Dixon's Kentucky heritage and because most of the range riders who worked the cattle came from Texas. Still, this woman's voice was different, lilting and musical and, to his ears, altogether charming, as was the woman herself. Her fair hair had pulled free of the silvery net that bound it at the nape of her neck, and shining locks hung in disarray about her face. But most striking of all her eyes, which were large and blue and somehow like Rose's, though he could not say how they were the same.

She was looking at him with a question in her eyes, and he realized she was waiting for an answer.

"I'm sorry," he said, feeling his face go hot. "Would you say again?"

She smiled, apparently accustomed to her effect on men. "I said, what is your name?"

"Billy Sun."

"Billy Sun. Thank you for saving my life, Billy Sun." Her tears had dried, but she was sniffling. He offered his handkerchief and said, "It's clean."

"Thank you." She accepted the red bandanna and wiped her nose. "I'll launder this and return it to you, Mr. Sun. Where —"

At this point her male companion reached them, red faced and panting. He took her gloved hands without a glance at Billy. "My God, Lady Faucett, are you all right? I am sorry, I am prostrate — I cannot think what made the horses take off like that! They've never done it before." The man spoke with a British accent, a thing Billy had never heard before moving to Wyoming Territory.

"It's all right, Fred. I'm fine," she said, "thanks to Mr. Sun here." She touched him lightly on the arm. "I was asking him where he lives. I'm sure Richard would like to recognize Mr. Sun's heroics in some manner."

For the first time, the man, Fred, turned his eyes on Billy. "Would that be Billy Sun?"

Billy nodded.

"Yes, I've heard of you. They say you're very skilled at breaking horses."

Billy said, "If you understand an animal there is no need to break his spirit. There are other ways to let him know what you want."

"Is that so?" Fred said. "Well, I suppose that's the Indian way of looking at it."

Odalie Faucett clasped her gloved hands. "Why, what perfect timing! Richard has just acquired a string of wild horses, and his man, Ringo, is having no luck. Richard could use someone with your talents, Mr. Sun. Are you available to come work for us?"

Billy could not believe his luck. Since coming to Wyoming he'd been living with the Dixon family, helping all he could, but the doctor had little work for him. "Yes, Lady Faucett," he said, addressing her as Fred had done. "I am available. Very much available."

"Oh good. That's settled then." She laughed and Billy thought of a mountain stream rippling over smooth pebbles.

Fred cleared his throat and turned to her, giving Billy his back. "Odalie — that is,

Lady Faucett — perhaps you had better check with your husband before making such an offer." He lowered his voice but Billy heard him clearly. "Consider, too, Ringo might not like it."

"Rubbish! Richard respects my opinion in all matters, and as for Albertus Ringo," she waved her hand dismissively, "who cares what he likes? Come by the house tomorrow, won't you, Mr. Sun? Do you know where it is?"

"South of town," Billy said, "near the confluence of the three forks. The place they call The Manor."

She smiled, showing dimples in both cheeks and small white teeth. "Yes, that's us. We'll look for you around five o'clock then, if that suits?"

Billy nodded. "It suits."

"Well, then, that's that." She offered her arm to Fred, who helped her back into the buggy. Billy walked to the right-side horse and held his headstall as Fred took the reins and climbed in after her. "Thank you, Sun," he said curtly, "but I've got things under control here. Your assistance is no longer necessary. Good day to you."

He slapped the reins against the horses' backs, and the buggy started with a jolt. Odalie turned and waved. "Good-bye, Billy

Sun. Until tomorrow!"

Billy waved back, though he thought this white-person custom silly and had never done it before. He swung into the saddle and watched the buggy grow small in the red dusk.

"What do you think?" he said, leaning forward to stroke Sugarfoot's neck. "Do you like her? Yes, so do I."

BILLY SUN

Billy arrived at The Manor the next day at exactly five o'clock wearing a clean white shirt and store-bought pants so stiff they rubbed raw places on his knees and between his thighs. The fabric of one leg brushed against the other as he walked, sounding like a wooden block going up and down a washboard. Two cowboys cleaning their tack in front of the bunkhouse stopped to watch — and listen — as Billy looped Sugarfoot's reins loosely around the rail and approached the big house. They grinned at each other as he climbed the porch steps, his boots loud on the green-painted floorboards, and lifted the knocker, a shining brass ring through the mouth of a lion. A full minute passed before an Indian woman in a calico dress and apron opened the double doors of heavy, imported oak.

She did not greet him but looked him over from head to toe. Billy smiled, surprised to see a fellow Indian in this fine place, but the woman did not smile back. He removed his hat and raised a hand to smooth his pomaded hair, neatly parted just left of center.

"Billy Sun to see Mr. and Mrs. Faucett," he said.

The corners of the Indian's woman mouth turned down. "Lord and Lady Faucett expect you?"

"They do. I was invited by Mrs. — by Lady Faucett."

"You wait." She closed the door in his face.

Billy stood for another four minutes, hat in hand, eye to eye with the brass lion and starting to hate the thing. Once he turned to look at the two grinning cowboys, suspecting their good humor was at his expense. Billy shifted his weight from foot to foot, turning his hat, wondering if he had been forgotten. He was about to knock again when the door opened and, instead of the Indian woman, or Lady Faucett, he found himself looking at Fred Jolly, the buggy driver from the previous afternoon. The Englishman appeared as disappointed to see Billy as Billy was to see him.

"Follow me to the bunkhouse," Fred said, brushing by him and descending the steps.

"I'll show you your quarters. You're a fortunate fellow, Sun. I was done with roundup hiring, I had no intention of adding another man."

Billy turned back to the house. "That's it? I'm hired? I thought I was supposed to meet with Lady Faucett and her husband."

Jolly shook his head. "She spoke to his Lordship for you, that's all you need to know. Your business is with me now, Sun. Lord Faucett has instructed me to offer you a position. In addition to the horse work, he insisted on giving you a place in the spring roundup. Your wages will be the same as the others' — that amount, plus seven dollars for each horse you break — or whatever you Indians call it."

Any disappointment Billy felt evaporated. Seven bones a head? He couldn't believe his ears. The going rate was five and often less.

As they neared the squat, unpainted frame bunkhouse, the two cowboys stopped oiling their tack. Jolly greeted them with a brisk nod of his head. "Nate, Jack, this is a new man, Billy Sun. I am your foreman, Jack Reshaw is your wagon boss." A stocky young man in his mid-twenties stepped forward and offered his hand. He had clear, blue-gray eyes, a steely grip, and a friendly smile.

"Good to have you, Billy," Jack said. "I hear good things."

"And this," Jolly indicated the second man, "is Nate Coday. He'll show you where to put your gear. Good luck to you, Sun." Before leaving the yard, Jolly stopped and turned back. "Work hard and stay out of trouble." His eyes cut to Coday. "Don't make Lady Faucett sorry she spoke for you."

Coday made an obscene gesture to Jolly's back, then offered Billy his hand. Coday was taller than Reshaw and a bit younger, but with an equally strong handshake. "Lady Odalie herself spoke up for you?" he said with a low whistle. "How the hell does a red Injun like you manage a thing like that?"

Billy pulled free his hand.

"Leave him be, Nate," Reshaw said. "Sun has special talents, or so I hear. I suspect he'll earn his pay. Come on inside, Billy. I'll show you where to put your gear." Reshaw looked over Billy's shoulder. "Where is it?"

Billy gestured toward Sugarfoot, standing patiently at the rail. All his professional belongings — spurs, quirt, lariat, and the short bits of grass ropes he used for hobbling — were in his bedroll and saddlebags.

"That's it?" Reshaw raised his eyebrows.

"Most of it. I got clothes back at the

136

Dixon place but nothing that won't fit in a suitcase."

Reshaw said, "Before you go for those, come on down to the corral. Me and Nate cut a horse out for you. We want to see what you got before the boys get back."

"You want me to finish a horse right now?" He looked down at his stiff new pants.

"Why not?" Reshaw said. "We got a gelding yonder." He nodded his head toward the round, pole corral where a single horse nosed one of his companions in the neighboring enclosure. He was big for a wild horse, at least fifteen hands, the product of interbreeding between Spanish mustangs and stray U.S. Cavalry animals, with thick, muscular shoulders and hindquarters. He was a bay, with a white star and coronets on three legs. He looked like he had plenty of fight.

Billy shrugged. "I'll need a blanket and a working saddle."

"We got those."

Billy cursed himself as he retrieved his gear from his saddlebags. He should have expected this. Now he'd have to finish a horse in pants that felt like they were made of iron. This would interfere with his use of his legs, his ability to feel the animal beneath him.

The bay eyed him warily as he entered the corral, then started trotting around its circumference, breaking into a run as Billy took the coil of rope from his shoulder. Reshaw and Coday perched on a rail, watching Billy rope the gelding around the neck on the first throw and snub him to a post in the middle of the corral. The bay's eyes showed some white, and Billy talked to him in a low voice, hoping he wouldn't have to throw him to get a bridle on. If he could get close, Billy would try to introduce himself by breathing in the horse's nose, getting him familiar with his scent, but Billy doubted the bay was going to cooperate.

But he surprised him. Though he pulled back and braced his feet as Billy came near, the wild horse was unprepared for the strangling effect of a snubbing lariat and didn't fight the bridle. For the same reason, Billy was able to cross-hobble him with the soft grass ropes. If he'd had more time, Billy would have tied an old pair of pants around the horse's belly, giving him a chance to get used to the sensation before he threw on a saddle, but that wouldn't happen today. The bay's eyes rolled when Billy came at him with the blanket and saddle, but he remained straight-legged and stiff when Billy threw them on and tightened the cinch. It wasn't until Billy freed him from the snubbing post that the bay showed what he was holding. Despite the hobbles, he fought like a tiger, hopping around the corral and dragging Billy like he was one of Lorna's rag dolls. Billy was vaguely aware of hoots and hollers coming from the pole bench where Reshaw and Coday had been joined by a third man, but he didn't take his eyes off the horse for an instant. The furious bay pulled Billy around for the better part of an hour when he suddenly stopped and hung his head, seemingly spent.

Billy approached him cautiously, sensing the animal still had some left. "What's this?" Billy smiled, his teeth white in his dirty face. "You think you can trick me?" The horse watched him with an eye that was wary but still bright. Billy reached out and grabbed the bronc's ear, giving it a hard twist. This distracted him long enough for Billy to swing aboard.

This was Billy's favorite part of horse work; it was an art form, as much as quillwork or beading or a white man's picturemaking with paint and brush. One of the secrets to keeping your seat came in knowing how much rein to give; too little and you go over the head, too much and you come off the other end. Billy liked to start off with the reins two fists' distance from the front of the saddle.

He'd learned to keep his feet high, so the stirrups were at or above the horse's shoulders, so when the bronc came down on his front legs, with his rear legs up high in the air, Billy was almost standing. He used his spurs and his quirt when he had to, because it was necessary to teach the animal that bucking and spinning would bring pain, but Billy took no joy in hurting a horse and seldom drew blood. Keep your seat in the saddle, your hips moving in time with the animal between your legs, and let him know you're not fooling and you're not going anywhere. In a way, Billy thought, gentling a horse was sort of like being with a woman. Certainly, there was beauty in both, beauty and feeling. It was a thing a person was born to. You could teach a boy to ride, but you could not teach him how to find the beauty and joy in it. You either felt it or you didn't.

Finally the bay had truly had enough. He came to a shuddering stop and hung his head, breathing hard. Billy always felt a breath of sadness when this moment came. The horse was defeated and he knew it. His days of roaming the rangeland, running free and unencumbered with the wind at his back, were over. Billy leaned forward and stroked the bay's sweating neck.

Other cowboys had returned while Billy was fighting the horse, and by the time it was over a crowd had gathered around the corral. One man took the bay's reins and led him to the enclosure that held the *remuda*. Coday and Reshaw came to Billy in the center of the ring.

"Welcome, Billy Sun," Coday said, slapping Billy's shoulder. "I picked that bay 'cause he looked the meanest, and you broke him in no time. Hell, you made it look easy."

"It's never easy." Billy wiped his cracked lips with the back of his hand. His mouth tasted of dirt, and his new clothes were filthy.

"That was good work." This was the third man, the one who'd first joined Nate and Jack on the rail. "How'd you learn to ride like that?"

"I just did." Billy disliked the question, one he heard often. Usually the person asking it seemed to think horsemanship was a talent that came with Indian blood.

The fellow smiled and offered his hand. "Tom Waggoner," he said with a thick German accent. He appeared to be about thirty, older than Nate and Jack, with long, greasy hair hanging below his hat and a dark complexion. Billy didn't like the look of him. His eyes were flat and lifeless, like black buttons, and his hands were sweaty. Billy resisted the impulse to wipe his palm on his pants leg after they shook.

"You take contract work, Billy Sun? I got me some mustangs need breaking. I'll pay five dollars a head." Behind Waggoner, Jack Reshaw was shaking his head.

"I've got all the work here I can handle," Billy said. "But thanks for the offer."

Waggoner smiled and half turned his head, as if he suspected Reshaw's silent signal. "Suit yourself," he said. "But let me know when things change — and they will."

DIXON

Though weeks had passed, Dixon had been unable to put the experience at the Crow village out of his mind. The old woman was Biwi, but she had not looked as he remembered and her voice had been different, too. And though he didn't think of it at the time, it was odd that she had spoken to him in English. When he knew her, she had no language other than Crow and relied on Billy to translate. She could have learned English in the years since last he saw her, though he thought this unlikely.

It would be easier to put the episode aside if not for her warning. Lorna was unusual, unlike any child he had ever known and certainly nothing like her brothers. Of the three, Dixon was closest to Harry, and he had been very pleased when his older son announced he wanted a career in medicine. Already, Dixon was writing the necessary letters, laying the groundwork for a training position in the East, either Philadelphia or Cincinnati where Dixon had attended medical school. Bookish and curious, Harry's personality was suited to a life of intellectual inquiry and a home in the city. Dixon had been aware of this for some time. Caleb was a quiet boy, small for his age and so retiring his father felt he hardly knew him. His sister dwarfed him, and had done since they shared the womb. Though both were small at birth, born weeks before their time, Lorna was healthier and stronger, her color more vibrant and her cries more lusty. It was as if she had overpowered Cal since conception and taken the lion's share of placental nutrients for herself. Dixon had been struck by this from the first moment he saw them. Though crushed by Rose's death, and — to his shame — repelled by the infants who took her from him, his detached, medically trained brain could not fail to notice the difference in the two newborns. Indeed, he initially doubted the boy would survive. That he did was due solely to Biwi.

Indeed, Lorna eclipsed both her brothers in strength of personality. Despite her youth, she dominated a room the instant she entered, even without speaking a word. With her white-blond hair, olive skin, and

144

pale, penetrating eyes, she was lovely to look at and elegant beyond her years in her movements. Harry and Cal adored her, and she them, though there was never any doubt who held the whip hand. Only one man commanded her respect and admiration, and that man was Billy Sun. The Indian boy had intrigued her since she was just a toddler, and this fascination had only deepened as she grew. Dixon had thought it merely a girlish infatuation, and Billy himself appeared indifferent, treating her as he would any other child.

Could Lorna be capable of harming Billy, or anyone? Dixon did not believe it, but try as he might, he could not dismiss Biwi's spectral warning. Even if he had been dreaming, which he doubted, her words had had an impact. They forced him to confront a reality he wanted to avoid. His children, the twins especially, needed more from him. Despite his proclamation that he feared no one, Cal showed signs of effeminacy. He needed a father's love and guidance, and Dixon resolved to give it to him. He had been a poor parent, and he was ashamed. If nothing else came of his ill-fated visit to the Crow village, his investment in his children would change.

It was a warm spring evening and Dixon,

returning to Buffalo from Fort McKinney, had been riding for more than an hour, lost in thought. Unnoticed by him, daylight had been replaced by a red twilight. He saw the lights of Buffalo twinkling in the distance. Again, his heart swelled with love for this beautiful country. No place in America matched Wyoming Territory for the purity of its air, the spaciousness of its skies, its natural majesty. He was fortunate to live here, fortunate to be raising three healthy children in such an unspoiled place, a land wrested with much violence from the Indians who loved it, too. Dixon raised his eyes to the fiery sky.

"Rose, I've been absent since you went, as if I left this world when you did. I've been self-indulgent in my loneliness and neglected our children." Alice turned her head at the sound of his voice. The horse knew her rider's habits, and it was unlike him to speak when they were alone. "This will change. The children need a woman in their lives — not a mother, only you will ever be that, but a softening, female presence. I must find another wife. Whoever she is, she will never replace you in my heart, but she must be worthy of love, or the purpose is defeated. Please understand, Rose. I believe you do."

He urged Alice forward, toward home. He had not felt desire for a woman since Rose died, that is, not until very recently. Odalie Faucett could not be his, but he wanted her, and that, in itself, was cause for hope. Maybe he wasn't dead yet after all.

BILLY SUN

"You looked stupid," Lorna said. They were in Billy's room, a small, windowless lean-to off the kitchen. It was dark, lit only by the coal oil lamp on the Star Crackers box he used as a nightstand. He neatly folded his clothes, including the dirty new ones, and stacked them in a cardboard case. "I can't believe Lord Faucett hired you — you looked like a nester in those clothes, an East Coast jake just off the train." She forced a laugh. "It was funny, that's what it was."

Billy kept his eyes on his packing.

"Didn't he look like a jake, Cal?" Lorna nudged her brother, silent at her side. "Didn't he just?"

"I guess," Cal said glumly. "Do you have to go, Billy? I thought you were going to stay with us. Don't you want to anymore?"

Billy put a hand on Cal's shoulder. "It's not about wanting, Cal. Your pa doesn't have enough work for me. Faucett has horses, and that's what I'm good at. Not only that, but he gave me a place in the roundup. I can make real money, put some aside to get my own place."

Lorna made a sound of disgust and folded her arms across her chest. She fought back tears. "You'll never have a ranch, Billy," she said. "They'll never let you run your own cattle. Don't you know that? Them big augers won't let anyone else raise cattle in Powder River country — and an Indian to boot! You're just fooling yourself if you think that's ever going to happen."

Billy wasn't going to argue with her. Lorna would never let anyone else win an argument. Not for the first time, he thought how unlike her mother she was. Though Lorna would be a beauty, like Rose, she had none of her mother's softer, more womanly traits. While Rose had been generous, sensitive to the needs of others, Lorna cared for no one but herself. When she grew to be a woman, she would give the man who loved her a world of trouble.

Billy knew she had feelings for him, he had always known, but he was not the low kind of man who would take advantage of a girl's amorous yearnings. The truth was that even if they were closer in age, Lorna would never be a woman he wanted. Kindness was important in a woman, as important as beauty, and Lorna would never be kind.

"It's because of her, isn't it?" Lorna said, her voice rising in anger. "Lady Faucett. She's the real reason you're going, isn't she? Oh, I see her around town, with her curled hair and fancy clothes, queening it in Raylan's Dry Goods like some sort of royalty, looking down her nose at the rest of us."

Billy said quietly, "That's not how she is."

Lorna stamped her foot. "Odalie Faucett is never going to look at you and you're never going to own your own ranch. Never! You're being an awful fool and everyone sees it. Everyone's laughing at you!"

Billy snapped the case shut. Odalie Faucett was one of the Bar C's attractions, but not the primary one. This was the best chance he would ever have to make something of himself. As for Odalie, he had no aspirations there — he wasn't a fool, despite what Lorna said — but he enjoyed looking at a beautiful woman. What man didn't? He lifted the case off the bed and turned to Cal, avoiding Lorna's eyes.

"Take care of yourself," he said, offering his hand. "And keep an eye on your sister. Maybe next Sunday I'll come for you, take you to the Bar C so you can help me with the horses. How does that sound?"

Call nodded, eyes on the floor. "Good."

Billy leaned down to whisper in the boy's ear. "Don't let her push you around. You're good as she is, don't forget that."

Cal nodded again and wiped his nose with the back of his hand as his father entered the room. Lorna stomped out and Cal followed his sister.

"So it's true," Dixon said. "You're leaving us for the Bar C?"

"Lord Faucett offered me work and a spot in the roundup. It's good money. I couldn't turn it down."

"No, of course not. You should go. I could never give you that kind of opportunity."

"I thank you for the work you have given me all these years and for setting me up with Nelson Story up north. Not everyone would do what you did for an Indian. I learned a lot from him, and from you, too."

Dixon put his hand on Billy's shoulder. "You don't need to thank me. You were — are — like a member of the family. Is Sugarfoot saddled?"

Billy nodded.

"I'll walk out with you."

They passed through the kitchen, where Mrs. MacGill was rolling biscuits. She insisted he sit down for a glass of buttermilk before leaving. When he stood to go, she

151

embraced him, leaving flour handprints on the back of his shirt. "Good-bye, laddie," she said. "Dinnae be a stranger now."

It was fully dark when they stepped outside, though the spring air was still warm. Sugarfoot raised his head and nickered as they approached.

"I feel we've come to the end of something," Dixon said. "We'll all miss you, Billy."

Billy smiled. "It's not like I'm moving to Missouri, sir. I'll be around."

"I know." Dixon looked toward the craggy mountains, and Billy sensed there was more the doctor wanted to say. "I never got a chance to talk to you about what happened in the village."

"You said it was empty. No one was there."

Dixon nodded. "Yes, I did say that, but someone was there. Biwi, your aunt. Only her, not another soul. We spoke . . . it was very odd. That is, she seemed to think we — all of us, my family and you, too — were in some sort of danger . . ." He could not bring himself to say from whom.

Billy frowned. "You saw Biwi in the village and she spoke to you?"

"Yes. As I said, she was alone; the whole thing was very peculiar. She spoke to me in English. She must have learned it quickly."

Billy shook his head. "Doctor, that cannot be. Biwi died the morning I found Cal and Lorna near the old soldier fort. I didn't say it then, because I didn't want the twins to know, but I wrapped her body myself. I carried her to the wagon."

"This makes no sense." Dixon looked at his thumb, where a scar remained. He remembered the glowing lodge, the powerful animal smell. "Then who was in the lodge with me? Who was I talking to?"

Billy smiled. "Visitors from the world behind this one sometimes appear to us. I have never experienced this myself, but I have known those who have and I do not question the truth of it. I believe such a visitor came to you. You have been given a gift. Honor it, Doctor. This is my advice to you."

ODALIE

Frank Canton chose not to seek a third term as Johnson County sheriff in the fall of 1886. Though he claimed to be on the fence about running, and confident of another victory, most people did not believe he could win re-election. He barely scraped out a victory in 1884, and he had lost popular support during those two years. There was a growing sense he and his deputies were no longer a good fit with the people of Buffalo, now a community of some one thousand souls. No one questioned Canton's skills or commitment as a lawman, but, more and more, he was seen to be overly impressed with his own importance. Worse, his deputies had acquired a reputation for ruthlessness. One of these, Chris Gross, a large, oafish Swede, mistreated a prominent citizen who fired off a letter to the local newspaper, the *Big Horn Sentinel,* complaining about the "unwonted zeal of that most enthusiastic officer." Later, Gross shot an accused horse thief in the head, killing him without benefit of trial. The death was widely regarded as unnecessary.

"Yes, I believe it's time to let someone else shoulder the load for a while," Canton said to Dixon one evening over glasses of beer at the Occidental Hotel restaurant and saloon. The two were not friends, but they had run into each other in town and Canton extended the invitation. Dixon accepted reluctantly. He had not been able to shake off his suspicions about the sheriff, suspicions that had only grown since the seeds were planted that cold winter night in Doriselaine Schmidt's barn. The image of the young widow stroking her dead husband's hair haunted him still, along with her words: *You've got a lot to learn about how things work in Powder River country.*

"It's not that I don't enjoy the work," Canton said. "I do, but I'm a married man now, with a child, and I believe I can do better for my family, financially speaking, in another line. In fact," he paused and leaned closer to Dixon, "I've already got something lined up. I'll be working again as a range detective for the WSGA, riding the entire Big Horn Basin." He dropped his voice to a

155

whisper, so low Dixon could barely hear him in the noisy room. "I'll be getting twenty-five hundred a year, plus expenses."

"That's a lot of money," Dixon said. "A lot of country, too."

Canton nodded with obvious pride and settled back in his chair. "All of Johnson and Crook counties, plus parts of five others, a bigger area than some Eastern states. Yes, Dixon, it's a big responsibility, but the organization will give me plenty of latitude to do the job as I see fit."

He looked down at the glass in his hand. "Still, I've got to say it was hard to give up sheriffing. Like I said, I'm sure I'd be reelected, and I gave another term serious thought, but the job can make a man crazy. The damn rustlers run hog wild, and when you try to do your job they cut you off at the knees. That Holmberg business stuck in my craw." On that occasion, Canton had traveled all the way to Kansas to bring accused horse thief H.H. Holmberg to justice, only to see him released without charge. "And One-Eyed Tex Cherpolloid — I had that cockeyed son of a bitch dead to rights, and even there I couldn't make the charges stick. Public indecency and a damn ten-dollar fine — that's all I could get on the bastard. I tell you, Dixon, I get hot just thinking about it. I can't get an honest jury, nothing but a bunch of lily-livered nesters who wouldn't indict Judas Iscariot." He shook his head and raised the glass to his lips. "How many men do you reckon I've sent to prison for livestock theft in my four years as sheriff?"

"I have no idea."

"Go ahead, take a guess."

"I don't know," Dixon said. "Forty?"

Canton nodded. "Should be that many. Hell, should be twice that. No, Dixon, I worked my butt off for four years to put eighteen rustlers behind bars. Eighteen. The job's a pitiful waste of a man's time. Pitiful."

"I'm surprised," Dixon said. There was plenty of thievery in Johnson County, everyone knew that, and whatever his other faults, Canton was not lazy. "Why would a jury not convict a man who is obviously guilty?"

Canton laughed. "Hell, Dixon, you know the answer to that well as I do. Those dirt-eaters on the jury don't shed any tears when Lord Richard Faucett or one of his sort lose a few horses or a dozen head of cattle. They're happy when the no-good trash gets away with it, and by no-good trash I mean fellows like Nate Coday and Jack Reshaw, those boys your man Bill Sun threw in with." Canton balled his fist and pounded the table, drawing looks from their fellow drinkers. "That Reshaw is a goddamn troublemaker. I hear he just bought himself the Lazy L and B from old man Hathaway over on the Red Fork. Bought the ranch and a dozen head of worn-out emigrant cattle. You hear about that?"

Dixon nodded. All of Buffalo was buzzing about Jack Reshaw's bold move and waiting to see what the ranchers were going to do about it. It would be messy, of that Dixon had no doubt. Reshaw had already drawn the ire of the WSGA as one of the leaders of a cowboy strike just before spring roundup. The trouble started when the men learned some of their colleagues were working for as little as thirty dollars a month. They refused to ride unless the bosses agreed to pay everyone no less than forty. "There's no justice in this," Reshaw told a gathering of cowboys and foremen. "We are brothers in this work. When you cheat my brother, you cheat me!" Eventually the cowboys prevailed, though Reshaw paid a heavy price for the victory. After the roundup, the association passed the word around that Jack Reshaw would never ride for a Wyoming outfit again.

In buying the Lazy L and B, Reshaw was sticking his finger in the WSGA's eye again. The association's members would not tolerate small homesteaders or ranching operations on land they perceived as theirs, and this was especially true if the aspiring stockman used to cowboy for them. Indeed, they vowed to blackball any puncher who started his own brand, saying it would increase thievery. Reshaw's latest act of defiance had drawn widespread attention, and everyone had taken a side.

Association members knew they would have to tread carefully. Reshaw, the son of a prominent Charleston, Virginia, planter was confident, well-educated, and a leader not only among the cowboys but in the community as a whole. Any injustice done to him would fan the flames of discord.

The controversy added to an aura of foreboding in the air that fall, beyond the usual tension between the stockmen and cowboys. Dixon felt it in his trips to town and in his conversations with patients, a sense that a hard winter was coming, bearing down on Powder River country like a giant, crouching bear. The October wind had a bite, and the ponies were laying down an unusually thick coat of hair. Old-timers spoke of an early migration of birds.

"He's a hard one, Jack Reshaw, and crook to boot," Canton said, drawing Dixon from his thoughts. "If I were you I'd tell Sun to keep away from him and Coday before someone gets hurt. Your girl, Lorna, she'd take it mighty hard, I bet, if anything happened to that good-looking Indian boy." He winked and finished his drink.

Dixon was annoyed. "Billy doesn't work for me anymore. In fact, we hardly see him. And not that it's any of your business, Sheriff, but there's nothing going on between him and Lorna. She's known him all her life. He's like a brother."

Canton shrugged. "Maybe so, but I don't think that would make a difference, if it was up to her."

Dixon got to his feet, fighting an overpowering urge to punch Canton in his drink-flushed face. "You talk too much, Canton," he said, putting on his coat. "You should be more careful about what you say."

"Take your coat off and sit down, Doctor. Don't get your pants in a bunch. I didn't mean any disrespect. Lots of girls around here are sweet on Sun. Like I said, he's a good-looking boy and the best horseman in the Territory. Everybody says so."

"Good night, Frank." Dixon started for the door.

"Just tell him what I said, all right?" When Dixon did not stop, Canton raised his voice. "Tell Bill Sun to keep away from Jack Reshaw and Nate Coday. Tell him I said so — for his own good."

Dixon decided to stop by the small office he kept in Buffalo, a single room above Raylan's Dry Goods, before heading home. He kept hours in town only one day a week, Saturday, and often arrived to find he had let supplies of linen bandages, plasters, and other materials run low. Canton's words echoed in his head as he walked along the boardwalk, eyes down, lost in thought. Of course Lorna was infatuated with Billy, this had been true as long as Dixon could remember, but that's all it was, a girlish adoration that would pass when she found her first real boyfriend. When would that happen? She was almost sixteen years old; most girls her age had already had a boyfriend by now, hadn't they? A friend from school or a neighbor? But Lorna didn't seem interested in other young people her age, and neither did Cal for that matter. They seemed satisfied with each other's company, as they had when they were young and spoke that gibberish to each other. Did they still do that, when they were alone?

Dixon shook his head. If only Rose had lived . . .

He fished the key from his pocket as he climbed the stairs. As he inserted the key, he felt a pricking on the back of his neck. He turned to find a woman in a dark, hooded cape standing behind him.

"I followed you," she said. "I've been hoping to catch you alone."

There was no mistaking the voice. "Lady Faucett?"

"Please open the door, Dr. Dixon. Hurry, before someone sees me."

The landing was dark and he had trouble with the lock. Finally the tumbler turned and she swept by him as he pushed open the door. Dixon followed her inside. Other than the pale gray light from the lone window, the room was dark. Dixon heard her sigh as he walked to his desk and lit the coal oil lamp he kept there. As he replaced the glass chimney, Odalie flew across the room and pulled down the paper shade. She removed her hood but kept her back to him and did not speak. When at last she turned, he was alarmed by her appearance. Her face was pale and there were shadows below her eyes, half moons of purple.

"Are you ill?" he said. "Please, sit." He took her arm and guided her to a chair.

"Can I get you some water?"

She shook her head. "No, thank you. I'm sorry to ambush you like this, you must find it odd."

"Not at all. If there's something I can do, I'm happy to help."

Odalie looked down at her hands and pulled off her gloves. "This is difficult. I don't know how to begin."

"Take your time, Lady Faucett. Remember, I'm a physician, there's nothing I haven't heard."

She smiled at him with gratitude. "Please, call me Odalie. Yes, I'm sure it would be difficult to shock you." She took a deep breath, then exhaled. "I do have a problem, you see, and there is no one else I could turn to. No one I trust, at any rate."

She hesitated, twisting her gloves in her hands. Dixon suspected he knew what she wanted to tell him and thought he would make it easier.

"Are you with child?" he said.

"Yes." She responded immediately, clearly relieved to be unburdened of her secret. "How did you know?"

"It was just a guess." But in fact he had detected faint brown spots on her forehead, splotches on her otherwise creamy skin that had not been present when he saw her last.

These spots, known as chloasma, were a sure sign of pregnancy, though more common in women with darker skin. When she removed her gloves he had also noticed a distinct redness on the palms of her hands. This was another sign, though usually not seen until twelve weeks' gestation. "But why is this a problem, Odalie?" he said.

She got to her feet and began pacing. "Because my husband is an odious little man and I do not want his child. In fact, I have absolutely no desire to be a mother at all." She stopped and looked him directly in the eye, smiling slightly. "There, have I succeeded in shocking you?"

He returned her smile. "Well, I admit I'm a little surprised to hear your opinion of Lord Faucett. Having seen you together, I wouldn't have guessed it. It must make your marriage difficult."

"And that's all that surprises you?"

Dixon sensed he was entering a minefield. He had never met a woman like this one, and he was uncertain how to proceed. "I know some women feel . . ." he searched for the right word, "apprehensive about pregnancy. It's understandable and there's no shame in it. I've known many women who believe they don't want children, who fear childbirth, but when their baby comes they feel quite different."

She laughed shortly. "You disappoint me, Dr. Dixon. I do not fear childbirth, and I assure you I will not become a crooning idiot when I hold my new baby in my arms." She resumed pacing.

"May I ask why you dislike your husband so intensely? Does he mistreat you?"

"Would you consider boring someone to death mistreatment?"

"Without a doubt. In fact, it may be legal grounds for murder."

She laughed again, this time genuinely. "So we agree."

"Really, Odalie, why have you come to me? Do you want me to deliver the child? I'll be happy to do that, of course, though I can also recommend several local women who are capable."

She made a sound of impatience. "No, Dr. Dixon, I do not want your help delivering the child. I told you, I do not want it. I want you to help me. I cannot have this baby — I will not have it."

Dixon was hoping she would not ask this of him. Though he was sympathetic, motherhood was an overwhelming responsibility, and the burden of caring for a child — even a much wanted one — fell heavily on a woman, she asked of him something he could not do.

"Do I disgust you?" she said.

"No, that's not what I feel. I'm sorry you find yourself in this painful situation. I'd like to say I understand, though I realize only another woman can fully appreciate what you're going through. But I cannot do what you ask. I'm sorry."

Her blue eyes sparkled with anger. "Oh, I see. It would violate your sanctimonious, self-righteous principles? Is that it?"

"Something like that, I guess. The truth is I couldn't live with myself. I already find that hard enough, I don't need to add to the weight."

Odalie returned to the chair and sat, covering her face with her hands. At first, Dixon thought she was crying, but when she looked up at him her eyes were dry.

"I'm sorry." She shook her head. "I shouldn't have said that. Of course, I understand your position. I guess I expected it."

"Odalie, you don't need to apologize to me. How far along are you?"

"About ten weeks."

He thought she was probably further along, judging by the signs he observed, but he did not share this. Instead he said, "It's still early. Pregnancies at this stage often end spontaneously, as I'm sure you know."

Dixon wanted to comfort her somehow, to take her in his arms, but could not. There was nothing he could do to ease her burden. "You must feel very alone," he said.

She stood and covered her fair hair with her hood. "I shouldn't have bothered you," she said. "I've got to go, Fred Jolly is waiting for me at the Occidental. I told him I was going to Raylan's to look at fabric with Etheline. He'll be half in his cups when I get there; he won't notice when I come back empty-handed. If he does, I'll make something up." She laughed without humor. "Fred's very loyal to my husband. He makes up in devotion what he lacks in intelligence." She pulled on her gloves and walked to the door.

"Let me walk you to the hotel," Dixon said.

"No, it's better you don't."

He reached for the knob but did not open the door. "It's none of my business," he said, "but does your husband know about your condition?"

Her pale face, surrounded by her black cloak, appeared to be suspended in the darkness. "No, nor will he."

"What are you going to do?"

"I've heard about an Indian woman who

deals in such matters. I — or rather, someone who works for me — will make inquiries."

"Please be careful, Odalie. What you are contemplating can be dangerous. Things can go wrong."

"Don't worry, Dr. Dixon. I wouldn't want you to distress yourself on my account." She brushed past him, leaving a faint scent of jasmine, and descended quickly to the street, her tread light on the stairs.

BILLY SUN

The fall roundup of 1886 was a harvest of disappointment, following a summer of extreme heat and drought. It was the same throughout the Territory, on lands watered by the Powder, the Belle Fourche, the Little Missouri. The spring grass burned away, and there was very little forage, while more cattle than ever were released upon the range. One single company drove thirty-two thousand steers up from southern states and turned them loose to fend for themselves. The cattle began to starve.

The overstocking, combined with the lack of rain, turned the rich Wyoming soil into a dry powder that was fine and choking as talc. The winds were hot, blowing mostly from the south that summer, instead of from the northwest and west as usual. The cowboys tied handkerchiefs over their faces to keep the dust and dirt out of their mouths and noses, and Raylan's Dry Goods sold out of its supply of sun goggles within two weeks. There were many prairie fires. Streams that normally ran year-round dried up, and the water that remained stood in small, stagnant pools that were so alkaline the animals would not drink. The summer's only bumper crop was one of poisonous weeds, which the desperate cattle ate and died. The survivors collected in the fall roundup were ribby and exhausted.

Cowboys working the roundup were stressed and buggy, too. If an owner didn't make money, neither would his men. Billy worked for Faucett that summer, though he was often away as area ranchers sought him out to break their green horses. At first, Lord Faucett was proud of his buster and let Billy keep his earnings, but he grew less charitable as Billy's reputation grew. By the end of the summer, Faucett was demanding one-fifth of Billy's pay. Billy understood Lord Faucett didn't need the money, that it was just Faucett's way of making sure Billy did not forgot who he worked for. Billy didn't mind; he'd rather spend his time working with horses than roping a terrified, bawling calf and dragging it to the branding fire. Their screams and rolling eyes disturbed him.

He was happiest on those afternoons

when, if the sun wasn't too hot, Lady Odalie would walk down to the corral from the big house and stand in the shade of her parasol watching Billy finish a green four-year-old. She didn't say much, but she didn't have to. Odalie admired Billy's skill, and he saw that in her eyes. Sometimes Billy thought she was like a wild horse herself, not fully tamed but stuck in a cage.

Nate Coday had moved to a larger ranch, the EK, where he was promptly appointed wagon boss. He and Billy saw little of each other that summer until the fall roundup when the cowboys came together in the evenings for eating, singing, and card playing. The EK's cook, Marcus Maupin, a barrel-chested Texan with a headful of wiry red hair and hands the size of hams, was generally regarded as the best cook in the Big Horn basin. His pies, cobblers, and doughnuts were the stuff of legend. On the last night of the roundup, Coday invited Billy to join the EK's grubline and Billy happily accepted. On that special night, Maupin served up his famous apple pie with walnuts and raisins, which he baked in tins carefully stacked in a Dutch oven strategically placed just off the fire. The scent of apples and cinnamon filled the crisp night air as Billy joined the line of men, waiting with bowls in hand for their hot pie served with a dipper of cream. The cowboy behind Billy bumped him hard in the back with his bowl.

"What you think you're doing, chief?"

Billy turned to see a man of about his height but heavier, with sloped, powerful-looking shoulders and a bald, bullet-shaped head. "You don't ride with us, you don't get none of coosie's pie. The EK don't serve Injuns." He glared at Billy with bloodshot, protruding eyes and yanked on Billy's grizzly claw necklace, but the leather cord held fast.

"Shut up, Ringo." This came from Nate, eating his pie on an oilcloth beside the fire. "Billy's here because I asked him." Nate called to the cook in a loud voice. "Marcus, serve my friend, Billy Sun, a piece of pie and make sure it's bigger than Ringo's."

Billy stepped forward and held out his bowl, conscious of Ringo's heavy breathing behind him. The cook gave him a thick slab and poured a dipper of thick, yellow cream over it. Billy took his bowl to sit cross-legged on the ground beside Nate, who handed him an opened can of condensed milk to lighten his coffee. Billy forgot about Ringo until his bowl was empty. When he looked up, he saw the cowboy glaring at him from across the fire. Ringo's greasy head shone in the firelight like a polished knob.

"Some people around here have forgot what you red niggers did to our people when we first come out here," he said. "Nate, I guess you're one of them, but me, I ain't. You Injuns killed my kin, and it weren't that long ago." The men sitting around the fire fell quiet, so the only sounds were the pop of the fire and the bawling of cattle.

"Ringo, I am your wagon boss and I am telling you to shut your gob hole," Nate said. "Anyhow, Billy's people were Crow. They never did harm to you or your kin."

Ringo kept his eyes on Billy. "Crow, Sioux, Cheyenne, it don't matter." His top lip curled back in a smile that showed yellow teeth and blood-red gums. "Injuns are all the same. They all smell the same, too." He threw back his head and made a show of sniffing the air. "You boys smell that? Phew, it's enough to make a man puke."

"That's just your breath blowing back in your face, Ringo," one of the cowboys said.

"I don't want to fight you," Billy said, putting down his bowl, "but I will if I have to."

"Haw haw!" Ringo laughed, looking around the campfire. "Did you all hear that? Chief, here, is ready to fight me." He turned to Billy. "You're a tough one, aren't you, chief? A real hard case."

"No. I said I would if I had to."

"Leave him alone why don't you, Ringo?" one of the cowboys said. "He's not bothering anybody." Others murmured their agreement.

"It's sad, that's what it is," Ringo said, getting to his feet, "and a good thing the old-timers aren't here to see it. Hell, has everybody forgot what them stinking redskins did to Fetterman and his boys, not far from this very place?" He looked at the circle of faces in the firelight and, when no one responded, shook his head and stormed off, muttering to himself.

"I'm sorry for that ugly galoot," Nate said. "I didn't know his feelings — it never came up before — but it doesn't matter. Nobody cares what Albertus Ringo thinks anyhow."

Billy nodded. Albertus Ringo. It was a hard name to forget.

Four inches of snow fell on the first day of November, but the sun stayed warm and it melted fast as it fell. Usually there'd been a sticking snow by this time of year, and some of the townfolk started to hope the Territory might be spared the hard, punishing winter old-timers prophesied. But then the storms started coming, one after another, heavy snowfalls accompanied by a bone-breaking cold. Hurricane winds blew day after day, from sunup to sundown, for fifty-four days. Fences and outbuildings were leveled; haystacks disappeared. Stages were unable to pass through snowdrifts six feet high and had to turn back. Trains were blown from the tracks or frozen in place.

The rivers and streams froze solid and cattle were driven mad by thirst. The cattle herds drifted toward the larger rivers, where they would always find air holes no matter how thick the ice, but while the leaders drank the followers closed in from behind, pushing the animals into the rapidly flowing water where they were swept away to drown under the ice. In a desperate attempt to escape the snow and wind, cattle by the thousands wandered onto the railroad tracks where snowplows had cleared a pathway, delaying trains for hours and sometimes driving passengers from their cars to drive the animals from the tracks. Starving cattle invaded towns, eating garbage when they could find it, tarpaper from the sides of buildings, straw and grain from the manure of horses. People complained of being unable to sleep at night because of the moans of the invading herds. Many animals died in the streets or in yards.

Cowboys tried to save their employers' suffering cattle, but it was futile as trying to empty the ocean with a teaspoon. They worked to keep the animals out of the valleys and draws, where the snow was deepest and they would die. Instead they drove them up into the hills, where occasionally the wind would expose a green patch of grass, or around to the south side of a mountain where they might find shelter from the scouring wind.

Billy left Faucett's employ to pass the winter with Nate Coday and Jack Reshaw on Reshaw's Red Fork ranch. Their job was less difficult than the cowboys working for larger outfits, but it was a struggle nonetheless, and Reshaw worried that even with his friends' help — Billy and Nate worked for no pay but a roof over their heads and food in their bellies — he would lose most of his herd. In the evenings, they retreated to the house, a three-room cabin made of logs of hewn pine. It had an earthen floor and, in the main room, a round-bodied, cast iron stove that had a surface to cook on and threw good heat, more than a fireplace. Billy worried that the stove would get too hot and start a fire, roasting them in their sleep. He solved this by hammering flat a bunch of food cans and covering the walls nearest the stove in tin.

All in all, Jack Reshaw's cabin was a good place to be that winter, sparsely furnished but comfortable, with a table and three chairs, a washstand, mirror, and a rough plank counter along the back wall. A bucket served as a sink. Above were rows of shelves lined with bags of flour, sugar, coffee, and tins of canned milk, vegetables, and fruits. The two back rooms had bed frames built into the walls at the corners, each tautly laced with ropes and covered with tick mattresses. Billy stuffed his with blue-green needles of Douglas fir that filled the room with a sweet, fresh fragrance. The scent reminded Billy of his childhood in the Crow mountain village when his mother would make him a tea of crushed fir needles whenever his stomach hurt.

In late January, they were blessed with a two-day thaw. The warm sun melted the top layer of snow, forming pools of water that the grateful cows drank greedily. The three men celebrated the thaw with a bottle of whiskey, hoping the worst of winter had broken but knowing in their hearts it had not. Indeed, they were punished for their short respite, for it was followed by a brutal freeze with temperatures plunging to forty below zero. The wind was constant and merciless. Billy, warm in his bed, heard the storm bearing down during the night, howling, screaming, and bringing death. He pitied the living things caught in its teeth, and knew that soon he and Sugarfoot would be out among them, trying to save Jack's brainless beeves. The animals turned their tails to the wind and let it push them wherever it wanted. Too often it drove them into a fence where they piled up, one on top of the other, and died; sometimes it forced them down into the gullies or railroad cuts where the snow was deepest and they froze to death. Horses were smarter; they understood it might be necessary to head into the wind to reach a better place. They could break through ice with their hooves to get water. Billy didn't know whether cows were stupid or just lazy, but, whatever the reason, they needed a man's help to survive.

"You awake?" Nate spoke from his bed across the room. Billy, who was entertaining impure thoughts of Odalie Faucett, and not for the first time, feigned sleep, so he could finish the sweet show playing out in his head. But Nate felt like talking.

"You ever think about giving this up?" he said. "You ever think about finding some other way to make a dollar?"

In fact, Billy had already decided this would be his last year of working cattle. "I'm done with this," he said. "Horses, that's what I'm good at. No more cowpunching for me. What about you? You thinking about ditching Jack and going to work in town for Tom Raylan, like he asked you? That don't sound like much."

"Hell, no! That Raylan's a scoundrel, a unhung thief. No, I like cowboying but I want a place of my own. Jack wants me to go shares in the Lazy L and B, and I thought about it, but no, I've got to have my own brand, my own herd, my own place. That's what I want, and I will have it."

"The WSGA won't let you, Nate," Billy said. "Not you, or Jack, neither. Faucett and Dudley and them, they let him get this far, but they'll put the kibosh on it soon enough. Jack's twisting their tail, and they won't have it. When I was in town last week, I heard Frank Canton's been saying Jack stole the steers we're running, says he's been slapping the Lazy L and B mark on mavericks, blotching other brands, you name it. Canton's getting folks stirred up. It's dangerous for Jack — me and you, too. But I'm not telling you what you don't know."

A blast of icy pellets struck the window, rattling the glass in its wooden frame.

"Canton," Nate said with contempt, "Faucett's favorite ass-kisser. He's made a full-time job outta that." There was a moment of quiet, then Nate said, "I don't know why you stick around, Billy. Me and Jack, we go back a long way. We're like kin. But you don't need this. You could go. I'd get out if I was you."

Billy had not told Nate about a letter he'd had from Nelson Story in the fall. *"I can't find a man with half your skill for busting ponies,"* Story wrote. *"I'll give fifty a month if you will come back."* But even if he hadn't promised Jack his help through the winter, Billy would not have taken Story up on his offer. He was in Powder River country to stay, he would never give up on his dream to make his way in Absaroka, the land of his forefathers.

"I'll stick it out," Billy said, "through the winter leastways. I told Jack he'll have to find someone else in the spring, when the new horses come in."

The banshee scream of the wind rose an octave. Soon it would be light enough to ride. Jack was already up. They heard him get out of bed with a groan, then shuffle from his room to throw wood on the coals still glowing in the stove's firebox.

"Well, you're right about one thing," Nate

said. "What we're doing is dangerous. I've gotten used to your red Injun face. I'd be sad to see anything happen to it."

Billy grinned in the darkness. "That's real white of you," he said.

BILLY SUN

Billy wore nearly every piece of clothing he owned, but even so he was chilled to the bone. Around noon the sun broke through the gray ceiling of clouds, and though it lessened the cold, the glare reflecting off the snow scorched his eyes. Billy blacked his high Indian cheekbones with soot from a lamp chimney, but still he was blinded. Sugarfoot suffered, too. The ice that had formed when the melted snow refroze cut the animal's legs when he broke through the crust. Billy wrapped them in strips of torn-up burlap feed sacks, but even so his horse left a bloody trail in the snow.

"Damn beeves," Billy said as he and Sugarfoot fought their way toward one of the herd's favorite gullies. If he found any alive, he would drive them to a more sheltered place, maybe the south side of a mountain, where he would shovel through four feet of snow with the hope he would uncover enough grass to keep the starving animals alive for one more day. Often as not there was none, the range having been grazed or burned bare during the long, scorching summer. Cattle were stupid, but Billy was soft on four-leggeds of all kinds and he hurt for them. He had never seen suffering on such a scale. One poor steer he found wandering on four bloody stumps. His hoofs, Billy reckoned, must have frozen and broken off. He put the animal out of its misery, then cut off and packed as much meat as he could carry and left the rest for the wolves. They were the only creatures getting fat in Powder River country that winter.

He raised his face to the sun. It was about two o'clock, and Billy was getting hungry. He was dreaming about a hot plate of elk stew with onions, carrots, and potatoes and a steaming mug of sweet Arbuckle's coffee when he heard the crack of a rifle shot as Sugarfoot's muzzle exploded in a spray of blood and teeth. The horse screamed and rose on his rear legs, blindly churning the air with his feet. Billy fought to keep his seat, at the same time scanning the treeless, snow-covered hills for the shooter. A second shot struck Sugarfoot in the head and he dropped, first onto his knees and then, with a groan, rolled over onto his side. Billy barely had time to jump free.

A third shot plunged into Sugarfoot's belly. Billy threw himself down on the snowy ground behind the horse's body and again searched the horizon. This time he saw him, a black shape on the line where the white of the ground met the blue dome of sky. "Damn you," Billy said. "Damn you to hell." He was lucky Sugarfoot had not fallen on his rifle. Billy slid the .38 Winchester from its sheath, levered in a shell, braced the barrel on the saddle, and squeezed off a shot. The black shape disappeared.

Billy waited. Had he killed the son of a bitch? Billy didn't know, but he would. He would find the cowardly horse-killing devil and put him through. He'd do it if it was his last act in this world. Billy's throat was thick, and he felt a rotten sickness in the pit of his stomach as he stroked Sugarfoot's muscular neck. "I'm sorry," he said. "I'm sorry."

The shooter did not reappear. Billy got to his feet and started walking, rifle fully cocked, toward the place where he had been, hoping to find a corpse. He kept a sharp eye out; the killer could have doubled back and gotten behind him. Could have, but Billy didn't think so. When he reached the base of the rise where the shooter had been, Billy stopped and listened. Hearing nothing, he began the climb, holding the rifle before him. Just before reaching the crest, he dropped into a crouch and moved forward crab-like, close to the ground. At the top, he saw blood in the snow where the assassin had lain in ambush. Billy smiled. Good, he had hit him. Farther down, he found the place where the coward had left his horse and deep tracks marking their departure.

The snow was starting again. Billy looked to the southeast, toward Jack's place a good fifteen miles distant. It was getting on to three o'clock. There was a pair of snowshoes hanging from his saddle, but even so there was no way he'd make the ranch before dark.

He retraced his steps to Sugarfoot's body and kneeled beside him, trying not to look at his destroyed face. He placed his hand on the horse's neck and closed his eyes, speaking to the animal's risen spirit. "You were a brave and loyal friend," he said. "We came together at a time when I doubted myself as a man. I could not find my place, not in the Indian world and not in the white man's world, but you showed me a path to

185

follow. You showed me that I was worthy of trust. You never failed me, you never disappointed me. You were my true friend. Thank you." Billy tasted his own salty tears. He had not wept since the day Rose was taken.

He went through his saddlebags, discarding everything he would not need but keeping two waxed paper–wrapped biscuits, each split in half and dipped in bacon grease with a thick slab of bacon in the middle, two cans of peaches, and an extra pair of socks. Even though it weighed a good thirty pounds, he would take the saddle, too. It was too valuable to leave behind. Before getting under way, Billy unsheathed his knife and cut long strands from the horse's black mane and tail and put them in the saddlebags. Later he would weave a lariat of the horsehair so Sugarfoot would be with him always.

He started walking, with a heart heavy but blood warmed by hate. He entertained himself with thoughts of how he would put the killer through; his relatives the Mountain Crows had been creative in this regard. He had grown up with stories of tortures the women inflicted on Sioux captives the men brought back to the village, and he took pleasure in remembering them now; fingers and toes removed one by one, hot coals dropped in ears . . .

The snow stopped after about an hour. It was at least two feet deep on the ground and in places much deeper. Billy trudged forward, awkward in his snowshoes and sheepskin coat but glad of them, glad also he had thought to stuff his boots with newspaper. It was a good thing too he brought his rifle, something he did not usually do when tending cattle, because a long gun interfered with access to his lariat. He only thought to bring it this time because of the danger he and Nate had spoken of the night before. Billy raised his eyes to the sky, thanking his protector in the Spirit World for looking out for him. If only the protector had done the same for Sugarfoot.

It was about four o'clock and the cold was cruel, at least twenty below. For the first time that day, Billy felt a chill that had nothing to do with the temperature. He was young and strong, but far from home. How would he survive the night? "Keep moving," he said aloud. "To stop, to sleep, is to die."

He walked steadily for hours but the snow was deep, and even with the snowshoes he did not make good progress. Thirst plagued him, but he had foolishly allowed the water in his canteen to freeze. Even now, though he carried it inside his coat, it remained solid. He felt it bumping against him with each step, heavy as a blow. From time to time he bent to take a mouthful of snow, and though this slaked his thirst it made him colder. He ate the bacon biscuits without pausing, though these, too, were frozen and he was forced to hold each bite in his mouth until it softened enough to chew. Despite their iciness, the greasy biscuits were delicious, perhaps the most delicious food he had ever eaten, though the saltiness of the bacon increased his thirst.

The time came when he could no longer carry the saddle, and he acknowledged he had been foolish to try. He told himself he could come back for it later, maybe it wouldn't be too damaged, but now all he could think about was getting closer to the round-bellied stove that threw good heat. He turned a circle in the moonlight, trying to find a protected place to hide the saddle, or at least a landmark so he would know where to look later. Finding nothing in the rolling mounds of sparkling white, he dropped it where he stood. That saddle cost him forty dollars, more than a month's pay. It was the first thing he bought when he started earning real wages. Nelson Story himself helped him choose it. Abandoning the saddle felt like defeat.

Before midnight Billy noticed a wolf following him, about fifty yards behind. He turned to challenge the animal, and though the wolf stopped as well, he made no move to run. Clearly, he saw in Billy no menace, only meat on the hoof. Billy walked on, followed by his gray, yellow-eyed companion.

When he came to the creek, and the skeletal cottonwoods that lined it, Billy knew he was fewer than five miles from the ranch, but it might as well be five hundred. His feet were numb, despite the newspaper and thick woolen socks. He wore a wool scarf over his hat and tied under his chin to cover his ears, but even so they were frozen, so cold they had stopped hurting a long time ago. As a boy in the Crow village, Billy and the other children had been fascinated and repelled by an old warrior who, as a young man, had been wounded on a horse-stealing raid against the Sioux and had lain in the snow for hours until his friends found him and carried him to safety. The warrior kept his fingers and toes but his frozen ears had rotted off, leaving red, angry mounds of misshapen flesh on either side of his head. Billy put his mittened hands over his ears and sent a plea to his protector in the world behind this one. *Please, do not take my ears.*

Without realizing it, Billy had stopped walking and stood swaying like a solitary tree about to fall. He caught himself just in time and looked over his shoulder at the wolf, inching closer. Billy forced himself to keep moving. *Maybe I should make for the trees, try to make a shelter, a wickiup, with downed branches. Maybe I could make a fire.*

Even as he considered, he knew any branches he could find would be wet, covered in snow; still he had no choice but to try. Otherwise he would freeze. He started down the slope toward the frozen creek. Gradually, he became aware of a sound, barely audible above the crunch of his shoes on the snow and the ringing of his ears. What was it? He hesitated, searching the dark stand of trees ahead. Was something — or someone — in there? Someone, like him, seeking shelter from the cold and, if so, friend or foe? He pulled his rifle from its canvas sheath and raised it to his shoulder.

"Billy!" He froze. Was his mind playing tricks or did someone actually call his name? No, it was real — the wolf heard it, too. He turned his head toward the sound, which came again. "Billy!"

A man on horseback came toward him, leading a second horse. Billy laughed with relief as the wolf, with one last, hungry look in Billy's direction, loped away.

"I'm disappointed in you, Billy," Nate said with a grin. "I thought you redskins were better at this type of thing."

Billy struggled to speak, his frozen mouth could barely form words. "Someone shot Sugarfoot. He got away, but I wounded him." He walked to the second horse and, after removing his snowshoes, tried to mount, but his foot was so leaden he could not lift it to the stirrup. Nate dismounted and vaulted Billy into the saddle.

"Can you ride?" Nate said. Billy nodded.

"We'll get you home and thaw you out. Then you can tell me what happened."

Now that he knew he was going to survive, Billy's thoughts returned to revenge, He would ask Dr. Dixon if anyone had come seeking treatment for a bullet wound. And when Billy found him, he would give him another.

ODALIE

She sat at her dressing table, still in her chemise, brushing her hair. Downstairs she heard the guests arriving, all of them lumpen, uninteresting people she would not bother to say hello to if she were in New York or New Orleans. The people of Wyoming Territory had no understanding of style, of glamour, and she had yet to meet anyone, male or female, with a sense of humor. She'd almost given up looking. She sighed and dropped her brush. Things weren't a complete loss, she thought. Some of the men, at least, were good to look at.

Richard would be wondering where she was; Odalie knew she should be dressed, already downstairs greeting the arrivals at her husband's side, but she was in no hurry. After all, she'd be putting up with them until the wee hours. These cow merchants never knew when it was time to go home.

She leaned forward to examine her face

more closely in the mirror. Were those freckles? God, they were. Soon she'd look like an Irish washerwoman or one of those high yellow girls who wove baskets in the French market. With a sound of disgust, she walked to the window where she concealed herself behind the white gauzy curtains to watch the scene below. Men in high hats and bowler hats escorted women in silks and brocades, some in pearls and diamonds that glittered in the lamplight. Odalie felt a wave of sadness wash over her. She had not bargained for this desolation, this crushing tedium, when she married Lord Richard Faucett four years ago, though her mother had tried to warn her. "He might have money, my dear, but he is not an interesting man. Think about the boys you've grown up with, the Landreneu brothers, Felix Robinett, Wyatt — think about Wyatt, Odalie! How could you be happy with Richard Faucett when you've had the love of a man like that?"

Her mother had been wise to mention Wyatt Tarwater, a childhood friend who had grown into a beautiful man, tall and athletic, with unruly brown hair that was forever falling into his eyes, full, pillowy lips and a wonderful, knowing smile. Yes, she loved him — indeed, he had been her first lover and she could not have hoped for better, in every regard — but the Tarwater family had fallen on hard times after the war, and Wyatt, charming though he was, would never be the kind of man to put his shoulder to the wheel. Much as she loved him, she had refused his offer of marriage. A life of genteel poverty was not in the cards for her — or so she thought. Had she made a mistake? She still pictured him in her mind's eye every time she was with Richard. With her eyes closed, it was still Wyatt's face she saw, his voice she heard. That is, until recently. There was another man who had something of Wyatt about him. Now it was sometimes his face she saw when she performed her wifely duty.

As she turned from the window she saw Daniel Dixon walking up to the house. She smiled, pleasantly surprised; she had not expected to see him this evening, but who was on his arm? A small, slender woman with blond — almost white — hair, simply but charmingly dressed in a pale yellow silk with a modest décolletage. Odalie smiled. This evening might not be a total bore after all, she thought.

She went to her wardrobe, putting aside the tasteful but sedate dress of London smoke she had chosen and selecting instead a low-cut gown of Nile-green silk that showed her slim figure to advantage. *I don't know who you are, my little darling, but tonight we'll show you how a grown woman does it.*

By the time she was dressed, the party, was in full swing. Richard had hired musicians — strings and woodwinds but no brass — from Fort McKinney who played nicely from the gallery. Arnaud, who had been working for days, had outdone himself. On the sideboard were oysters packed on ice, Columbia River salmon au buerre, and an arrangement of cheeses and cold meats. Once the guests were seated, they would be served their choice of consommé aux champignon or chicken gumbo, followed by roast loin of beef, an entrée of fricandeau of veal with vegetable glace, and, to finish, Richard's favorite, an English plum pudding with hard sauce. Throughout the evening, wines and champagne would flow freely.

When Odalie floated down the stairs, the revelers fell quiet. Well, she said to herself, the Nile-green must have been a good choice after all. At the last minute, she had decided on the emerald necklace Richard had given her for Christmas. It was an expensive, overly decorative bauble she rarely wore, but it went well with the green silk. She was annoyed to see Frank Canton hurrying to the foot of the stairs to offer his arm, smiling up at her like an itinerant quacksalver. As she placed her hand on his sleeve, Odalie caught sight of Canton's wife, Anna, across the room, flushing an unbecoming red. She saw jealousy in the woman's eyes and wished she could tell her not to worry. *I wouldn't have your cruel beast of a husband if he were king of England.*

"Thank you, Sheriff," Odalie said. "I'm so glad you and Mrs. Canton could join us this evening. I think after the winter we've been having we're all due a bit of celebration. Don't you agree?"

"Indeed, I do, Lady Faucett, though I'm afraid it may be premature. Your husband and the other cattlemen won't know whether celebration is in order until spring comes for real and they know how their herds fared. The roundup won't tell the whole story, scattered as they are. We may not know until summer. For some, I expect the losses will prove ruinous."

Odalie rolled her eyes. "How dreary," she said. "Let's talk of happier things tonight."

"I agree," Canton said. "And in that vein, may I say you look especially lovely this evening? You are the most beautiful woman in the room."

"I suppose you mean to be kind, Sheriff, but a man should not say a thing like that if his wife is in the room as well. It's disrespectful."

Canton smiled and said, "I am an honest man, for better or worse. I have often suffered for it."

"Have you? I rather think your wife will suffer for it, too." She took her hand from his arm. Poor Anna, she thought, she has tethered herself to an ass and, if Odalie's suspicions were correct, an immoral man. Though she did not concern herself with her husband's business, she knew Canton did the WSGA's bidding, no matter what its members asked, as long as the pay was right. And they paid him very handsomely indeed.

She searched the crowded room for Dixon and his mysterious blond companion and found them talking to William Angus, a Buffalo bar owner and businessman better known as Red. Canton followed her eyes and, spotting Angus, laughed with derision.

"There he is, mayor of Laurel Avenue," he said, referring to the street where Buffalo's taverns and brothels were located. "Red Angus, cattle thief, pimp, and gambler, friend to whores, thieves, and cutthroats —

and now I hear he plans to seek the Democratic nomination for sheriff next year. Ha, that's rich!" Unsure of Odalie's politics, Canton paused, giving her a chance to respond. When she said nothing, he continued, reassured. "Frankly, I'm surprised you and Lord Faucett would have a man like that in your home. He is not a person of your quality."

Odalie decided to make Canton squirm. "Yes, I did know Mr. Angus is considering a run for office, and I think he would make a fine sheriff. He's smart, well liked, and, far as I know, beholden to no one. If he made some mistakes in his past, well, so what? Who hasn't?" She turned to look Canton directly in the eye. "I certainly have — haven't you?"

Canton loosened his shirt collar with a forefinger. Sometimes he got the feeling Odalie Faucett knew things about him no one in Wyoming Territory knew, not even his wife. But no, it was impossible. How could she know his birth name was not Frank Canton but Joe Horner, that in his Texas youth he had robbed banks, stolen livestock, and served time in the state penitentiary in Huntsville, from which he escaped in August 1879? Did she know of the men he had killed? No, there was no way she could, but still, a certain light in her eyes troubled him.

"Sheriff, who is that with Dr. Dixon? I don't believe I've seen her before."

Canton was relieved by the change of topic. "That's his daughter, Lorna. She and her twin brother must be sixteen or seventeen by now. Their mother died when they were born."

"Oh?" Odalie knew the doctor had a son attending medical school in Cincinnati, but she did not know about the twins. "She's a very pretty thing, isn't she? Such remarkable coloring. Come, I want you to introduce me."

Years had passed since the unpleasant encounter he and Tom had had with Billy and the twins on the road to Buffalo. Their paths rarely crossed since, and Canton hoped she had forgotten, but when Lorna saw him crossing the room with Lady Faucett on his arm, he knew that she had not. After making the requested introduction, Canton offered his excuses, and Angus soon followed.

"So nice to meet you, Lorna," Odalie said, admiring, with more than a pang of jealousy, the girl's youthful beauty. It was rare indeed to find hair so fair paired with an olive complexion and eyes that shade of blue. "I understand you have a brother, a twin? Is he here this evening also?"

"No, ma'am," Lorna said. "Cal doesn't like parties. He's at home with Mrs. MacGill and his books."

"Mrs. MacGill?"

"Our housekeeper," Dixon said.

"I see. And do you like books, too, Lorna?"

"No." The girl regarded Odalie with a bold frankness that was disconcerting, as if to say, *"Don't bother with dull female chatter. I won't go along."*

Dixon broke in. "Lorna, would you ask Chang to pour Lady Faucett a glass of punch?" Lorna obeyed, with a small, secret smile, leaving Dixon and Odalie alone.

"You look well," he said. "It would seem your . . . problem . . . has resolved."

Odalie colored. "Mercifully, it happened naturally, as you said it might. I suppose the goddess of motherhood found me unfit to join her ranks — and rightly so."

"You may feel differently one day."

Odalie felt herself grow warm. "How patronizing. Please, don't presume to know me better than I know myself."

"I'm sorry. I didn't mean to offend you."

Dixon looked uncomfortable and Odalie immediately regretted speaking so harshly.

When would she learn to control her tongue? "No, I'm the one who should apologize. I was rude. I was happy to see you here tonight, and this is not the conversation I was hoping to have with you. Let's speak of something else — your daughter, for instance. She's quite lovely. What does she do?"

He sighed and looked at Lorna across the room. "Not much, and that's the problem. She has no interest in schooling, as you heard, unlike her brothers. My older son, Harry, is training for a career in medicine and my younger son, Caleb, may do the same. I had hoped Lorna might be a schoolteacher one day, but I no longer see that in the cards. Oh, she's very bright, no mistake about that, but she doesn't have the temperament for teaching. Frankly, I don't know what Lorna has the temperament for."

"And why not medicine for her, too? It would be more interesting than teaching surely. You say she's bright. A woman can be a fine surgeon, equal to a man. Or do you — with your patronizing attitude toward us — doubt it?" She smiled to show him she was teasing.

"No, not at all. I've known some skilled female physicians, but I don't believe Lorna has the dedication and scientific curiosity she would need to succeed in that field. Not only that, but she'd have to go East for training, to Philadelphia, unless other medical schools are now accepting women, and she wouldn't want that, either. She loves the west, has no need to live in the States. Nor would she be equipped socially. I'm afraid I've not done her justice in that regard."

They watched Lorna return, carefully carrying a glass of ruby red punch. Odalie said, "Yes, I'm sure it's hard for a father to raise a daughter alone, without the benefit of female companionship and instruction." A thought came to her. "Why don't you let Lorna stay with us for a time, with Richard and me? Does the poor girl ever have any female company other than your housekeeper, Mrs. — I forget her name? No, I didn't think so. I could teach Lorna the things a lovely young lady should know. She would be my protégé. We would travel, see the world. I would like that, truly I would. I believe she has great potential."

Dixon was surprised. "I thought you had no maternal instinct. Why would you want to saddle yourself with a child who is not even your own?"

"She is not a child, Dr. Dixon. She is a young woman who needs to be given an opportunity to make the most of herself, to enjoy the fine things in life. Not that you could not provide that, of course," she added quickly. "But Richard and I are in a unique position to help, if you will allow us to."

Dixon was reluctant, though he could see the idea had merit. He did not understand his strange daughter, and he had no idea what to do with her. "Thank you, Lady Faucett," he said. "I'll discuss it with her. Of course, I would pay for her room and board."

Odalie shrugged her shapely shoulders. "If that's important to you, but I assure you it isn't necessary. Richard and I have more money than we know what to do with."

That may be true now, Dixon thought as Lorna arrived with Odalie's drink. *But your husband's financial picture could change dramatically in a few months, once winter's toll is fully known.* The newspapers predicted light losses, of no more than five percent, but Dixon was convinced the damage would be much greater, in the neighborhood of seventy-five to eighty percent, if not higher. Overstocking, the lack of forage and feed, and winter's fury may have spelled disaster for the Wyoming cattlemen and their open-range system.

Later, as he and Lorna climbed into the buggy, Dixon noticed Frank Canton and another man, tall and wearing a Mexican-style hat, deep in conversation by the stables. Lorna saw them, too.

"I hate him," she said. "That man with Sheriff Canton. I hate them both."

"You know him?" Dixon was surprised. "How?"

"Cal and me and Billy met them on the road to Buffalo that day, you know, when you went to the village."

"You didn't tell me. Did something happen?"

Lorna shrugged. "They were mean to Billy. The one in the hat especially, treated him bad on account of he's Indian. I miss Billy, Pa. I do. I wish he could come work for us again. We haven't seen him for so long."

In fact, Dixon had seen Billy only a few weeks before. He had come to Dixon's Buffalo office to ask if he had recently treated anyone for a gunshot wound. Dixon told him he had not.

"The man with Canton," he said. "Did you catch his name?"

"The sheriff called him Tom."

Dixon slapped the reins down on the horse's back and started the buggy. The night was cold and Lorna wrapped herself in her dark cloak, pulling the hood over her shining hair. Canton and Tom stopped talking as they passed, and Tom raised his hat.

"Good evening, Miss Lorna," he said with his wide smile, his lips red under his full mustache. "It's nice to see you again. I declare, you just keep on get getting' prettier and prettier."

"Keep going, Pa," she said. "Keep going."

But Dixon reined in. "And who might you be, sir, to address my daughter in such a familiar fashion? Do we know you?"

He stepped forward and lifted his wide-brimmed hat. "The name's Horn, Dr. Dixon. Tom Horn, at your service."

BILLY SUN

I may not see a hundred
Before I cross the Styx,
But coal or ember, I'll remember
Eighteen Eighty-six.

The stiff heaps in the coulee,
The dead eyes in the camp,
And the wind about, blowing fortunes
out, As a woman blows out a lamp
                    — Author unknown

A merciful chinook finally blew down from
the eastern slopes of the Rocky Mountains,
arriving well behind schedule and hard on
the heels of the last blizzard of that cruel
season. The people were grateful, now that
the worst of the winter was over, but at the
same time they knew the retreat of the ice
and snow would reveal the true horror of
that terrible time, which would be long
remembered as the Winter of Death.

With mighty groans and shudders, the great rivers began to break up, the Rosebud, the Yellowstone, the Tongue and Powder, the Big Horn and Cheyenne, the Little Missouri, overflowing their banks and sending giant cakes of ice crashing and grinding downstream, leaving wreckage in their wake. Valleys and gulches that had been bone-dry the summer before now filled with rushing water that carried the corpses of countless cattle, tumbling and rolling over one another along with downed trees and other debris in the muddy, churning flood. Hapless ranchers and cowboys stood by to watch the deadly flow while the air throbbed with the water's endless roar.

Though the extent of the devastation would never be fully known, it was immediately obvious the large ranchers had lost the most. Richard Faucett lost at least fifty percent of his stock and Moreton Dudley, eighty percent. Early in the roundup, a grim-faced Faucett surprised his men by occasionally riding with them, his face lengthening as they discovered piles of rotting corpses in the creek bottoms, gullies, and the other low places that had offered the miserable creatures false promise of shelter from the iron wind. The air stank of death.

The worst carnage was suffered by the un-acclimated steers that were driven up from the south in the fall and dumped, already bony, onto the range. A Texas company that released fifty-five hundred head in August found only one hundred animals, barely alive, in the spring. The owners did not bother to claim them.

Though none emerged unscathed, the smaller operations, such as Jack Reshaw's, lost less. Their cowboys were better able to manage the herds, moving them to sheltered places in the foothills where they could uncover enough grass to keep them alive and, if not, feeding hay — if they had it. In another cruel twist of fate, a legion of raven-ous grasshoppers had descended on the range late in the fall, consuming all uncut hay.

The spring roundup was a bleak affair. In the Upper Powder region alone, the number of wagons dropped from twenty-seven, the fleet at the height of the beef bonanza, to only four. Grasslands that once supported ten thousand animals now accommodated only a few hundred. Cowboys would ride for hours, to find only a few bony steers, scarcely able to walk.

One by one that summer, many of the big-gest companies started closing out. Horace

Plunkett shut down his outfit and returned to his native Ireland. Britisher T. W. Peters sold his interest in the Bar C, and his countrymen Alston, Winn, and Windsor departed also. The Wyoming Stock Growers Association saw its membership plummet as the cattle market bottomed out, partly because of the poor quality of the surviving stock and partly because of an oversupply as the owners liquidated their holdings.

Those who chose to stick it out, including Faucett and Dudley, were more determined than ever to succeed, though they could no longer enforce their ownership of the public rangelands. An era of ill will followed the Winter of Death. The few remaining cattle barons faced stiff competition for graze lands and water rights from scrappy homesteaders and small ranchers who flocked to the territory as the European lords departed. Faucett and Dudley repeatedly accused these "nesters" of theft, of marking mavericks that "by rights" should be theirs, blotching or otherwise altering brands and, worst of all, stealing horses. Juries, however, refused to indict the accused, men like themselves trying to scratch out a living in a beautiful but hostile land. Jurors were sympathetic to the so-called thieves, hardworking cowboys like Jack Reshaw, who had been black-balled by the association during the bonanza years.

Indeed, newcomers to Powder River country found a champion in Reshaw, who was boisterous, full of fight, and a natural politician. He wrote funny, literate letters to the newspapers, skewering the big ranchers and praising the "little man." In 1888, he took on four partners, giving each man a one-fifth interest in his Lazy L and B outfit. Billy Sun and Nate Coday did not buy in, though they remained tight with Reshaw and his boys, or the "Rustler Elite" as Faucett and his associates called them. Though they never filed on a homestead, Nate and Billy set up an operation on the headwaters of the Middle Fork, in a protected valley shielded by trees and brush on the north and red sandstone walls on the southwest. There was only one way into the valley, and it was along this narrow trail that Nate and Billy built their cabin, a rough, two-room pine-log affair set up on foundation stones buried in the earth to keep out the restless Wyoming wind. It was barely big enough for two built-in bunks and a stove, but, because of Billy's horse work, Nate was alone there most of the time. He managed their growing cattle herd of about two hundred head.

Billy spent the warm-weather months riding from ranch to ranch on Sugarfoot's successor, a piebald paint named Heck. Billy's skills were much in demand, for he was able to gentle even the wildest, meanest horse in a single afternoon and never injured the animal, or turned him into a man-hater, in the process. People said he was successful because of his Indian blood, because only red men had such ancient understanding of four-leggeds, but whatever the reason he had a reputation as a man of merit, a man who could be trusted. For the first time in his life, Billy felt his future held promise, not simply days to mark off on a calendar. Billy Sun had money in the bank, a place to call home, and he was in love.

The killings started the next spring, though the first one took place outside of Johnson County, so it wasn't immediately recognized at the beginning for what it was, the opening salvo of the Johnson County War. The victim was Tom Waggoner, the German rancher who kept horses in the north, near Newcastle. For a long time Billy refused to work for him. It was a far ride up to Newcastle, and there were no ranches where Billy could stop and pick up extra work along the way. But the main reason Billy said no was because of the man himself. Waggoner brought a darkness with him, an aura of gloom and misfortune. People avoided him, and laughter stopped whenever he joined a circle. He was unclean in his personal habits and carried an earthy, animal scent like the smell of the grave.

Eventually, however, Billy agreed to break Waggoner's horses, but only when the German agreed to pay seven dollars a head. Even for that kind of money, Billy did not like going there. Waggoner did not take pride in the look of his place. He lived in a filthy, two-room cabin with a dirt floor and no furniture other than empty wooden crates and boxes. His common-law wife was a small, frightened-looking woman, who struck Billy as not right in the head, with three dirty children including a newborn. The woman and her babies were pitiful to look at, so Billy tried not to.

Despite his lack of personal charm, German Tom Waggoner had one thing and that was plenty of horses. How he got them Billy didn't know, and he wanted to keep it that way. Most bore Waggoner's mark, but some — if Billy looked close — appeared to wear a brand that might have been blotched or had new elements added. As with the woman and her babies, Billy made it a point not to look too close.

He rode to Newcastle in late May for a job that had been arranged the previous fall. When Billy arrived at the ranch he saw right off things weren't right. The cabin door was hanging crossways on its leather hinges, and one of the children was sitting bare-assed in the dirt, bawling.

"Tom?" he called. "It's Billy Sun. I'm here to work your horses."

No answer. He looked around the dusty yard. There was a water barrel beside the house, a child's wagon with only three wheels, an empty chair rocking in the wind. Though it was nearly noon, Billy saw no sign of industry, no sign of the simple-minded woman, no sign of Tom. The wailing child appeared to be alone.

He dismounted and walked toward the house, his gun at the ready. Stopping beside the open door, he peered into the darkened room. "Tom?" He heard a scuttling, like a desperate animal in its hole, and saw a shadow flit across the window on the far wall. "Who's there? Show yourself!"

He pressed his back against the side of the house and waited. Finally he heard a strangled sob and the woman shot out the door. She made straight for the child and took him in her skinny arms, holding him close. Immediately the boy stopped wailing. Billy smiled. A boy loves his mother, no matter what. The woman turned to Billy with wild eyes.

"Where's Tom?" he said. "What happened here?"

She shook her head but said nothing. Her eyes cut to the door. Looking in, Billy saw the other two children, including the newborn, lying motionless on the earthen floor. He hoped they were sleeping.

"What happened?" he said again. "Can you talk?" He realized he had never heard Tom's woman say a word. "Where is Tom?"

She held the child and rocked side to side. Billy had just about decided she was mute when she said, "They took him."

"Who took him? When?"

"Them — three men with black hoods. They took Tom two days ago. He didn't want to go with them, but they made him." Once she started, the words came rushing out. She walked to Billy and, though still holding the child, grabbed his arm with a bony hand. "Tom told me to wait, he said he'd come back but he ain't, and we're hungry. We ain't got nothing to eat. Will you find Tom for us, mister? Please!"

Billy looked at the low, sage-studded hills and felt the hair lift on the back of his neck.

About a half-mile over one of those rises was the valley where Tom kept his herd. That's what this is about, Billy thought, the horses. He was sure of it, the same way he was sure Tom Waggoner would not be coming back. He was out there somewhere, hanging from a tree or rotting in a shallow grave.

"Will you, mister? Will you find Tom?"

The woman's plaintive voice pulled Billy from his thoughts. He looked at her; her running eyes and nose left muddy tracks on her face. Had he ever seen a more pitiful creature? Billy wanted nothing more than to climb onto his horse's back and put miles between himself and this hellish place.

"I'll look for him," he said. "Do you and your children have a place to go? Is there anyone who can stay with you?" Billy knew the answer before he asked the question. People like Tom's woman never had a place to go. She looked at him with blank eyes and shook her head. Billy walked to his horse and emptied the contents of his saddlebags — jerky, crackers, canned peaches, coffee, a can of condensed milk — and offered them to her. "It's all I have," he said. She put the child on the ground with great gentleness, took the armload of food, and ran into the house where the other children were beginning to stir. At least they weren't dead, Billy thought, but then again, maybe they would have been better off in the world behind this one . . .

Billy had a good idea where he would find Tom, or what was left of him, and even if he didn't all he had to do was follow the trail left by the three horsemen. One set of prints was deeper than the others; this would have been the horse carrying Tom and one of his killers. Another animal, Billy noticed, was "barefoot," or unshod. He followed the trail north two miles, heading for the sheltered valley where Waggoner's horses were. There was good pasture there and a pole corral with a snubbing post in the middle.

He was unprepared for the sight that met his eyes when he crested the last hill. The last time he worked for Tom, he owned maybe two hundred head. Now Billy was looking at close to one thousand horses. Some were mustangs fresh off the range, but most clearly were finished, saddle-ready animals that were not bothered when Billy rode among them. He saw a variety of brands and some he recognized, including the U.S. mark. Billy had long suspected Tom was a rustler, and here was proof. He'd heard whispers that Waggoner's ranch served as a way station for highwaymen working out of Montana Territory and Nebraska, but Billy had no idea the scale of it. Tom must've had money — hell, with this many horses he must've been rolling in it — so what the blazes did he do with it all? Billy shook his head. If German Tom wanted to live in filth, that was his choice, but what kind of man made his woman and children live that way, too?

Gray clouds sailed in, obscuring the sun, and a cool wind blew down from the mountains. Billy turned Heck's head toward the creek that ran the length of the valley. The summer before it had gone dry, but now it was full, overflowing its banks. Waggoner's meadow was lovely as a park with lush green grass and a bumper crop of cone-flowers, red clover, and white, yellow goatsbeard, bluebottles, dandelions, and devil's paintbrush orange as pumpkins. Heck picked his way daintily through the wet, marshy ground as they moved along the valley floor. The place was so beautiful and the air so pure, Billy did not want to believe anything bad had happened here, but he knew different. They rounded the shoulder of a low hill and there was German Tom, good and dead, hanging from the stout branch of a cotton-wood.

Heck wanted nothing to do with the strange, stinking fruit and refused to go farther. Because he and the horse were still getting to know each other, Billy figured it wasn't worth a fight. He slid to the ground and walked forward, jumping when an enormous black crow flapped up out of the tall grass below the body, where it had been feeding on Tom's droppings. The smell got worse the closer he got. Billy covered his mouth and nose with his handkerchief, but it didn't help.

Tom's face was black and so swollen he was scarcely recognizable as a human being. His neck was grotesquely stretched so that his feet, small for a big man, almost touched the ground. The rope cut deep into the rotting flesh, and Tom's eyeballs protruded obscenely from their sockets. German Tom had died hard and slow. Billy didn't like the man, but even so it was hard to picture him ending that way, twisting in the desperate throes of asphyxiation, while his killers watched. And they did watch. Billy found the place where they sat their horses, side by side. One had enjoyed a smoke as Tom twisted; there was the burned end of a cigarette on the ground by the feet of the barefoot horse.

It started to rain. Fat drops fell like tiny bombs, leaving perfect craters in the dusty soil. Heck was jumpy and wanting to quit the place and Billy didn't blame him; he felt the same. He cut Tom down and stretched his decaying body on the ground, but he would not bury him. He didn't owe him that.

"Don't worry, boy," he said to Heck as he settled in the saddle. "This ain't our trouble and I will not make it so." But even as he spoke the words, Billy knew the trouble would come to him and all of Johnson County, and it was just getting started.

LORNA

Christmas, 1890

Lorna sat at the dressing table while Odalie stood behind her, brushing her hair. Music played below, mingled with the murmur of voices. Their eyes met in the mirror.

"Always remember," Odalie said, "the moment you walk through the door, you are the most beautiful woman in the room. No man will look at anyone else, only you."

"What if you're in the room?" Lorna said. "Who will they look at then?"

Odalie laughed. "Sugar, I guess we'll have to wait until I'm feeling better and then we'll see, won't we? But it won't be tonight. Tonight is all yours." She put down the brush and braided Lorna's shining hair into a long coil, twisted it into a simple chignon, and pinned it in place. She was careful to leave a few tendrils loose, to curl about Lorna's face and soften her features. "There," she said, stepping back to admire her handiwork. "Lorna, I can truly say you are an absolute vision, an angel descended from heaven. The dress is perfect, mauve suits you, my darling; it brightens your complexion and highlights your eyes. Pinch your cheeks so." She demonstrated and Lorna did the same, bringing a becoming pinkness to her skin. "Do this from time to time throughout the evening, when no one's looking, of course."

"Of course."

"Now," Odalie continued, "for your jewels." She opened the dresser's top drawer and took out a large enameled box, pale green in color and decorated with cabochons of garnet and turquoise. Lorna's eyes widened as Odalie lifted the lid and withdrew a rope of lustrous pearls, all perfectly round and of a generous size. The strand was long enough to twice encircle the girl's slender neck, its clasp an opened rose of solid gold with a brilliant diamond in the center.

"So beautiful," Lorna whispered, touching them. The pearls were smooth and cool against her olive skin, silvery in their luster. "Are they real?"

Odalie laughed. "What do you think, honey? Of course they're real. But if you want proof, rub them across your teeth. Feel that grittiness? Imitations are smooth. You can always tell the difference." After fastening the necklace around Lorna's neck, Odalie reached again into the enamel treasure box and selected a pair of diamond and pearl earbobs, which she held to Lorna's ears. "Perfect. These, too."

Lorna slipped the thin gold wires through the tiny holes in the lobes of her ears — Odalie had pierced them with a sewing needle, after first numbing the skin with ice — then stood to regard herself in the mirror. She smiled at her reflection. Was this sophisticated woman looking back at her really Lorna Dixon? It was all so wonderful: the brocade dress of mauve silk, the gleaming pearls, the way Odalie had slightly darkened Lorna's eyebrows with a kohl pencil to make her pale eyes more dramatic, the Parisian scent she dabbed behind her ears and on the underside of her wrists — who could believe that such simple things could change skinny Lorna Dixon with the scabby knees to the woman in the mirror? *Oh, if only Billy could see me now.* Her cheeks colored without pinching.

Odalie smiled to see the pride and excitement in the girl's face. "Are you happy, Lorna? Are you excited for your debut?"

"Oh, yes!" Lorna turned to the older

woman and threw her arms around her in an impulsive embrace. "Thank you for this, Odalie, for all of it. I'm so very grateful, but I don't understand why you've done this for me. Why did you?"

Odalie, still in her dressing gown, returned the girl's embrace. "Why, I told you, honey, I saw potential in you. I couldn't sit back and watch such a lovely young woman go to waste in this . . . this," she waved her hand, "this desert. And I must say, I was right. Everyone will be astonished when they see you tonight — I'm just sorry I won't be there to see your father's face." She laughed. "Oh, how I would love that. Won't he be surprised?" She glanced at the clock on the mantelpiece. "It's time to go down. Have a good time, sugar, enjoy yourself, but remember to be careful with the punch. Chang makes it strong. I've hold him a hundred times and he won't listen because Richard likes it that way. You may have one glass, but one glass only. Nothing — well, almost nothing — is more ruinous to a woman's reputation than drunkenness."

Lorna nodded. "I won't drink any punch. I don't need it." She kissed Odalie lightly on the cheek and walked to the door, then turned. "Is there any chance Billy will be here? All the ranchers think well of him;

he's finished their horses."

"Billy Sun? Goodness, no. Why would you think so?"

Lorna dropped her eyes. "I was just wondering . . . I haven't seen him for a long time, that's all."

Odalie stepped close to Lorna and took her hands. "Sugar, forget him. Haven't you been listening to what I've been telling you about Peter Dudley, or Lord Stanton's son, Robert, and his cousin, Will? They are educated young men with property and, yes, money, and they will be here tonight. You will dazzle them!" She squeezed Lorna's hands. "You would have a brilliant future with any one of those fellows, and if you don't like one of them there's plenty more where they come from! Not in Wyoming, maybe, but in New York, New Orleans, London, the real world! Forget you ever knew Billy Sun. He's goodlooking, I grant you that, and a fine horseman. I doubt any of those boys I mentioned could even come close to him on that score — but, sugar, he's a cowboy and an Indian to boot! No, the world is your oyster now, Lorna. You are a beautiful young woman, and there is no more powerful creature in God's great world. It's a gift from Mother Nature, her little joke — why, a beautiful woman can turn the strongest, most important man into a complete fool if she wants to — but it's a power that fades quickly, no matter how one tries to preserve it. So, take advantage of this gift you have and use it! Do not sell yourself short. No cowboys, sugar. No Billy Sun." She released Lorna's hands and gave her a gentle push. "Now go downstairs. I need my rest. I'm going to take a sleeping powder, but I'll want to hear all about your great triumph in the morning."

The evening unfolded just as Odalie said it would. Peter Dudley and the Stanton cousins, three handsome young men — Will Stanton, especially — followed Lorna around like puppies, and even their fathers pursued her with hungry eyes as she moved about the room. She caught a glimpse of herself in the mirror above the sideboard and was pleased with her reflection, especially the way Odalie's diamond earbobs sparkled in the candlelight.

When her father arrived, Lorna laughed aloud at the astonishment on his face.

"How beautiful you are," Dixon said, bending to kiss his daughter on the cheek. "I hardly recognized you. It's amazing, really. You look like a different person."

Lorna laughed. "I'm not. Odalie has

taught me how to dress, how to do my hair, but I'm still Lorna. Where is Cal? I was hoping to see both of you tonight."

"He's home with Mrs. MacGill. She hasn't been feeling well. I'm getting worried about her. She keeps getting weaker and weaker, and I can't figure out what's wrong. But enough of that. How was London?"

"All right," Lorna said. "I'm glad to have seen it, but the city was filthy, the streets, the air, all of it. Two weeks were quite enough. I loved the ocean crossing though. I wasn't sick once, not for a moment, not even during a storm. The voyage was my favorite part of the trip."

Dixon smiled. "Your mother was the same. When we went overseas I spent two days in the cabin, hanging over a bowl and wishing I was dead, but Rose loved every minute of it." He drifted a moment, remembering her hair blowing in the sea air and the bronze kiss of the sun on the bridge of her nose and cheekbones. "We visited London in sixty-nine — did I ever tell you that? — and Scotland, too. We spent hours wandering the medieval streets of Edinburgh's Old Town." He paused, regarding his daughter with an odd expression.

"What is it?" she said. "Why are you looking at me like that?"

"It's strange. You look very different, but at the same time you're more like your mother than I've ever seen you. It's your eyes."

Talk of her mother made Lorna uncomfortable, so she changed the subject. "So, how does Harry like Cincinnati? Are his studies going well?"

"I believe so, though he misses Wyoming. He says he feels closed in by all the trees, and the sky isn't big enough. But he enjoys his classes and the company of people his own age. He's never had much of that. Neither have you and Cal, for that matter. It's not right."

"Who cares?" Lorna said, tossing her head. "I wouldn't trade one day in Wyoming for a whole week in Ohio with 'people my own age.' How tedious that sounds." Suddenly her mood dimmed. She sighed and snapped open her fan, scanning the room for Billy. Despite what Odalie had said, she hoped he would show up. He was self-confident and well liked, even by these wealthy landowners. Most of all, Billy Sun did what he wanted to do, even if others did not approve. His boldness was one of the things she most admired about him. She surveyed the crowd with impatience. Her three suitors were hovering nearby. As she raised her hand to call them over, her eyes met those of Tom Horn, watching her with a predatory smile. Apparently in his cups, he started walking unsteadily toward her when, to her relief, he was waylaid by Lord Faucett.

"Mr. Horn!" Faucett said, pumping his hand. "Good to see you, man! I hear you may be joining our team. Great news, I must say. We could use a man with your particular skills. I'll certainly make it worth your while. Meantime, how's it been for you in Denver? Enjoy your time as a Pinkerton?"

"Hello, Sir Richard," Tom said, reluctantly pulling his eyes away from Lorna. "I thank you for the recommendation. Your word carries a lot of weight with Mr. McParland. He might not have hired me for a Pinkerton otherwise."

Faucett waved his hand dismissively. "No need for that, Horn. You've proved yourself time and again. I say, you and Doc Shores did especially good work with those horse thieves down in Arizona. Two of those stallions you recovered were mine, you know. The brigands stole them from a fellow in Colorado just days after I'd paid for them, and a pretty sum it was, too."

Horn smiled with a show of modesty. "Well, sir, I'm glad I could help. Me and

Doc, we partner up pretty good. Later this month Pinkerton's sending us up to Oregon on a job — well, me anyhow. I'm not sure about Doc on this one."

"Is that right?" Faucett said. "What is the assignment, if I may ask?"

"I'm sorry, Lord Faucett. I'm not at liberty to discuss it."

"No, no, 'course not. Good man."

Lorna, discreetly eavesdropping, was shocked. Tom Horn, a Pinkerton? She had pegged him for a criminal, and she fancied herself a good judge of character. Well, she thought, Pinkerton or no, Tom Horn was not to be trusted, she was sure of that.

Will Stanton asked her for the waltz, and as they glided about the room, Lorna felt Horn watching her. His eyes seemed to throw heat; they were penetrating and very dark, almost black, against his sunburned skin. Some women might find him attractive, Lorna thought, but not she.

Later that evening, as she danced again with Will, she spotted Horn and Frank Canton deep in conversation with Faucett, Moreton Dudley, and two other men, including Will's uncle.

"I wonder what that's about?" she said, smiling up at Will. "Looks like something important."

Will looked at her with adoring eyes. "Oh, it is. I know all about it, but I'm not supposed to talk."

"Not even to me?" She moved closer, briefly pressing her body against his. Will folded like a two-dollar suitcase.

"It's the rustlers," he said in a low voice. "Lord Faucett, Sir Dudley, my uncle, and others of the association, they've finally had their fill. The law won't go after them, and when Sheriff Angus actually does arrest someone, the courts won't convict. It's been going on long enough." Will's eyes glittered as he warmed to his topic. "The cattlemen, men like Lord Faucett and my uncle, they're the ones who've made this territory, and they're going to put an end to the stealing once and for all."

Lorna's heart raced. "And how will they do that?"

Will smiled knowingly and nodded toward the cabal in the corner. "Do you see that man talking to Sir Richard, the tall one with the mustache?"

"Tom Horn?"

Will nodded. "Tom Horn, Tom Hale, he goes by both names. Anyhow, he and some others, they'll be brought in to deal with the rustlers. Jack Reshaw and the Lazy L and B boys, Nate Coday, Billy Sun, and that lot, just you wait. They'll be food for the worms come spring."

ODALIE

Billy and Odalie lay together on his narrow bed, under a striped traders' blanket. Though it was midday, the room was cool and dark. Her head was on his shoulder, and he stroked her unbound hair.

"You should always wear it this way," he said. "Loose, down on your shoulders. You should stop pinning it."

She laughed. "A woman can't walk around with wild, blowing hair, like some kind of savage." Immediately she regretted her choice of words. "That is, it's not done."

"Too bad," Billy said. Then, after a pause, "How did you get away this time?"

"I said I needed to exercise my horse. Richard wanted Fred to accompany me, but I said I wanted to be alone. I must head back soon or they'll start looking for me."

"Don't go." Billy pushed himself up on one elbow, then leaned down to kiss her on the mouth. "Don't ever go. Stay with me forever. I want you to."

With a sound of impatience she pushed him away, threw off the blanket, and got out of bed. Billy watched her walk to the room's only chair, where her clothing was draped, and begin to dress, starting with her silk chemise.

"What is it?" Billy said. "What did I say?"

She did not answer. Her back was to him, and he could not see her face.

"Odalie?"

She buttoned her dress, then sat in the chair to pin up her hair. Billy's room had no mirror so she did this by touch. He remained in the bed, waiting for an answer.

"We agreed what this would be when it started," she said at last, raising her eyes to meet his. "It's ruined when you talk like that."

Billy's face darkened. "I didn't know I was violating our treaty."

"Well, you were. You should know that." She leaned down to button her boots, fawn in color and of the softest kid. Billy had noticed their softness when he pulled them off Odalie's small, well-formed feet. He thought he would have to finish ten horses to afford a pair of boots like that.

"I'm leaving now," she said, standing and smoothing her skirt. He leaned down for his pants, but she raised her hand. "No, stay where you are. I'll let myself out."

"Odalie," he said. "Don't go away angry. I won't see you for a while. It's been good today, don't spoil it." He ran a hand through his hair, pushing it back from his eyes. "You said I need a haircut. You were going to cut it for me, remember?"

"I don't have time." She turned to him, and any anger she felt melted away. He looked like a boy, a lovely boy, with his lean, copper body, hairless chest, and remarkable green eyes. She had even grown to like the heathenish bear claw necklace he wore around his neck. She smiled. "Besides, I like it long. It suits you."

Odalie did not blame herself for what had happened between them. How could she? Any normal woman in her position would have done the same, but even so she could not let this bit of self-indulgence complicate her life. She did not fear disgrace, but she did fear poverty. Richard, she knew, would not be generous if her secret came out. The time had come to end this with Billy, though she would have liked to continue a bit longer. She crossed the room to sit beside him on the bed.

"Billy, I care for you, you know I do, but there was never a chance it would be more than this. We discussed it, remember? Besides, I'm older than you. Old enough to be your mother, or close to."

He looked injured. "That's not true. Anyhow what difference does it make? Our years, that's not what this is about."

"No," she said, "of course you're right. It's not about our ages. I'll be honest. I could never spend my life with a cowboy, not even you." She reached out to touch his face. "Surely you realize that. I'm too spoiled, too accustomed to my comforts, and I'd be miserable without them." She looked around the spare room, with its bed, lone chair, and rickety table. "I'd make you miserable, too."

"No —"

She interrupted. "Of course I would. But there is someone else who cares for you, someone who would make you much happier than I ever could." She hesitated. Just a short time ago she was counseling Lorna to forget Billy, to choose someone from a higher station in life, but now she thought maybe she had erred. True love was a rare thing, and Lorna loved Billy. With a bit of support from Richard, a generous wedding present perhaps, Billy could get a good start and eventually, with his skills, make a comfortable life for them, maybe not in

Wyoming, but somewhere. For a moment, Odalie envied her protégé. Billy was a wonderful lover, by far the best she had ever known, and she had known her share.

"I'm speaking of Lorna, of course," she said. "She is a beautiful woman, more beautiful than I ever was, even in my youth. You must know she has feelings for you, Billy. Why not accept them? Many men would, and quite happily, too."

Billy sat up and, gingerly, put his feet on the floor. The day before a horse had stepped on him, breaking his big toe, which was bound to its neighbor with a dirty strip of gauze. He picked his jeans up off the floor and stood to step into them. "I know how Lorna feels. I've known for a long time. I do not feel the same for her."

"Why not? You should have seen her at her debut. She owned the room. No man could look at anyone else, or so I'm told." She smiled and reached out to take his hand. She and Billy had been together that night, for a dangerous, stolen hour in the loft of the horse barn. They were almost discovered by Fred Jolly, a brush with danger that only made the experience, for her, all the more exhilarating.

"Lorna is good to look at," he said. "But her spirit does not speak to me."

Odalie raised her eyebrows. "And mine does?"

"Yes," he said. "Since the first moment I saw you. You have a good heart, but you hide it. I don't know why. You are kind, more kind than she is."

She shook her head, feeling strangely exposed and embarrassed. "You don't know me."

"I do know you."

Billy looked into her eyes, and Odalie turned away, feeling her face go warm. This is ridiculous, she thought. She got up and walked to the window. There was something else she had to say to him.

"Richard and the association are planning something. I don't know what exactly, but it involves Frank Canton and that other fellow, Horn. You must know Richard suspects you of rustling — you, Nate, and Jack. You must be careful."

"Odalie —"

She raised her hand. "I don't know if you steal cattle, and I don't want to know. Frankly, I don't care, but Frank Canton's been coming by the house more than he used to, and he usually has that Horn fellow with him. They meet in Richard's study with the door closed. Moreton Dudley and David Stanton are part of this, too. I have a bad feeling. I know how angry and cruel Richard is. You and your friends must be careful."

Billy's expression grew serious when Odalie mentioned Canton's companion. "Tom Horn. The man is a killer. I hear he places a stone under the heads of his victims, like a pillow. His heart is black."

Odalie put her hand on Billy's hairless chest. "Take care of yourself, Billy. You're a good man, and you matter to me. We won't be together like this again, but I don't want to see you get hurt." She walked out of the cabin, closing the door softly behind her.

DIXON

Daniel Dixon sat in the parlor in his favorite chair, holding a new copy of the novel *Anna Karenina* by his favorite writer, Leo Tolstoy. He'd been looking forward to this moment ever since he read of the book's English publication in a dog-eared copy of the *New York Times.* He'd ordered the novel directly from the publisher, Thomas Y. Crowell & Co., and paid with a "check," a new means of commerce by mail that did not require the posting of actual currency. The book had taken some time to arrive, but finally appeared in the post today. Now all was at the ready; the coal lamp was lit, and he had a sharp knife at hand for cutting the pages along with a glass of red wine on the table. With a sigh of satisfaction, he opened the book, its leather-bound spine cracking in complaint. If this one was anything like *War and Peace,* Dixon thought, he had a splendid journey ahead.

He was finishing the first page when someone knocked. With a sigh of disgust, he put down his book and opened the door to find Sheriff Red Angus leaning against the frame. He was bleeding from a cut on his head and cradled one arm awkwardly against his chest.

"Thank God you're home, Dixon," he said. "I'm about all in."

Dixon helped Angus to the chair he just vacated. "What happened?"

"Somebody took a shot at me," Angus said. "Spooked my horse. I think I broke my arm when I fell."

Dixon hoped he was wrong. Broken bones were time consuming, and he planned to spend the evening with his new book. He examined Angus's head wound first. Like all such injuries, it bled profusely but would not require stitches. A cleaning and a plaster would suffice. Then he turned to the arm, carefully pulling off the sheriff's jacket. As he loosened his shirt, Dixon noticed an older, well-healed wound, perhaps caused by the graze of a bullet, on Angus's shoulder. "What's that?" he said.

Angus re-covered the scar. "It's nothing. Just a little accident I had a while back. Didn't amount to nothing."

Dixon noticed the sheriff's fingers, they

240

were swollen and discolored — a bad sign.

"How did you fall?" Dixon said. "Which part took the impact?"

Angus demonstrated with his good arm, extending it palm down toward the floor. "I landed so," he said. "There was a loud pop."

Dixon rolled up the sheriff's torn sleeve to find the classic bayonet-shaped deformity characteristic of a Colles fracture. "The bones of your wrist are broken," he said. "I'll need to set them and splint your arm." He helped Angus to his feet. Though the summer evening and the house were cool, Angus's thin, ginger-colored hair lay in wet, sweaty strings across his head.

They walked through the darkened hallway to Dixon's surgery in the back of the house. It still smelled of Dixon's dinner: fresh mountain trout, dredged in cornmeal and fried in olive oil. He opened the surgery door and lit the lamp, then walked to the waist-high exam table in the middle of the room and pushed a low stool in place so the short, stocky sheriff could climb up. After Angus was settled, Dixon unlocked the supply closet and took out splinting materials, gauze, and tape.

"This will hurt, Red, but it'll be over in twenty seconds." In Dixon's experience, few bones were as painful to set as the radius and ulna. "Are you ready?"

Angus set his jaw and extended his misshapen arm. "I guess I am."

Dixon gripped the sheriff's lower arm with both hands, placing one just above the breaks and one below, pulling with one hand while pushing with the other. He felt the bones move beneath the skin and heard a small click as they slipped back in place. "There," he said. "It's done."

Angus's face was completely drained of blood, so even his lips were white. He kept his eyes firmly closed as Dixon bent his elbow to a ninety-degree angle and wrapped his forearm in white gauze with a sugartong splint.

"You have any idea who the shooter was?" Dixon said when he saw the sheriff's color returning.

"I do," Angus said. "And if it wasn't him, it was the other or maybe the two of them together. They are an unholy pair."

"You didn't see anyone then?"

Angus opened his eyes and looked at Dixon. "No, but I know who it was just the same. I want you to know, too, Doc, but I'm asking you to keep the information to yourself. This thing is going to blow wide open soon enough, and I want to try to contain it as long as I can. People are going to get hurt."

Dixon returned the unused supplies to the closet and locked it. He wasn't sure he wanted to hear what the sheriff was about to tell him.

"It was Frank Canton," Angus said. "Him or his scaly friend Tom Horn, one or the other. Canton's been out for me ever since I announced for sheriff. I know what he's been saying about me and about my friends, how it's disgraceful that a man like me should be Johnson County's top lawman. Well, you know what? I may have made some bad choices in my life — who hasn't? — but I don't give a damn what Canton says about me. The good people of Johnson County don't, either. I'm an honest man and I do the job, not the bidding of the WSGA."

Dixon raised his eyebrows. "You think Canton tried to kill you tonight? That's a serious charge."

"That son-of-a-bitch is still doing the dirty work for Faucett and Dudley and them, just like he always has. They're gunning for me because they know I'm on the side of the nesters and little men. This is public land, goddamn it, they got no right to claim it. It's all coming to smash now, Dixon, and everyone, you included, will have to pick sides."

The desperate winter of 1886–87 had worsened the competition for rangeland, and now the bad blood had boiled to the killing point. Dixon's first thought was of Billy, who, along with his friends Nate and Jack, the so-called Rustler Elite, was smack in the thick of it. He thought also of Lorna, still living with the Faucetts in The Manor. It was time to bring her home.

Angus was waiting for some kind of response. "I have no dog in this fight," Dixon said, realizing as he spoke them how cowardly his words sounded. He felt vaguely ashamed but at the same time, he was angry. After all, he was a fifty-year-old man and he'd seen his share of war and bloodshed and hatred. Wasn't he entitled to a little peace? "Here," he said, taking Angus's coat off the back of a chair, "let me help you with this."

Disappointment showed on the sheriff's face as he gingerly slid his arm into the sleeve. "Like it or not, you are in this fight, Dixon. Men like you, with a role in the community, you got to take a stand. Everyone who lives in the free state of Wyoming will be involved in this war that's coming. One thing for sure you could do, Doc: you could convince Billy Sun and his friends to leave Powder River country for a while. Persuade them to go up north to Montana for a bit, maybe. That would go far to keep the peace."

"I could try," Dixon said, "but I doubt he'll listen. I don't have that much influence."

"Too bad," Angus said, climbing down from the table. "People are going to be hurt. What do I owe you?"

"Ten dollars. There's no rush; pay me when you can."

"I'll be on my way then but remember what we talked about tonight, Dixon. Try to get Billy and them to clear out. And if you hear anything you think I should know, come see me. I expect that of you."

Dixon nodded. "Of course."

As they walked the length of the house to the front door, Dixon wondered if Canton and Horn were waiting outside, hot for a second chance at Angus or whoever appeared in their rifle sights. Angus noticed his hesitation and smiled.

"It's times like these show a man what he's made of," he said. The sheriff threw open the door and stepped out into the darkness.

BILLY SUN

Jack Reshaw surprised everyone by taking a wife. She was a tiny, redheaded widow from Cheyenne, mother to a six-year-old boy. Billy and Nate were slack-jawed with astonishment when Jack brought mother and son home in his wagon, she sitting stiffly beside him on the bench and the boy riding in the back with their few pieces of furniture and several boxes of groceries.

"Hell, Jack," Nate said after introductions were made and the bride had gone inside to survey her new home. "We didn't even know you was courtin.' How did this happen?"

Jack grinned bashfully. "It just did. Her name is Sara and the boy is Davey, and I aim to make a good home for us. A good, solid home. Nate, when he gets a little older I want you to teach the boy how to handle a gun and, Billy, you can show him how to ride."

"Sure, Jack," Billy said. But looking at Davey, Billy thought he'd have his work cut out for him. The boy was thin as a rail and jumpy as a flea in a skillet. Growing up with a ma like Sara, Billy could see why. What she lacked in size, she made up for in meanness. Jack's new wife was the queen of hair-pulling and name-calling, and neither he nor Nate could understand what their friend saw in her. One afternoon she boxed Davey in the ears for accidentally kicking over a pail of new milk. "You are a trial to me, boy!" she said. "A trial and a vexation, just like your pa." Davey ran to the barn. Sara stormed into the house and slammed the door.

Jack kept his eyes on his boots, his face flushed with embarrassment. "She can be short tempered sometimes," he said, "but she has other talents. You'll just have to take my word for that."

Billy and Nate exchanged glances. "All women get cross now and then," Nate said. "I never met one who didn't. Your Sara's a fine woman, anyone can see that." It was true Sara kept the house neat as a pin, put curtains on the windows, swept the floors every day, and sanded them once a week. The grounds around the cabin and barn were free of litter, and she'd started a kitchen garden in the back.

"She does go hard on that boy, though," Billy said. This was not the first time he had seen her strike him.

Jack nodded. "I know it. I intend to have a word with her about that, but I am not looking forward to it. The woman does not brook criticism." He cast an anxious eye toward the house. "I swan, I ain't never seen such a temper."

"And I bet you didn't see it when you was courtin', neither," Nate said.

Jack turned on him with a face like thunder. "Have a care when you speak of my wife, Nate Coday. I'll hear no disrespect." He walked to the house, carefully scraping his boots before going inside.

Nate shook his head. "It brings me no pleasure to say it, Billy, but Nate's wife is a termagant. I pity him. Jack will rue the day he swore his vows."

"If a termagant is a mean, spiteful woman whose heart would get lost in a thimble, then that's what she is," Billy said. "But I figure Jack will deal with her when he's had enough. It's the boy I feel for; he's had nothing but her meanness all his life. It's no way for a boy to come up."

Nate mounted his horse. "I've had enough of this place. You coming back?"

Billy shook his head. "No, you go on. I'll be along later." He walked to the barn and stuck his head in the open door. "Davey?" he called. "You in here?"

His greeting was met with silence, but he went in. The barn was dark and Billy's eyes had not yet adjusted from the bright sun. "Davey?" He heard a dry shuffling in the loft. "Come on down here," Billy said. "I want to show you something."

"What?" The small, pale face appeared above him, at the top of the loft stairs. The boy had his mother's red hair, though his was uncombed and full of cowlicks.

"Only a honey tree I found yesterday. Thought maybe you'd like to get some with me."

Davey leaned out a little farther. "A honey tree?"

Billy nodded. "Ain't that far, neither."

The boy hesitated, then pulled back out of sight. "You don't have to, mister. I'm all right."

"I know that. Sure I do. Only I'm headed that way and I'd like company. Say, you know who else likes honey? Jack. Maybe he'll ride out there with us."

"He won't," Davey said glumly. "Ma wants him for chores, and he's afraid of Ma. Everybody's afraid of Ma."

Billy shook his head. "Your ma has a sharp tongue, and that's a fact. My ma was the same and she was Indian. Why, her tongue was so sharp she could clean a buffalo hide with it."

Davey's face appeared again at the top of the stairs. "You a full-blood Injun?" he said.

Billy pulled the grizzly claw necklace out of his shirt and held it out for Davey to see. "Pretty near. My Pa was white but I grew up Mountain Crow. That's why I'm so good getting honey away from bees. Like I said, I'm going and if you don't come down, you'll miss out."

"Ma won't like it," Davey said. "I got chores."

"You bring honey home, and I bet she won't mind. Might even sweeten her up some."

Davey considered, then scrambled down the ladder. "What's your name, mister?"

"Billy Sun."

"You're a friend of Jack's?"

"Yes. We go back a ways."

Davey offered his hand. "Okay then, let's go." Billy was not expecting this; it had been a long time since he'd held a child's hand. When he took it, it felt like a bag of small, fragile bones.

■ ■ ■ ■

They rode three miles to the fallen cotton-wood where the bees had made their hive. Davey followed Billy and Heck on his calico pony, Dale.

"He's named for my pa," Davey said. "He died when I was four. Pa cut his hand when he was chopping firewood and we wrapped it real tight but poison got in anyway." Billy recalled a freezing winter night when an injured cowboy and his friend came to Dixon's surgery. The cowboy had an infected hand that the doctor could not save. He amputated but it was too late; the fellow died that afternoon. Later, Dixon explained to Billy the injury itself was not that bad, the flesh had mortified because the friend had bound it too tightly. "Sometimes an overabundance of good intentions is more dangerous than neglect," Dixon said.

Billy looked back at the boy and saw sadness on his face. Remembering his pa had made him blue.

"I'm going to tell you a story about the first person to bring honey to my people," Billy said. "It was a boy about your age who lived a long time ago. He was poor and had no relations. A bear had killed his mother and father and clawed the boy's face when he was a baby, so the people called him Scarface. He didn't care about that, he believed in himself anyhow. He knew he would do something great someday. When he grew up, Scarface fell in love with the beautiful daughter of a chief, but all the other young men wanted her, too. She liked Scarface but she would have none of them because the Sun-God decreed that she could not marry.

" 'This is a heavy burden,' Scarface said to her. 'Is there no way you may be free of it?'

"She said, 'There is one way only. I will be free only if a brave man goes to the Sun-God and asks him to release me.' Scarface said he would go to the lodge of the Sun-God immediately.

"The daughter said, 'And when you see him, ask him to remove the scar from your face as a sign so I will know you truly spoke to him and he has given me to you.'

"So Scarface rode for many moons seeking the home of the Sun-God. He rode across prairies and deserts, rivers and snow-covered mountains, but he could not find the Sun-God's lodge. Then one day he met a handsome warrior sitting dejected on a rock. When Scarface asked what troubled him, the handsome warrior said he had lost his bow and arrows.

" 'I have seen them,' Scarface said. 'I found them by the lake and they are there still. Although they were very fine, I did not take them because they did not belong to me.'

"The handsome youth praised Scarface for his honesty and asked where he was going. 'I seek the lodge of the Sun-God,' Scarface said. And the handsome youth said, 'I am Morning Star and the Sun-God is my father. Come with me.'

"But on the way, Scarface and Morning Star were attacked by the savage birds that lived beside the Endless Waters. Scarface saved them both from the monsters and together they traveled on to the lodge of the Sun-God, who was very grateful for the rescue of his beloved son.

" 'How can I repay you?' the Sun-God said. And Scarface told him of his love for the chief's daughter. 'I shall free her,' the Sun-God said, 'and as a sign of my goodwill, I shall make your face handsome and smooth.' Scarface thanked him and turned to start his journey home. But then the Sun-God said, 'Stop!' and Scarface trembled for fear he had changed his mind. But the Sun-God said, 'Take this also, for the chief's wife is a sour woman and this will sweeten her foul nature.' Do you know what the Sun-God gave Scarface?" Billy said, turning in the saddle.

"Honey?" Davey said with a smile.

Billy nodded. "So Scarface took the honeycomb to the chief's wife and she smiled on him, and all was good for Scarface and his beautiful bride for the rest of their days."

They rode the rest of the way in silence until Billy reined in his horse and pointed to a downed tree in a dry creek bed. "There's our honey. It won't be long now."

While Davey tied down the horses, Billy squatted next to one end of the hollow tree and made a smoky fire of old burlap bags and green pine needles. Davey approached cautiously for the bees were beginning to stir.

"Don't worry," Billy said. "The smoke will quiet them. If one lands on you, keep calm. Bees are like horses and dogs; they sense your fear and take advantage of it. If you do get stung, scrape the stinger off but do not pull it. If you pull, the little sack of poison on the end will break and then you will feel it."

Davey nodded. By now the fire was producing thick gray plumes of smoke. Billy gave him a saddle blanket. "Fan the smoke toward the opening." As the boy fanned, Billy rolled down his sleeves and buttoned the cuffs, tied a handkerchief over the lower half of his face, and pulled on a pair of leather gloves. Then he took a small ax from his pack-along and made two holes in the tree about three feet apart. After this he connected the two holes with a series of shallow cuts, marking a long, rectangular slab. "Add more pine needles, Davey," he said through the kerchief, "and keep the smoke coming."

Very carefully, Billy pried loose the slab, exposing the colony. Bees flew up at him, landing thickly on his arms and face. He did not swat at them or fight them but kneeled and, with a small shovel, lifted out a thick sheet of honeycomb and placed it in a deep metal bucket, covering the top with a piece of cheesecloth. Davey noticed Billy left half the comb in the log. Finally, he put the rectangular slab back in place, recovering the colony. Together, he and the boy extinguished the fire, smothering the flames with dirt until there was no more smoke. Then they sat under a tree and ate honey with their hands, comb and all, until they'd had their fill. Still, there was plenty to take home.

■ ■ ■ ■

It was late afternoon by the time they got back to the house. The sinking sun struck Sara's red hair as she stood on the porch, looking for all the world, Billy thought, like a wooden kitchen match. She ran to meet them as they rode up. "Davey, you get down this instant!"

As soon as Davey's feet hit the ground she hauled off and hit him on the side of the head. "Ma!" the boy cried, cowering and covering his reddening ear with his hand.

"I been worried sick about you," she said, her face contorted with fury. "How dare you take off without my say-so!" Sara was preparing to strike him again when Billy sprang from his horse and caught her hand.

"Don't hit the boy, Sara," he said. "It was my fault. I asked him to come with me. He didn't do wrong."

She wheeled on him. "And what do you know about it?" He realized he still held her hand and dropped it like a red-hot coal. In the midst of this confrontation Jack came out of the house.

"What's happening here?" he said.

"I'll tell you what!" Sara said. "Your Injun friend took Davey off without my say-so and now he's trying to tell me how to discipline my own son." She lunged at the boy again, but this time Jack grabbed her arm.

"No, Sara," he said. "I want you to stop hitting the boy. My feelings on this are strong."

Sara turned her fury on her husband. "And since when do I take instruction from the likes of you on the business of child-rearin'?" They stood face to face in the gathering twilight, chickens scratching in the dirt at their feet.

"Since you became my wife and Davey my stepson," Jack said.

"He's my boy, not yours," she said, "and I'll do with him as I please."

With his open hand, Jack struck her soundly on the face. Sara gasped and covered her cheek with her hand. Her face drained of color.

"How do you like it?" Jack said quietly. "I won't mistreat you, Sara, and I'll not let you mistreat the boy. I'm telling you how things will be."

Sara stepped back but the fight was not out of her. "I love my son," she said, "but I will not spoil him. Davey's got to learn the way of the world, the overall fitness of things. Otherwise, he'll turn out weak and shiftless like his pa."

"He wasn't!" The three adults turned to Davey. They had almost forgotten him in their anger with each other. "Pa was not weak and shiftless!" His lower lip trembled, but he soldiered on. "He worked hard but you never thanked him — you never thanked him for nothing! He never did anything good enough for you. I miss Pa — I wish I was up in heaven with him." With this the dam broke and Davey's face collapsed into tears. Again, he ran to the barn.

Without another word to Jack or Billy, Sara walked into the house and slammed the door.

Billy filled his cheeks with air, then exhaled loudly. "Jesus, Joseph and Mary!" Though not a Christian, Billy swore like one. "I don't know what set her off like that. Davey was low after that business with the milk this morning, so I took him out to a honey tree I found. We brought some back." He pointed to the tin bucket hanging from Heck's saddle horn.

"Don't fault yourself, Billy," Jack said. "It was coming anyhow. I ain't never hit a woman before, but damn, I do not countenance the way she beats on that boy. Things will be different now. Will you stay for supper?"

"No," Billy said quickly. "I've got to get

back. I'll leave the honey by the door. You and Davey can have it on hot buttered biscuits tonight, if she ain't too mad to make 'em."

Jack looked to the house. "Oh, she'll make 'em. Like I said, things are going to be different around here, for all of us."

ODALIE

Dixon, Lorna, and Odalie sat in the front room of the Faucetts' sprawling mansion. The Big Horn Mountains filled the floor-to-ceiling windows that opened onto a covered deck that encircled The Manor. The mountains' snowy crests appeared bright against the dark clouds behind them. The sun cast a stormy light.

Lorna wore a petulant expression as Chang poured tea. "I don't see why I have to go," she said, "especially since we were just about to leave for New Orleans. I've been learning so much, Pa — just ask Odalie about how my French is coming. Don't make me come home!"

"It's true, you know," Odalie said. "Your daughter is a very apt pupil, and we were planning a trip. My husband won't be able to come with us. Richard is much caught up in his business just now, and I don't like traveling alone."

Dixon cleared his throat. Part of him would be happy to leave his difficult daughter with Odalie, but if trouble was coming — and he thought it was — the Faucetts would be in the eye of the storm. Lorna's place was not with them. Also, it was high time his daughter learned to make herself useful, time she thought of someone other than herself for a change. Since the sudden death of Mrs. MacGill — he had returned from the Faucetts' party that evening to be met by a wild-eyed Cal, who described finding her dead in her bed — he and Cal had all they could do to keep the household functioning. "Thank you, Lady Faucett," he said, "for all you've done, but it's best that Lorna come home. We miss her and, frankly, we need her help. I will hire another housekeeper, but it'll take a while to find one."

Lorna rolled her eyes and muttered something under her breath.

"Yes, of course you're right," Odalie said. "I'm afraid I've been selfish with your daughter's time. You need to be with your family now, Lorna. After all, your nanny has passed. Or . . ." Her eyes brightened and she extended a slender hand toward Dixon. "Perhaps there is another way. Why don't you and your family come with us to New Orleans? I haven't told Lorna about this yet, but I've arranged a side trip to Grand Isle, a lovely place on the Gulf where Richard and I often spend the summers. It's so restful there, with the sun and the ocean breezes. It would do you a world of good, and your children, too."

Lorna jumped to her feet and clapped her hands. "Yes, Pa, it's perfect — you know it is. Please say you'll come!" She turned to Odalie, urging her to continue.

Odalie nodded. "Doctor, you once told me you haven't been to New Orleans since the war. Well, as I said then, it's changed a great deal since then, and not for the better, I'm afraid, but there are still places along the Vieux Carre where you can find the old magic." She smiled. "You just have to know where to look."

Dixon had no doubt Odalie could find magic wherever she was. She seemed to create it, with just her presence. Still, he would not give in. Dixon shook his head apologetically. "Thank you, but my family and I can't go on taking advantage of your hospitality. Lorna must come home."

Lorna stamped her foot. "No! I'm going to Grand Isle with Odalie and that's all there is to it."

"Lorna," Odalie said sharply, "that's no way for a young woman to speak to her father. Say you're sorry at once."

"I won't. He doesn't care about me, he never has. He wishes Cal and I had never been born. He blames us for our mother's death. There, you see? He doesn't deny it."

Dixon sat stunned, as if nailed to the chair. He had never admitted such a thing, not even to himself, but his parental responsibility was the same, regardless. "I'll be back tomorrow, Lady Faucett," he said, "with the wagon for her things. Again, thank you for all you have done."

"You can save yourself the trip," Lorna said with a toss of her head. "I won't be leaving with you."

Odalie leaped from her chair and, before Lorna could anticipate what was about to happen, slapped her hard across the mouth. The girl's eyes filled with tears and she ran from the room.

"I hope I haven't made you angry, Doctor," Odalie said, "but that's how a woman deals with a disobedient child where I come from. If her mother were here, I believe she would approve. Lorna will be ready tomorrow when you arrive."

JACK RESHAW

Most years Jack Reshaw was sorry to see the cold weather set in, but not this year. He and his partners had worked hard, building the Lazy L and B's herd from two hundred to four hundred head over the course of the summer. Now he was ready to kick back and enjoy the holidays with his new family. Sara was still high spirited, but she no longer raised her hand to Davey. And the boy seemed happier, less timid, and more willing to spend time with his step-father.

The fall roundup had been contentious, with Lord Faucett and other members of the WSGA accusing Jack and his men of splotching brands and claiming mavericks in violation of the 1884 law. Jack countered these charges in a letter, written with Sara's help, to the *Buffalo Bulletin.*

I have been accused of building my Brand

with the long rope and the running iron. Anyone who knows me and my partners knows this is not true. My title to the cattle is clear, and no man acquainted with the facts could say otherwise. We owners of the Lazy L and B are free men, entitled to the fruits of our own labors, and we will not be unmanned by a club of tyrants who claim as their own public lands that by rights belong to all of us! For years, these despots have confiscated "mavericks" that belong to us and will not let us reclaim them or even buy them back when they come up for sale. No more!

It is time the hard-working small cattlemen of Johnson County unite and stand up to our oppressor! It is time we take matters in our own hands. Furthermore, I suggest we start our spring roundup early, on May 1. This will protect our property from the devastation brought by the large herds moving through and, most importantly, prevent the continued confiscation of our cattle.

I ask you: *Are we not, as free men and women, entitled to the fruits of our labors?*

Small ranchers were emboldened by Jack's letter. The newly formed Northern Wyoming Farmers' and Stockgrowers' Association, which included women among its members, enthusiastically endorsed the early start date and appointed Billy Sun roundup foreman.

The WSGA was unexpectedly muted in its response. In a reply to Jack's letter, written by Richard Faucett, the association noted that only the state livestock commission (whose members belonged to the WSGA) had the legal authority to start and conduct roundups. Jack's move, Faucett alleged, was nothing more than an attempt to steal all the mavericks on the range before the legitimate owners could claim them. *"Rest assured,"* Faucett wrote, *"the association's lawyer will ensure that this obvious attempt at thievery will be dealt with promptly and appropriately."*

Jack and Sara lay in bed, her head on his shoulder. It was a cold night in late November and both were tired. Jack had spent the day shoeing horses, while his wife did the heavy laundry — britches and blankets — working long hours in the hard autumn sun.

"I'll be taking the wagon into Buffalo tomorrow," Jack said, stroking her hair. "Make a list of the things you need. I'll be gone a couple days." He enjoyed his trips to Buffalo this time of year, when folks from all over Powder River country came to town to buy supplies for the winter, transact business, and catch up on the latest news. Best of all, court was in session in late November and early December and the judicial goings-on were always a rich form of entertainment.

"Who knows?" Jack said. "If you stay sweet, could be a little surprise in the wagon for you when I come back." He kissed the top of her head. Things had been good since that trouble the day of the honey tree. "I saw a toy drum in Raylan's last time I was in town. If it's still there I thought I'd buy it for Davey."

Sara raised her head to look at him. "A toy drum? Jack, Davey's too old for that. I've been thinking you should get him a gun and start showing him how to use it. It's time he learned."

"Honey, he ain't but seven and barely that. He's not ready for a gun."

"Pappa got my brother a gun when he was six and nothing bad came of it. In fact, Luther was the best shot in five counties."

"Well, it's a personal thing. Could be some boys are ready at six, but most are not. Davey isn't."

Jack felt Sara stiffen. Sensing an argument on the horizon, he gave in. "All right, all right." He pressed her head back down on his chest and resumed stroking her hair. "I'll look into it."

He left after breakfast, but progress was slow. Recent rains had turned the road into a sticky red gumbo, and his team could manage no better than a slow walk. Several times the iron wheels sank nearly to the axle and Jack had to climb down and push. Though the trip to Buffalo was only twenty-three miles, it was dark by the time he finally made town. After stabling his horses and the wagon, he walked to the Occidental Hotel. He was drinking beer in the bar, when Orley "Ranger" Jones came in. Jones was building a cabin for himself and his wife-to-be on the Red Fork, a few miles downstream from Jack's place.

"Hello, neighbor," Jack said. "Take a seat." He called to the bartender for a bottle of sarsaparilla, as Ranger Jones never took a drink. "I haven't seen you in some time. What brings you to town?"

Ranger folded his long, rangy body into the chair and put his hat on the table. Like most cowboys and men who lived in the saddle, his forehead was whiter than the rest of his face. "The house brings me. I'm here for floorboards and windows. The house, she's really coming along. I'll be finished by

Christmas, easy. Come by and take a look."

Jack smiled. "I'll come by when it's done. Otherwise you'll have me shingling the roof or laying floors." Jack liked Ranger. The young man had come to Wyoming Territory from Nebraska in 1887 and quickly made a name for himself as a reliable cowhand and top-notch bronc-buster, second only to Billy Sun. Like Jack, he had run afoul of the big ranchers when he stopped riding for the EK brand and announced plans to start his own place. Also like Jack, Ranger had been blackballed by the WSGA. He and Fred Jolly had a special dislike for each other.

"So when are you and your lady tying the knot?" Jack said.

"We're waiting till spring," Ranger said, eyeing a comely young woman entering the restaurant with her beau. "That's how Susanna wants it."

Jack smiled and sipped his beer. He could tell his young friend a thing or two about marriage, starting with what happens when a fellow looks at another woman, but he'd let Ranger learn these things on his own. "It's always best to let a woman have things the way she likes them," Jack said.

"The hell," Ranger said.

"It's not that bad," Jack said. "Though you might have to remind her who wears the pants every once in a while." But Ranger was not listening. His eyes were on two men who had just entered the saloon. One was dapperly dressed in a fine woolen overcoat and bowler, and the other was a cowboy with a bald head and sloping shoulders. Fred Jolly and Albertus Ringo walked up to the bar.

"Son of a bitch," Ranger said, pushing back his chair. "Fred Jolly is a gaudy liar and I'm of a mind to tell him so."

"Hold off," Jack said, holding Ranger's arm. "Let's have our drinks in peace. It's been a long day."

Reluctantly, Ranger settled back in his seat. "Well, maybe this ain't the time. But that human skunk is going around town calling me a rustler — and you, too, come to that. You, me, Nate, Billy Sun, he says Faucett's lawyer is going to get all of us arrested and thrown in jail. Haven't you got wind of this?"

Jack shrugged. "It's just talk, Jolly flapping his lips. I'm not afraid of Faucett or his lawyer; Nate and Billy aren't, either. Nothing's going to happen tonight anyhow, so settle down." But by now Jolly and Ringo, each with a glass of whiskey were coming their way. Ringo had acquired a limp.

"Well, well, look who it is," Jolly said with

a smile, nodding his head. "Good evening, Jack, Ranger. I say, d'you mind if we join you?"

"We mind," Ranger said, "but why would high-falutin gentlemen like yourselves want to sit with a couple of low-down rustlers like us anyhow? Ain't that what you been saying about us, Jack and me? That we're nothing but no-account range bums and rustlers? Ain't that what you been telling everybody, Jolly?"

Jolly chuckled and waved his hand, as if shooing a fly. He and Ringo pulled out chairs and sat down. "I don't recall anything like that, Mr. Jones, but, I grant you, there has been a good deal of" — he searched for a word — "unpleasantness around here lately. That ill-advised letter of yours in the *Bulletin,* Mr. Reshaw, that was the cause of it. Emotions are high; there is strong feeling. People will be hurt before it's all over, but you fellows don't have to be among them." He turned in his chair so he was facing Jack. "In fact, you could save yourself and your friends much pain, Mr. Reshaw, and very simply, too."

Jacked sipped his beer. Jolly was delivering a message from Faucett. He wouldn't talk so boldly otherwise. "And just how would I do that?" he said. "This unpleasantness, as you call it, it's been going on a long time. I don't see any simple fix, nothing that involves me anyhow."

"Please, don't be so modest, Mr. Reshaw. Why, you and your friends are squarely in the middle of our local drama. You put yourself there with your letter writing, but you could undo the damage by dissolving your little association, the Northern Wyoming Stockgrowers or whatever you call it, and stopping this talk of an early roundup. It's not going to happen anyway, and everybody knows it. The law is against you and your sort — remember, Wyoming is a state now. A civilized country. You and your friends must stop your rabble-rousing or you'll find yourself making brooms in Laramie." Jack understood this to be a reference to convict labor in the Territorial prison. "Throw in with us, Reshaw. You, Nate Coday, and Billy Sun — even you, Mr. Jones. Join us and all will be forgiven."

"Forgiven?" Now Jack's blood was up. "Why the hell would I need forgiveness from the likes of you? You or Faucett, that mollycoddle you toady for? I wouldn't ride with your outfit if you promised me one hundred thousand dollars and every goddamn cow in Wyoming. Join you? What kind of man do you think I am?"

Jolly sipped his whiskey, wiped his mustache with a thumb and forefinger. "I think we've established the kind of man you are, Mr. Reshaw. I'm offering you a chance to improve yourself. Think of your family. You have a wife and child now, don't you? A stepson? You wouldn't want them to suffer, would you?"

Jack jumped to his feet with balled fists. Now it was Ranger's turn to hold him back.

"You shit," Jack said. "Don't you threaten my family."

Jolly yawned. "Oh, sit down. This bellicosity is becoming tiresome."

Jack shook off Ranger's grip and stood in front of Jolly, who remained seated. "Stand up," he said.

"I won't," Jolly said. "I shall sit and finish my drink, and I suggest you do the same."

"Jolly, even if I was snake enough to take you up on your offer, the Northern Wyoming Stockgrowers don't take orders from me anyhow. It speaks for the little man, the hardworking farmer and rancher who's out there every day, breaking his back to make a home for his family. Faucett and them, they don't give a damn about the people of Johnson County; all they want is money in their pockets, more big houses, and fancier clothes for their fat wives. Paugh! You and your bug-eyed pal get out of here. I'm sick of looking at you."

"That's quite a speech, Jack," Jolly said quietly. "We'll go, but in the meantime, think about my offer. Lord Faucett is trying to do you a favor." As he spoke, Ranger saw Ringo reaching for his gun under the table. Ranger grabbed the cowboy's arm and the two scuffled, knocking over their chairs and spilling onto the floor. The bartender took his shotgun from behind the bar and held it across his arm, waiting as Jack separated the fighters.

"All right," he said. "This won't do any good." Jack took Ranger's hand and pulled him to his feet as Jolly did the same for Ringo, who struggled with his right leg. Only then did Jack remember Billy Sun's near-death experience, when someone killed his horse and left Billy afoot in bitter cold.

"Say, Ringo, how'd you get that hitch in your step?" he said. "Wasn't there last fall during roundup. Maybe you got tagged doing some dry-gulching last winter, eh?"

"I don't know what you're talking about." Ringo glared at Jack with bulging, bloodshot eyes.

Jack was walking to the bank in the morning when Ranger passed him on his way out of town, his wagon weighed down with floorboards and window frames. Ranger reined in his team and waved him over. Jack had just had his boots shined and wasn't keen to wade out into the muddy street, but Ranger wouldn't call him if it wasn't important.

A yellow puppy with a pink nose sat beside Ranger on the bench. "Who's your new friend?" Jack said. He put out his hand and the pup bit down on a finger.

"I call her Josie. I got her from George Munkres this morning when I bought the lumber. He said I need company when I'm out there working, and I guess he's right. Gets pretty lonely sometimes." Ranger gave the pup's ear a gentle tug. "The bitch had nine pups, so George has more if you're interested."

Jack shook his head. "That why you called me out here?"

"No." Ranger looked up and down the street. When he spoke, it was in a lowered voice. "It's something I heard this morning, over to Munkres's store. The Allen brothers were there, them and Jimmy Anable. Jimmy got to talking about a list, a kill list, he called it. He says we're on it, me and you. I came straightaway to the hotel to tell you, but you were out. Just luck I saw you now." He pointed at a shotgun laying at his feet. "I bought it this morning, just in case. You best make sure you're well heeled before heading home."

Jack laughed. "A shotgun? You'd be better off with a rifle."

"I'm not accurate as you. I feel better with this." He tapped the gun with his foot.

"Who wrote this list?" Jack said. "Jimmy Anable tell you that?"

"They don't know who wrote it, but it's the names of people marked for death. Jimmy saw it with his own eyes." Jimmy Anable was one of Sheriff Angus's deputies, as were, occasionally, the Allen brothers. "Your name's right at the top, just after Billy Sun's. Nate's up there high, too; I'm farther down. Jimmy said most of the boys are on it."

"Where'd this list come from?"

Ranger raised his hands, palms up. "It turned up the other night at the Occidental. Somebody found it on the floor and took it to the sheriff. 'Kill List' was right there at the top above the names. Could be someone dropped it on accident or —"

Jack interrupted "— left it on purpose, to get us running around like a bunch of old women." Jack leaned over to rub the pup's yellow head. "Don't get your pants in a bunch, Ranger. It's bullshit, that's what it is. Some fool's idea of a joke. Forget it. I'll come by the house soon to see how you're getting along. Maybe me and Davey can help you with that floor." Jack turned and picked his way to the boardwalk, cursing the mud that clung to his shiny boots.

Ranger called, "Jimmy said the writing could be Frank Canton's."

Jack raised his hand over his shoulder but did not turn. Ranger's news had bothered him more than he let on. *What the hell, I could use a new gun. Maybe I'll pick one up before I leave town.*

Jack Reshaw

Jack left Buffalo on a Wednesday morning, the first day of December. He'd finished his business on Monday and spent Tuesday shopping for supplies and Christmas presents. He got a fine new coat for Sara — a green plaid because the color looked pretty with her red hair — and a toy drum for Davey. She wouldn't be happy but the boy was not ready for a gun, though Jack bought one for himself, a Winchester carbine. It felt good in his hands, well balanced and with a good heft but not too heavy. He put it at his feet in the wagon, just as Ranger had done. He thought he might be acting overly cautious, but what the hell. No one ever died of that.

The day was sunny and warm for December. Jack was in high spirits but maybe a little sorry he hadn't stopped by George Munkres's place for one of those yellow pups. Davey would love a pup, and it would be good for him to take responsibility for another living creature. Might help him grow up some. The boy still cried easily and had a worrisome habit of hiding behind his mother's apron strings, but Jack didn't fault him overmuch. Davey'd never had a pa around to show him how a man should act. Well, Jack would see to that.

He'd been on the road for several hours when he encountered Sigge Alquist, a fat, cheerful Swede who carried mail back and forth between Buffalo and settlers at the head of Powder River. Jack pulled his team off the road so the mail wagon could pass.

"Good to see you, Reshaw," Alquist said. "I ain't seen another soul on this road for days. Damnedest thing."

Jack took off his hat to wipe his brow. "Didn't you see Ranger Jones? He left two days before me, traveling this very road. He'd a been moving slow, had his wagon loaded down with lumber."

"No, didn't see him. Haven't seen nobody. Like I said, it's peculiar."

Jack felt a tickle of alarm. The road to Buffalo was well traveled, especially at this time of year. Alquist should have passed several teams along his route; certainly he should've seen Ranger.

"So how's things in town?" Alquist said.

"Hoppin' I bet you. I read your letter in the *Bulletin* a while back. Haw! I reckon that shook 'em up some, and good for you, I say. You boys just keep stickin' it to 'em. Yep, that's what I say." He slapped the reins down on the horses' backs and went rattling on his way. Jack moved his team back on the road, feeling uneasy. *Why didn't Alquist see Ranger? Where was everybody?*

Jack was not making good time. His spring wagon was heavy and traveling no more than four miles per hour. He tried whistling, "Turkey in the Straw," to keep his spirits up, but it didn't work. In fact, the sound was so thin and small it made him feel even more alone, so he stopped. He squinted up at the sun. It was mid-afternoon and he was barely halfway. It was going to be a long day.

He headed down an incline, so steep he had to ride the brake all the way to the bottom. The first shot came as he was urging the team up the other side. It hit him in the fleshy part of his upper arm, passing through his body and striking the off horse in the crop. The animal screamed and lunged but did not fall. As Jack hunkered down and grabbed for the rifle, a second shot hit him in the side of the head, taking off most of his cranium. He died instantly, falling back onto the bed of the wagon where his bloody head came to rest on Davey's drum.

A young boy riding a saddle trail found Jack's body days later. The killer had led the team off the road and down into a gully where he shot both horses, still in harness. He did not steal any of Jack's supplies, which were still in the wagon. It had rained since the murder and the cargo was wet and mud splattered.

Sheriff Angus and Deputy Anable discovered Ranger's body the day after Jack was found. The weather had gone cold, and Ranger's body was frozen solid though it was clear he had been dead longer than Jack. He, too, had been shot from behind with a rifle at close range, twenty feet at most. The floorboards for his bride's new home were still in the wagon, along with the body of a yellow pup.

Anable released a low whistle. "What you think, Red? Is it the list?"

Angus walked around the wagon, eyes on the frozen ground. He found the prints of a single man, a number eight boot, but the tracks of two horses, one of them barefoot, or unshod. There had been only one set of tracks, man and horse, at the site of Jack's murder, but if he went back he felt sure he would find signs of a second rider on an unshod horse nearby, perhaps a lookout. "You don't want to know what I'm thinking, Jimmy," he said. "I don't want to say it and you don't want to hear it."

RED ANGUS

The murders of Jack Reshaw and Ranger Jones put the people of Buffalo in an uproar. Killings were not uncommon, but most of these were drunken shoot-outs in town or in front of witnesses. Unsolved killings were rare. The last one anyone could remember was August Schmidt's years before. Many rumors were flying around, and Sheriff Angus heard all of them. Breathless citizens came to his office to report things they had seen that were unremarkable at the time but now seemed suspicious. Mail carrier Alquist reported his meeting with Jack on the Buffalo road the day of his death. "He kept askin' me if I seen Ranger, and he seemed bothered when I said I hadn't. Not only that, but he seemed nervous, not himself. Like he was scairt of somethin'."

The most interesting report came from Mrs. Spicer, a ranch wife from south of Buffalo who had been on her way to town with her young daughter the day Jack was killed. Mrs. Spicer was on the alert because she had two hundred dollars with her that day, money she would use to purchase the family's winter supplies. She also had a gun concealed in the loose hay her husband had spread on the wagon floor to keep their feet warm.

"I saw two men, Sheriff," she said, "riding hard from the south. They were pretty far off but they wore handkerchiefs over their faces, I could see that clear enough, and it struck me as odd as there wasn't much wind that day."

"Thank you, Mrs. Spicer." Angus was only half listening. He was doing paperwork and anyway he and Deputy Anable had heard many such reports in the past few days, none of them useful. "Lots of men wear kerchiefs against the elements," he said. "I do it myself." But as she stood to leave, Mrs. Spicer said something that caught the sheriff's attention.

"One of the men sat his horse in an unusual manner. Straight as a rifle barrel. It was peculiar."

Angus looked up from his paperwork. "Did you get a look at him?"

"I told you, they wore handkerchiefs. Weren't you listening?"

"What about their horses? Did you notice them?"

"Well, as a matter of fact, I do remember one of them. It was a sorrel, very fine looking, with a blaze and white stockings on his hind feet."

Angus and Anable exchanged a look. Mrs. Spicer had just given a perfect description of Frank Canton's horse, Fred.

"And their hats? Did you notice those?" Angus said.

She gave him a look of disgust. "Horses don't wear hats."

"The men," Angus said impatiently. "Did you see their hats?"

"Oh, yes. One of them wore a big, round hat like the greasers wear."

Tom Horn, Angus thought. Horn and Frank Canton. As he suspected, it had finally started in earnest; the WSGA had unleashed its assassins upon its enemies. "I see," he said, getting up and escorting Mrs. Spicer to the door. "Thank you for coming by. I have no doubt the men you describe are long gone by now, long gone. Don't worry yourself about them." He gave her a reassuring pat on the shoulder. "Still, I wouldn't mention this to anyone else, if I were you."

She regarded him with narrowed eyes.

"Why not?"

"I just wouldn't. I'm going to keep an eye out for them, in case they come back. If they do, it wouldn't be good to let them know they'd been seen, would it? Killers like that? I'm only thinking of your safety, Mrs. Spicer." He opened the door and hurried her out into the late afternoon cold.

"Sweet Jesus!" Anable said. "She described Canton and Horn to a fare-thee-well. What are you going to do, Sheriff? Do we arrest them?"

Red Angus sat in his chair and covered his face with his hands. He was a hard man, who'd left his Kansas home at age twelve to enlist in the Union Army. He had worked as a freighter through west Kansas when it was Indian country, fought the Cheyenne with the Nineteenth Kansas Volunteer Cavalry, labored as a teamster in Guatemala and as a cowboy in California and Wyoming. Red Angus was no weak sister, and he'd tried everything, including things he was not proud of, to stop the trouble coming, but it was here. He was no match for Frank Canton and Tom Horn, and he knew it. Canton and Horn were killers, natural born. He did not want to tangle with them, and he sure as hell didn't want to arrest them.

"Sheriff?" Anable said. "What are you —"

"I heard you, dammit! Let me think." Angus was still thinking when the door opened and Billy Sun stood in black silhouette against the red and salmon sky.

"Hello, Billy." Angus spoke as if he had been expecting him. "Come in, sit down. We need to talk."

Billy removed his sheepskin coat and hung it on the wall. With a nod to Anable, he took a chair across the desk from the sheriff and placed his hat, brim up, on the desk.

"You look tired," Anable said.

"Deputy, you can go on home now," Angus said. "We're done for the day here. Thanks for your help."

"Sheriff, I'd like to —"

"No. Just go on home, Jimmy. Me and Billy want to talk, the two of us. I'll see you in the morning."

Reluctantly, the deputy took his hat and coat and left. Angus pulled his soft leather bag of makings out of his coat pocket and offered the bag to Billy, who shook his head. Angus started rolling himself a cigarette.

"What are you going to do, Sheriff?" Billy said. "You know what happened to Jack and Ranger. You know who killed them and why."

Angus drew on his cigarette and exhaled a cloud of blue smoke. "I don't know who killed Jack and Ranger, and neither do you, Billy. Let's not be going off half-cocked on this thing now. Let's not be throwing around unfounded accusations. This is a serious business."

"I was afraid you were going to say that," Billy said.

The two men looked at each other across the desk. The room was growing dark. When Angus drew on his cigarette, its glowing orange tip matched the color of the setting sun, its fiery glow filling the room's lone window.

"Now Billy, I know Jack was a friend of yours, and Ranger, too. They were good men, both of them, and I'm damn sorry for what happened. Everybody is. You might think you know who killed them, but —"

"Frank Canton and Tom Horn."

Angus slammed his open hand down on the desktop. "There, you see? That's what I'm talking about — don't go around saying that, Billy. Do not do it! Jesus Christ, man — you're going to get yourself killed and a lot of other people, too."

"Not if you arrest them and put them in jail where they belong. If you don't, you're probably right. They'll try to kill me, and Nate, too. People will die."

Angus got to his feet and walked to the

window. He spoke with his back to Billy. "Sun, why don't you get out of Johnson County for a while? Go back up north. That's where you came from, right? You used to work for Nelson Story up Bozeman way? Go back there. Man like you, with your talents, you could find work in no time."

He turned from the window to look at Billy, who said nothing.

"Take Nate Coday with you, come back to Wyoming in a year or two," Angus continued, "when things cool down. We got us a big old mess here, and you don't want to get caught up in it." Angus took two steps toward Billy and looked into his eyes. "I'm saying something important to you, Billy. I hope you'll take my advice."

Billy smiled. "So, you're in Faucett's pocket, too? You're going to stand by and watch while his hired guns take out his enemies one at a time?" He shook his head. "I thought better of you, Red. So did Jack. I'm glad he isn't here to see this." Billy stood and went for his coat.

"Now just you wait one god-damn minute!" Angus's face was red with anger. "I'm not in Faucett's pocket — I'm not in anybody's pocket. But what's happening here is bigger than one man, even a sheriff. Suppose I did bring them in, Canton and Horn? I couldn't make charges stick. What proof do I have? Faucett's fast-talking Philadelphia lawyers would have them out like that." He snapped his fingers. "And then what? Dammit, Billy, do like I said. Go away for a while. You and Nate, don't make any more trouble."

"We're not the trouble, Red." He shrugged his shoulders into his coat. "We're trying to make a place for ourselves in this country just like everybody else. You know that. I'm only sorry you don't have the sand to do your job. I thought you were a better man."

Billy walked out, closing the door firmly behind him. Angus watched him cross the street to the livery stable. The sheriff felt low, lower than a snake's belly. *If only I'd been successful last winter. If only I'd got Sun instead of his horse, none of this would be happening. That damn Indian.*

Angus walked back to his desk and rolled another cigarette.

ODALIE

Odalie and Richard Faucett ate dinner alone at the long mahogany table. Never, she thought, were she and her husband further apart than during these lonely meals. They had never had much to say to each other, but Richard had been unusually preoccupied with business lately, and Odalie was happy not to talk about it. As far as she was concerned, the less she knew, the better.

She was surprised by how much she missed the girl. It was true, she had only issued the invitation to Lorna with the hope that she, Odalie, would see more of Dr. Dixon, but things had not turned out that way. Father and daughter were as distant as she and Richard, but, to her surprise, Odalie found she enjoyed the girl's company. Oh, Lorna had many annoying qualities — she was self-centered and greedy — but Odalie saw a lot of herself in her young charge.

Perhaps that was why she found the girl so amusing. She could always predict Lorna's reaction to people and things because they were exactly her own. They liked the same food, the same music, the same clothes, the same kind of men. Lorna made no secret of her love for Billy Sun, even though he did not reciprocate her feelings. Most women would not be so forthright. Odalie admired and encouraged the girl's boldness; in fact, she sometimes felt that in Lorna she was creating a newer, fresher version of herself. If she'd had more time, maybe she could have made the girl the woman she, herself, might have been if only she had not been tethered by financial necessity to a man like Richard Faucett . . .

"I say, did you hear me, Odalie?" Richard was looking at her, fork in midair.

"I'm sorry, darling." She smiled, showing her dimples. "I'm afraid I was miles away. What were you saying?"

"I said I will be leaving for Cheyenne tomorrow. I've got business in the statehouse. I'll be gone all the week."

"All right, dear. That's fine. You've been working so hard, you deserve a break. Enjoy yourself."

"You should go to Denver. I'm sure things get tiresome for you here, especially with me away. It would be a nice trip for you. You can shop, see a play. Do all those things women like to do."

Odalie smiled. If Richard only knew how she looked forward to his absences. "Yes, that would be lovely," she said, "but I don't think I will go to Denver. It's quite a distance and I've got plenty to do here. Remember, dear, I have the Christmas party to prepare for."

Richard frowned and continued eating. After a time he said, "No, Odalie, you shall go to Denver. I insist. Ask Lorna to go along if you like. You'd like that, wouldn't you?"

Odalie placed her hands, palms down, on the table. "What is this about, Richard? Is there trouble? Does it have anything to do with the deaths of those two men?"

Richard reached for his wineglass. The crystal sparkled in the candlelight. "No, of course not. Why would you even say such a thing? Don't worry yourself, Odalie. Oh, I guess there is a spot of difficulty, but it doesn't concern you. I simply don't want you to be exposed to any, shall we say, ugliness."

"I see." Odalie touched her napkin to her lips. Though she tried to remain uninvolved in Richard's affairs, she kept her eyes open and she was not stupid. Her husband and his friends were ruthless, violent men, and she had some notion what was brewing. "Very well, then. I'll go into Buffalo tomorrow and ask Lorna to come with me. I imagine she'll be only too pleased to do so, assuming her father will permit it. Shall we leave right away? When might this 'ugliness' be expected?"

Lord Faucett looked at her sharply. He suspected his wife of mocking him, but she smiled innocently. "Soon," he said. "You should leave soon, the day after tomorrow at the latest."

Early the next morning Fred Jolly found Odalie in the stable saddling her favorite palfrey, a gray gelding she called Lord Byron, after her favorite poet. When he asked, she said she was riding to town.

"Alone?" Jolly was skeptical. "I believe Lord Richard would prefer that I drive you in the buggy, madam. After all, bad things have been happening in Johnson County lately. You'd best let me take you in the buggy."

"No, Fred, I want to ride." She spoke firmly. "It promises to be a lovely morning, and I haven't been for weeks. Byron needs the exercise. Don't worry, we'll be fine." She began leading the horse from the stable, but Jolly stepped in front of her.

"Lady Faucett, I insist you let me drive you."

Odalie slapped her kid riding gloves against her open hand. "I do not take orders from you, Mr. Jolly. You may be my husband's preferred toady, but you are nothing to me. Less than nothing. Now, get out of my way."

Jolly smiled in the patronizing manner Odalie despised. "Very well, Lady Faucett. As you wish." He stepped aside and Odalie brushed past him, using a low stool to step into the ladies' saddle. She flicked her crop, and Byron took off at a gallop, throwing clumps of mud onto Jolly's coat.

Odalie urged the powerful gray forward at a breakneck pace, and, though she was an accomplished rider, Byron was so full of energy she had to grab for leather to keep her seat. Her only thought was to reach the turnoff that led to Billy's cabin before Jolly came after her, for she had no doubt he would. Time and again she turned to look over her shoulder, but she did not see him. So far so good, she thought, although she realized Byron's prints would reveal her destination if Jolly was suspicious enough to track her.

At last she came to the narrow trail that

curled up the mountain to Billy's cabin. By now Byron was lathered and beginning to labor, but she urged him on, though the road was steep. Like the horse, she was breathless and her heart boomed in her ears. *What am I doing? Billy Sun is nothing to me, only an amusing interlude in the crushing boredom of my life. I don't want to see him hurt, but what do I lose in the event? On the other hand, if I am discovered, Richard will divorce me and I will lose everything. I will be cast out in the hedges.* Odalie saw herself in rags, begging for food on the streets of New Orleans, but she did not slow. Her husband and his men killed Jack Reshaw and Ranger Jones, and she believed they meant to kill Billy and Nate, too. Anyone who stood in their way would be eliminated. She was not in love with Billy, but she could not let any harm come to him. Odalie had done many things in her life she was ashamed of, and thus far she had managed to forgive herself, but if she let a good man die because of her cowardice, a man who loved her, then she might as well be dead herself.

The cabin came into view, lit by a shaft of morning sunlight slanting through the pines. She rode full speed up to the door and slid from the saddle. Her hair had come unpinned and hung to her shoulders, and, like Byron, she was winded. She ran to the door and entered without knocking. The one-room line shack was empty, the bed where they had passed many delightful hours unmade. She ran to the pole barn and found it too unoccupied. Billy's horse was gone. *Where was he?* She returned to the cabin and sat on the bed, feeling desperate. *Where would he be this time of day?* Only one possibility came to her. He had to be at the line shack he and Nate shared farther down the valley, but could she ride there without being discovered? Richard's henchmen may be watching; they may be outside Billy's cabin even now. Wildly, she looked around the primitive room as if seeking an answer from the rough log walls. She felt light-headed and the room began to swim. Stay calm, she told herself, breathing deeply. *Stay calm and find a way to warn him. There must be a way to warn him.*

BILLY SUN

Billy and Nate were sleeping when the killers came. One kicked in the door while two others ran in with guns drawn. One man stopped at the foot of Billy's bed, the other at Nate's. They were black shadows in the gray, predawn light.

"Get up, chief." The gunman closest to Billy kicked the bedframe. "You boys are going for a ride."

"Where are we going?" Billy said. "What do you want?"

"I said get up. Put your pants on, but don't bother with your boots. Where you're goin' you won't be needin' 'em."

Billy's mind raced. There were these two, the one by the door, and probably more outside. There was a chance, slim, but a chance. "All right," he said. "Give a man a minute to wake up." He yawned and extended his arms over his head as if stretching but in fact reaching for the loaded

298

revolver hanging in its holster from the bedpost. Billy's attackers detected his purpose just as his fingers closed around the cold, wooden grip. The gunman by Nate's bed fired first. Billy felt the wind from his bullet on his cheek as he pulled the trigger, striking his would-be killer squarely in the shoulder. By now Nate had grabbed his sidearm from under the bed and opened fire on the other intruders, one of whom shot wildly, sending a bullet into the wall with a spray of splinters. The failed assassins tried to flee but arrived at the door at the same instant, getting jammed in the frame. Billy shot again, hearing the thud of a bullet striking flesh, before they managed to break free. Billy and Nate jumped from their beds and continued firing from the cabin door as the three men ran, stumbling, toward a fourth, barely visible in the tree line, holding the horses. Billy counted four animals, including a distinctive sorrel with a star and stockinged hind feet. Nate groaned beside him.

"Are you hurt?" Billy said.

Nate's face was ashen and shining with sweat. "I'm shot," he said, falling back against the wall and sliding to the floor, his hand on his left shoulder. A stain was spreading on his red undershirt.

"Bad?" Billy would not desert his friend, much as he wanted to ride after their attackers.

Nate shook his head. "No. Maybe. I don't know."

"Take off your shirt." Even as he spoke Billy heard the horses crashing through the brush.

Nate unbuttoned his shirt clumsily with one hand. "Who were they?" he said. "Did you recognize them?"

Billy shook his head. "I didn't see their faces, but I know who they are or who sent them and you do, too. At least we hit a couple of them." He pointed to a black spray of blood on the door frame and adjoining wall. "They were stupid. They should've done us in our sleep like the cowards they are." Billy walked to the door. "Say, what's that?" Still in his stocking feet, he went outside and picked up a long gun, a carbine, leaning against the side of the cabin. He turned it over in his hands. Engraved on the walnut stock were the initials FC. He held the gun out to Nate, now shirtless, sitting on the earthen floor.

"Well, that makes it simple, don't it?" Nate said. "Hell, we knew it was Canton anyhow. Question is, what are we going to do about it?"

Billy nodded. "That's the nut. It's up to us. The law won't do nothing; Red Angus told me as much." He kneeled by Nate to examine his injury. Blood oozed from the red, meaty hole and there was no exit wound. The bullet must be lodged in the bone. "Do you think you can ride?" Billy said.

Nate's face was white and getting whiter by the minute. "What choice do I have?"

"We've got to get you to Doc Dixon." Billy took his canteen from the same bedpost that held his empty holster and gave it to Nate. "You rest up while I saddle the horses. We'll get you right and then we'll get the men who did this. This, and Jack and Ranger too."

LORNA

One candle burned on the table. The darkness suited the diners' moods. Lorna had made lentil soup with pork hock and corn bread, but the meal had not been met with enthusiasm. Bean or dried vegetable soups had been on the table every night since her return because those were the only recipes Lorna could manage.

"Does it disappoint you?" Lorna said, glaring at her father and Cal, both of whom looked down at their bowls. "I'm sorry if my cooking isn't up to your standards." She burned with resentment, which she did not try to hide. Just a few short months before she had been in London, wearing fine clothes, eating splendid food, and keeping company with sophisticated people. Now her days were nothing but hour after hour of endless toil — boring, grinding women's work. She suspected that was the reason her father brought her home, to be his char.

She could be in New Orleans, or Grand Isle; instead she was here, cooking, cleaning, washing dishes, scrubbing clothes. It was intolerable. She was meant for better things.

Cal dropped his spoon into his bowl. "Didn't Odalie Faucett teach you anything about cooking in all that time you were with her?"

Bright spots of color appeared on Lorna's cheeks. "Lady Faucett didn't know she was preparing me to be the family charwoman, and I didn't, either." She paused, then banged her fists on the table, rattling the dishes and flatware. "I hate the kitchen, I have always hated it. I hate scrubbing floors, I hate washing and mending clothes, I hate tending the vegetable garden. I am not meant for this drudgery, and I will not do one more day of it!" She threw her spoon across the room, where it clattered against the window glass. "You'll have to hire someone else to do your slave work, Pa, and there's an end!"

Dixon looked across the table at his daughter's angry face. She was a beautiful woman, but she was a shrew. He was furious, but at the same time he felt he had no one but himself to blame. He had never showed her a father's love, never given her

303

the attention a daughter deserved.

"Lorna," he said, trying to keep the anger from his voice, "I know you've had a heavy burden since Mrs. MacGill died. I was unprepared for that; I had no idea the poor woman was so ill. In fact, I rather thought she was improving. I never intended that you should —" He was interrupted by a firm knock, once and then again. Dixon got to his feet and his eyes met Cal's. These were dangerous times for unexpected callers. After a short hesitation, he crossed the room and opened the door. There stood Billy Sun, supporting a second man who was barely conscious.

"Billy!" Lorna stepped toward him, but Dixon raised his hand to stop her.

"I'm sorry to come to you with this, Doctor," Billy said, "but Nate has been shot. Can we come in?"

"Of course," Dixon said. "Come with me." Dixon led the way as Cal and Billy half carried Nate through the house with Lorna following. They took Nate to Dixon's surgery and placed him on a sheet-covered table. Dixon took Nate's wrist and felt his pulse, then began cutting off his shirt with scissors. The wool fabric stuck to Nate's shoulder wound, which oozed blood as Dixon pulled it free. When he asked Lorna to go to the kitchen to heat some water, she responded immediately.

"Who did this, Billy?" Dixon said.

"It was Frank Canton. Him and three others ambushed us this morning at the cabin. They broke in when me and Nate was sleeping. Meant to kill us but we got the drop on 'em. We managed to hit at least two before they got away."

Dixon raised his eyes from his bloody work. "Are you sure it was Canton?"

Billy nodded. "I'm sure. He left his gun behind. Not only that, I recognized his horse. It was him all right."

Lorna returned carrying a steaming basin and a stack of white linen rags draped over her forearm. She set them down, then turned to Billy with shining eyes. "At least they didn't hurt you. That jealous little tyrant. . . ."

Billy looked at her sharply. "Sounds like you got someone particular in mind."

Lorna flushed and touched her throat. "Well, no. I don't, that is, no."

Billy smiled, but there was no warmth in his green eyes. "Do you know something about this? If you do, you've got to tell me."

Lorna shook her head, color rising, as Billy and her father waited for a response. She was saved when Nate released a low moan, drawing their attention. Dixon began searching the wound with a Nelaton's probe, an ingenious device with an unglazed porcelain head that released an audible clink when it hit up against a bullet or other bit of metal. Many times in his career Dixon had sent thanks to the dead French surgeon, Auguste Nelaton, who invented it. It had helped him find and remove scores of bullets and iron arrowheads. In this case, though, it had yet to yield the desired result.

"Will Nate make it?" Billy said. "He don't look good."

"Coin's still in the air," Dixon said. "I need to get the bullet, and I'll have to put him under for that. Billy, you and Lorna wait in the house. Cal, I want you to help me." Dixon fished a key from his coat pocket and gave it to his son. "Get the chloroform."

Cal unlocked the medicine cabinet and took out a blue glass bottle.

"Lorna and Billy, wait in the house," Dixon said. "Please, do as I ask." He uncorked the bottle and soaked a handkerchief. The room filled with the scent of ripe apples.

Billy put a hand on Nate's undamaged shoulder. "Good-bye, my friend," he said. "I'll see you on the other side." He held the door as Lorna passed through, and they stood together in the dark hallway, listening through the closed door as Dixon gave his son instructions. "Cover his mouth and nose with the handkerchief and keep your head turned. Be careful not to breathe in any yourself."

Billy took Lorna's arm. She stood close to him, but it was too dark to see her face. "Let's go to the kitchen," he said. "You can make coffee and tell me what you know about what happened today."

"I don't know —"

"Stop it!"

His gripped tightened and she flinched at the anger she felt in him. He repeated the words in a softer voice. "Stop it, Lorna."

They sat at a small table. The kitchen was dark but for two candles burning in tin wall sconces on either side of the room. Lorna sniffled and blew her nose in a white, lace-trimmed kerchief. Her eyes were wet and red rimmed from crying.

"So Faucett knows about Odalie and me?" he said.

Lorna nodded.

"How do you know this?"

Lorna squeezed shut her eyes. It was an exquisitely painful memory, one she could

307

barely stand to recall, even now. "I overheard them talking in the library. Fred Jolly followed Odalie one day when she went to your cabin."

Billy remembered a spring afternoon when she was so late he thought she wasn't coming, and his overwhelming joy when at last Odalie appeared, windblown and happy. "I thought maybe I was being followed," she said, "so I took the roundabout way, just in case. No one could've followed Byron on that run!" And they had fallen onto his bed with their arms around each other, laughing.

"Did you tell Odalie about what you heard?" he said.

"No. I thought about it. I should have told her, I know I should have, but I was angry." She twisted the handkerchief in her hands, and when she spoke it was a whisper. "I couldn't stand the thought of the two of you together. I still can't."

Billy barely heard her, his thoughts were racing. *Was Odalie in danger too?* Jealousy might have been the reason for the attack on him and Nate that morning, but he didn't think so. If that were his motive, Faucett wouldn't have tried to kill Nate, too. Beyond that, Odalie didn't mean that much to her husband. He wouldn't go to the trouble of killing for her. No, it was the range war that stirred Faucett's passion, hatred for "squatters" who encroached on "his" land. Still, Lorna should have considered Odalie's safety.

"Did you ever think of her?" he said. "If Richard was angry, he might hurt her, too."

Lorna shook her head. "No. My only concern was for you." She covered her face with her hands, and Billy saw by the heaving of her shoulders that she was weeping again.

"Don't cry," he said gently. He felt pity for this young woman he had known since the very moment of her birth. "What happened today wasn't because of me and Odalie. I'm pretty sure of that."

Lorna dried her eyes with the back of her hand and raised her face. His tone had given her hope. "Billy, let's get out of here, just you and me, no one else. Those men meant to kill you — for whatever reason — and they'll try again. What happened today will only make it worse. Please, Billy, please — before it's too late." She pleaded with her eyes.

Billy laughed shortly. "Everybody keeps asking me to leave. I'm not going, Lorna. You go if you want to — you probably should — but this place, Absaroka, is my home. I won't let men like Richard Faucett and Frank Canton drive me away. I'm staying."

Lorna's face changed. "You are stubborn and prideful. Go ahead, get yourself killed, and you will, too. See if I care!"

Their eyes met across the table. The kitchen was even darker now; one candle had burned out, the other was guttering. "I'm sorry, Lorna. I never wanted to hurt you, never, but it seems like that's all I've ever done. From the very beginning."

"Oh, please, spare me your pity." Lorna fairly spat the words. "Plenty of men would be happy to have me. I've had many offers, I can tell you, even from the sons of British lords!"

"I don't doubt it."

"I hate you."

"I don't doubt that, either."

Lorna's bitter smile became a sneer. She wanted to hurt him. "If you think Odalie cares for you, you're a fool. She may have made love to you, but you mean nothing to her. Believe me, I know her very well. If she cared about you, she would have told me."

Billy was quiet, his face in shadow.

"Odalie Faucett would never cast her lot with an Indian," she continued. "That's all you were to her, a good-looking half-breed who broke her husband's horses." She paused but still he said nothing. Lorna pounded the table with her fist. "Say something, damn you!"

Billy pushed back his chair and got to his feet. "I'm going to the barn to see to our horses. Tell your father where I am, when he's done with Nate."

ODALIE

Early in January, Richard Faucett had sent Fred Jolly south to Colorado to buy conditioned horses for his army of cattlemen. They had to arrive ready to ride and primed for hard going, for it would have aroused suspicion if he and the other ranchers were seen preparing their horses so far in advance of spring roundup. Faucett also dispatched a cowboy from Texas back to his home state to assemble a legion of gunmen, twenty-two to twenty-five in number, with the story they were being hired to track down a band of outlaws.

Faucett took for himself the two most prickly tasks. First, he arranged with Union Pacific Railroad officials for the transport of fifty armed men and horses from Cheyenne to Casper, which would be the launching point for Faucett's expeditionary force. Starting in northern Johnson County, the regulators, as they called themselves, would march southward, eliminating rustlers along the way. From there, they would continue south and east, through Converse County, and then west, through Natrona. Once the transportation was arranged, Faucett turned his attention to negotiations with Amos Barber, Wyoming's acting governor, to ensure that city and country officials would not be able to enlist local militias to halt the invaders' advance.

All this planning kept Faucett at his desk. One warm evening Faucett was sitting in his study by an open window, writing intently, when Odalie entered in a draft of jasmine-scented perfume. She rarely disturbed him at work. In fact, they rarely occupied the same room. The tension between them was palpable, yet never discussed. But this afternoon she had learned of the attack on Billy and Nate Coday at the line shack in the mountains. Only now did she fully realize how dangerous Richard was, the depths to which his hatred would lead him.

"What are you working on, darling?" she said, affecting her usual airy manner. He covered his writing when she came to kiss his cheek.

"Some figures Jolly wanted for spring roundup."

She sat on the black upholstered sofa and

gave a great yawn. "How dreary. You know, Richard, I believe I'll return to Denver. I need a few items to finish my spring wardrobe. You won't be needing me for anything just now, will you?"

Richard returned to his work. "No, of course not. In fact, that's a splendid idea, Odalie. Yes, do go, as soon as you like, and stay as long as you like. I'm busy and I know how easily bored you are."

The Chinese serving man tapped lightly on the door and entered with a small bow. "Mr. Canton here to see you, sir."

Odalie wrinkled her nose. She had never tried to hide her dislike of the former sheriff. "I'll go now and start packing. I'm sure you and Frank have much to talk about." She passed Canton in the doorway, stepping to the side to give him a wide berth. Canton made a show of examining the sole of his boot.

"Did I step in something?" he said, smiling.

"I don't know, Mr. Canton." She spoke softly, returning his smile. "Did you? Perhaps that explains it."

"Well, I guess we can't all smell sweet as your Indian buck, if that's what you like — and I suppose you do. What I hear anyhow."

Richard, still at his desk, looked up from

his writing. "What are you two talking about?"

Odalie laughed though her heart was pounding. "We were just discussing men's colognes."

The two men sat in armchairs, separated by a low table, before the window. It was still open though the late winter evening had gone cold. Faucett held a snifter of brandy, Canton a glass with three fingers of whiskey. Reaching across the table, Faucett handed the former sheriff the document he'd been working on when Odalie interrupted him.

"This is it?" Canton said.

"Yes," Faucett leaned back in his chair. "Seventy names. I don't care whether they die by the noose or the gun, so long as it's done."

Canton's eyes ran down the page. "Seventy? I didn't think there'd be so many. Sheriff Angus and his deputies, all three county commissioners, Joe DeBarthe at the newspaper. I know these men." He took a mouthful of whiskey. "I didn't think the list would be this long."

Faucett crossed his short legs, jiggling his foot impatiently. "Are you losing your nerve, Frank? Because if you are, it's not too late to back out. Just return the money I gave you, and I'll enlist someone else. There's no shortage of candidates."

Canton cleared his throat. "No. No, Lord Faucett, I'm not backing out. We can't let the rustling go on like it is, but what happens if the locals call out the militia or the national guard? What happens then?"

Faucett waved his hand. "Don't worry about that. I told you to leave those things to me. Barber has issued an edict saying no armed force may be mobilized until he gives authorization. And he won't. I have his word."

"And what happens in Buffalo? All the people, how do we manage that?"

"First, you take the courthouse and seize the weapons there." Faucett gestured with his snifter toward the paper in Canton's hand. "Then tend to your list, disable the opposition. The telegraph lines will be cut, of course. Once our opponents are out of the way, once the people see the lay of the land, they will rise to support you. Already we've had many pledges of allegiance, many offers of wagons and horses and supplies. The honest cattlemen of Wyoming are hot to reclaim what is rightfully theirs! Things will be as they were meant to be, as they were when I first arrived here. This country was not created for grubby little men with dirty hands and dirty families who get by on stealing the livestock and holdings of others. It was not!" Faucett banged his fist on the upholstered arm of his chair.

Canton said, "I'm surprised to see Dr. Dixon on the list."

"Are you? And why's that? That red renegade, Sun, is his protégé, is he not? Are they not, as you Americans say, in cahoots?"

"Well, they're friends. But Dixon has never been involved in rustling, far as I know, and besides, he's a good doctor, the only one we got. We need him."

"Paugh!" Faucett got to his feet. "Physicians are a dime a dozen. He supports Sun and that lot and he's got to go — I advise you not to argue with me on this, Canton. Anyway, you needn't deal with him yourself. I've arranged for someone else to take care of the good doctor."

Faucett went to his desk, selected a cigar from a gold-plated humidor, clipped and lit it, turning it in his fingers and drawing until it glowed to his satisfaction. Its aroma filled the room but Faucett did not offer one to his guest. Instead he walked to Canton's chair and stood before him, looking down as he spoke. "You and your men made a mare's nest of that business at the line shack, Frank. You were supposed to take care of Billy Sun and Nate Coday, and instead you let them get away," he said. "How did that happen?"

Canton had been expecting this but, even so, beads of perspiration popped out on his forehead. "It just did."

Faucett shook his head. "I'm disappointed, Frank. I thought you were an able man."

"I am. I don't know what happened; maybe Sun knew we were coming. Maybe someone warned him."

"And who would do that?"

Canton shifted in his chair. Only one candidate came to mind, but he wasn't prepared to introduce that line of conversation with her husband. "I don't know."

"You say that often, don't you, Frank? 'I don't know, I don't know,' over and over." Faucett turned and went back to his chair. "All right. I'm a reasonable man. You're allowed one mistake. You hear me, Frank? One."

Odalie, listening breathlessly on the flagstone terrace outside the window, had heard enough. She turned and ran on cat's paws to the kitchen door, praying Chang did not see her. She made it through the kitchen undetected and flew up the stairs to her room. Soundlessly, she pulled her suitcases from under the bed and began to pack. The time had come.

BILLY SUN

Dixon finally got the bullet but not without a lot of digging. The slug was lodged firmly in the bone, and Dixon had to employ the screw, a difficult instrument and one he turned to rarely, to work it free. He dropped the bloody, misshapen chunk of metal in a basin, where it landed with an oddly cheerful clink. No artery had been severed, but bits of Nate's nightshirt had been driven deep into the wound and these had to be removed with forceps along with shards of splintered bone. As was his custom, Dixon talked to the unconscious Nate during the operation. This was a habit he had acquired during the war and, more than once, a patient told him he had heard and been comforted by Dixon's voice during the procedure. At first, Dixon was skeptical, but many times the man had been able to repeat words or phrases Dixon had spoken.

After the operation, Dixon and Cal moved

Nate to a bed in a darkened corner at the rear of the surgery. Dixon glanced at the clock: two thirty. His eyes burned and felt as if the lids were lined with sandpaper. He wanted sleep and the cool comfort of clean white sheets, but first, he had to talk to Billy.

"Stay with him, Cal," Dixon said. "When he wakes up, give him morphine sulfate, one-half drachm. Later, when he's able to take it, beef tea every two hours, or as he tolerates. You know what to do."

Cal nodded. "Do you believe Frank Canton did this?"

"I don't know what to believe. When we moved, I thought the killing was done here. I've always loved Powder River country, ever since your mother and I first saw it twenty-six years ago. I've always thought of it as a place where our children could grow up in peace. Now the killing has come again, only this time we don't have the Indians to blame it on." Dixon shook his head. "It's such a waste. Things could be so different." He noticed Cal was wearing his gun.

"What's that for?" he said, gesturing toward Cal's hip.

Cal touched the holstered weapon. "It seemed like a good idea, what with Billy and Nate showing up like that. You never know who's going to be next."

"You're probably right. Where is Billy?"

"I heard him tell Lorna he was going to the barn."

Dixon nodded wearily and walked to the door. "I'll ask her to relieve you in a few hours." Before leaving he turned back to his son, sitting at Nate's bedside in the darkness. "Thank you, Cal. You were a big help to me tonight. I do count on you, you know."

"Do you? You've never said." Dixon could not see Cal's face but he heard a strangeness in his son's voice.

"I haven't said many things to you and your sister I should have," Dixon said. "I'm sorry for that. I hope it's not too late to make things better."

Silence followed.

"Good night, Pa," Cal said. "Don't worry, I'll see to things here."

Dixon found Billy in the barn, sleeping soundly under Heck's saddle blanket on a mound of fresh hay. He thought about letting Billy rest — he and Nate had been worn out when they arrived — but Dixon decided he'd want to know the result of Nate's operation. Dixon leaned down and shook Billy gently by the shoulder. He woke with a start, sitting up with straws of hay clinging to his long black hair.

"What — oh, Doctor, it's you. How's Nate?"

Dixon sat beside him. "It took longer than I expected, but I got the bullet and cleaned the wound out well. Coin's still in the air, infection is always a risk, but I'd say his chances are good."

Billy's shoulders sank with relief. "I'd take it real hard if anything happened to Nate. He's like a brother to me."

Dixon looked down at his hands. "Are you sure it was Canton who attacked you this morning? I mean, are you sure enough to say it?"

Billy turned to him with surprise. "Doc, you know what's going on. There's no way around this. It was Canton, and Faucett sent him. It's the range war Faucett and them are forever gassing on about. It's started."

"Could be," Dixon said. "But, as you say, Faucett's been 'gassing on' for a long time now. It's never been clear to me he'd actually go through with it." He hesitated. "Is that what this is about, a range war, or is there something else between you and Richard Faucett?" He raised his eyes to meet Billy's. "Something personal maybe?"

"You mean me and his wife? Is that what

you're asking?"

"I guess I am."

Billy stood, brushing the hay from his clothes and hair. "Are you going to counsel me about getting in bed with another man's wife? How bad things come of it?"

Dixon shook his head. Rose was married to another man when he fell in love with her, so he didn't feel qualified to lecture Billy on that particular topic. "You're a grown man, you don't need any advice from me. But there is talk, and Odalie Faucett is the kind of woman a man might kill for. It occurred to me that might be the cause of what happened today."

Billy's face went dark as Heck's blanket. "I don't talk about Odalie, Doctor. Not with anyone, not even you. Anyhow, what happened to me and Nate this morning wasn't about that. I'm sure of it. It's about the roundup, about rights to the range. I figure Faucett and them plan to pick us all off, one at a time, pop! pop! pop! and with our early roundup coming, things are heating up. Way I see it, nobody's safe. Again, not even you."

Dixon had had the same thought. Everyone knew Billy Sun was practically a member of the Dixon family. If it really was the range war, if Faucett and the WSGA planned to get rid of the "rustlers" and their associates, Dixon could well be a target.

"I'm going to the Lazy L and B," Billy said. "I'll call the boys in. We'll go on getting set for the roundup, but our guns will be ready. If Faucett and his hired shooters come for us, they'll have a fight on their hands. They don't scare me. Besides, we have the law on our side."

Dixon said, "Billy, I wouldn't put much store in Red Angus and his deputies. You'd best go into this clear-eyed."

"I understand," Billy said. "But it's the sheriff's job to get involved. That's why the people of Johnson County elected him. Maybe he'll surprise us."

"Maybe."

Outside, the rooster crowed. Dixon got to his feet and knocked the hay off his trousers. "I'm going to get some sleep. Are you leaving now?"

Billy nodded. "Can Nate stay with you till he's ready to ride?"

"Of course. We'll take good care of him. Come and get some breakfast before you go."

The men were walking to the house when Lorna ran out the door, flushed and breathless. "Pa!" she said. "Oh, Pa! I was just now coming for you. I went to the surgery to relieve Cal, like you told me, and Nate, he was down on the floor all in blood. He's dead, Pa — Nate's dead. And Cal's gone!" She gestured toward the tracks left by Cal's horse, a hard-hoofed animal he kept unshod.

Frank Canton

The six-car train left Cheyenne late on the afternoon of April 5. On board were fifty-two men, including Faucett and a dozen of his fellow cattlemen, twenty-two hired gunfighters, and enough guns and ammunition to kill every man, woman, and child in the new state of Wyoming. The horses traveled in three stock cars, and three new Studebaker wagons were tied down to a flatcar. The train would take Faucett's regulators as far north as Casper, a distance of one hundred and fifty miles. There they would disembark and begin their southward march on horseback, cleaning out the rustlers on the way.

Faucett, cigar in hand, addressed the men as they rolled northward: "Gentlemen, our time has come at last. We shall claim this state for the good, honest people of Wyoming, who are sick and tired of the rustlers' brazen lawlessness, sick and tired of the tyranny of these godless criminals. They shall swing at the end of our ropes!" This was met with cheers which he acknowledged with a smile, then quieted with a raise of his cigar hand. "My only fear, and I have but one, is that the miscreants will somehow get wind of our purpose and flee to the mountains, where we will pursue them still, though our work will be made more difficult. But mark my words: not one of them — not one thieving soul — shall escape our wrath!" He pumped his fist in the air, drawing another chorus of cheers.

Later, he and Fred Jolly sat in a corner of the smoke-filled car, drinking brandies. "Do they know where the Indian is hiding?" Faucett said.

Jolly nodded. "Sun and a few others are at the Lazy L and B, holed up in a line shack. Frank and some of the Texans are there. They won't get by him."

"When we get to the Lazy L and B, I shall kill Billy Sun myself. Canton knows that, but make sure it's widely understood. I don't want anyone to deprive me of the experience."

"Yes sir." Women were a lot of trouble, Jolly thought, and the better looking they were, the more trouble they brought. No doubt about it, his father gave him good advice when he said, "homely women make the best wives." He had his eye on a widow woman in Buffalo who was just homely enough.

ODALIE

Odalie got off the Denver train at the first stop: Olympus. Despite its grand name, Olympus was a desolate outpost on the Fremont, Elkhorn, and Missouri Valley line that consisted of a covered platform and ticket office, telegraph station, livery stable, and hotel. After instructing the porter to remove her bags, Odalie stepped out onto the rickety platform where the cold April wind robbed her of her breath and almost of her hat. With one hand on her head, she approached the ticketing agent's window and requested a ticket to Buffalo.

"You just came from Buffalo," the agent said.

"Yes, and now I want to go back. When does the next train leave?"

"Not till tomorrow morning, miss. Ten o'clock, but it's usually a half hour late."

It was just noon. Odalie sighed and looked at the hotel — a hand-lettered sign above the door identified it as The Excelsior — a two-story frame building with peeling paint the color of sulfur and a trio of unclean characters lounging in chairs on either side of the entry. Could she bear nearly twenty-four hours in such a place? No, she could not.

"I want to send a telegram," she said.

The agent took a set of keys from the drawer. "Follow me." He led her across the platform to the telegraph station on the opposite side, where he unlocked a door and held it for her as she entered. "Now," he said, sitting before the machine and handing her paper and a pencil. "Write down what you want to say and to whom you wish to say it."

Odalie considered. By sending this telegram she was crossing a line that could not be uncrossed. She was, in effect, passing the point of no return. Resolutely, she gripped the pencil and began to write: *"To Sheriff Red Angus, Buffalo. Lord Richard Faucett and the WSGA cattlemen of Johnson County have formed an army. They will seize the courthouse and its weapons. They intend to murder seventy men, including Dr. Dixon and Billy Sun. Frank Canton is one of Faucett's men."* She handed the paper to the agent. "No signature."

The agent gave a low whistle as he read. "How do you know this, miss?"

"Never mind that. Just send it please."

The agent tapped out the message, but as he worked, Odalie heard her husband's voice speaking words she had forgotten until now: *"The telegraph lines will be cut, of course."*

"Can you tell if the message goes through?" she said. "Is there any way to know if Sheriff Angus has received it?"

The agent did not respond until he was finished sending. "No, miss." He took off his visor and raised his face to hers. She saw that he was quite young, clean shaven with a pleasing face. "I asked him to respond straightaway, but until he does there's no way to know if the lines are down. I assume that's what you're worried about."

Odalie's thoughts raced. She paced the room and tried to think clearly. *I can't wait for the train. Tomorrow may be too late. Daniel and Billy may be dead by then.* She pictured Dixon's hazel eyes and thick unruly hair, now mostly gray. She remembered the way he smiled when their eyes met at her Christmas party, the way he held her when they danced. *I can't let Richard hurt him, or Billy. I won't.*

"Do you have some reason to think the

lines might be down?" the agent said. Odalie, lost in thought, did not answer. After several minutes of restless waiting, she said, "Can I rent a horse at that livery stable?"

The agent showed surprise. "Well, Horace Stubbs has a horse to let, but she's an old bag of bones. I hope you're not thinking of riding back to Buffalo, miss. It's nearly forty miles. You won't make it before dark."

Odalie picked up her bags.

"Miss," the agent called. "You'll freeze!"

But she was already out the door.

BILLY SUN

Billy Sun and Pat Comstock were enjoying a meal of bacon and beans when Hi Kinch and Nestor Lopez rode up to the line shack in the late afternoon. It was spitting snow when they arrived, and by the time the beans and bacon were gone it was coming down hard. The men passed the cold evening before the fire. Kinch and Comstock played cards, Lopez cleaned his gun, and Billy wrote in his journal.

"Russ and Carlos and the boys will be here Friday, before maybe," Lopez said, squinting down the barrel of the Smith & Wesson army revolver he had won at cards off a drunken deserter from Custer's Seventh Cavalry years before. "Then when Faucett and his nabobs come, me and Carlos will show him what a couple of Mexicans can do. He won't be calling us greasers no more." Lopez smiled to himself as he pushed an oily rag through the barrel.

There were only two bunks in the shack. Billy and Kinch took those while Comstock and Lopez spread their bedrolls on the dirt floor. At dawn, Billy was first to wake. As he stoked the dying fire, Kinch climbed out of bed, pulled on his boots and picked up the bucket.

"I'll get us some water," he said, pushing aside the feed sack that darkened the window and peering out. "Damn me. There must be two foot out there." Snowdrifts twice that deep were banked against the cabin walls. Kinch had a fight just to get the door open because of the snow piled high against it. When at last he succeeded, he admitted a blast of cold air that made the two men on the floor groan and turn in their blankets. Kinch whistled to himself as he crunched through the frozen crust toward the creek, about fifty feet down the hill. As he passed the barn, where the horses were stabled, he heard a voice.

"Who's that?" Kinch said. "Someone in there?"

"Shut up and keep walking, old man, and you'll live another day."

Kinch kept on toward the creek, feeling a worm of fear crawl down his spine. As he walked he heard footsteps following, close behind. Once he turned his head halfway to see a young man, with white-blond hair and a thin, beardless face, carrying a rifle. "Don't try anything stupid," the young man said. Kinch thought he looked familiar, but he could not place him. Once they arrived at the creek he found two others, wrapped in colorful Mexican blankets, in a miserable, cold camp. One rose and spoke to the gunman.

"He the one we're after? This old buzzard?" Kinch recognized a Texas accent. Kinch hated Texans.

"No," the young man said, jabbing Kinch in the back with the business end of the rifle. "Is Billy Sun in that shack, old timer? You'll tell the truth if you know what's good for you."

"Yeah, he's there."

"Who else?"

"Pat Comstock and Nestor Lopez."

"Any others?"

"Just them."

"They on the list, kid?" the Texan said. "Say, maybe this old buzzard's on the list. What's your name, Granddad?" The Texan gave Kinch a tobacco-stained smile.

"H.I. Kinch. Folks call me Hi."

"Do they now?" The Texan's grin widened.

The boy consulted a folded paper from

his pocket. "Those names aren't on it," he said, shaking his head. "None of those. It's only Billy Sun we want."

"Well, damn, let's go take the son of a bitch," the second Texan said. "We shoulda done it last night while they was sleeping, like me and Jess said. Jesus H. Christ."

"No," the boy said. "We're not supposed to kill him, just hold him till Canton and the others get here."

"The hell," Jess, the first Texan, said. "You two are all warm and cozy in that barn while me and Andy are freezing our balls off down here. We don't care what Frank Canton and Lord what's-his-name say. C'mon, let's go finish it."

"No," the boy said. "When this one doesn't return, Billy Sun will come looking for him. That's when we'll take him." He turned to go back to the barn.

"So me and Jess keep on freezin' our balls off down here, with Granddad for company?"

The boy did not reply but raised a hand over his shoulder as he walked back up the hill. Kinch watched, trying to think where he had seen him before.

Jess looked up at the lowering sky. "Looks like more snow, Granddad. Damn, if I'd a knowed how damn cold and snowy it was up here I wouldn't a come. It's like the god-damn North Pole. Jesus H. Christ."

"Keep thinking on the money, Jess," Andy said. "Just you keep thinkin' on that."

"I guess." Jess settled back on the ground and wrapped himself in his blanket. "May as well sit, Granddad," he said. "You're gonna be here a spell."

Billy looked out the line shack's lone window. Hi should be back by now. Even if he'd stopped to answer nature's call, he should at least be on his way. Billy had a bad feeling.

"Something wrong?" Pat spoke from his bedroll on the floor.

"Could be. Kinch went for water and it's taking too long."

"I'll go see what's keeping him. I gotta take care of business anyhow."

"I don't know," Billy said. "Maybe me or Nestor should come with you?"

"Naw," Pat said, pulling on his boots. "I don't need company for what I gotta do. You just get coffee going and fry up some bacon. Me and Hi will be back in no time. Mind if I borrow your coat? Mine's still wet." He shrugged his broad shoulders into Billy's sheepskin and stepped out into the cold morning air. He took three steps when a bullet whistled past his head and smashed into the side of the cabin. Pat turned back, wild eyed with fear, when the second shot came. The back of his head exploded in a red spray of blood and brains.

ODALIE

Odalie's heart sank when she saw the rental horse available to her, an elderly, sway-backed mare with one milky eye. "Have you nothing else, Mr. Stubbs? I doubt this one will go the distance."

Horace Stubbs spat a jet of brown tobacco juice on the hay-covered floor. "Bella, here, is a fine, gentle palfrey for a delicate lady like yourself, Miss . . ." He waited for her to offer her name, but when she did not he continued. "Anyhow, what kind of distance are we talking about?"

"I need to get to Buffalo tonight."

"Haw!" Stubbs laughed. "Buffalo to-night!" He wiped his wet mouth with the back of his hand. "Do ye now?" He turned to two other men lounging in the stable, inviting them to share his amusement. They were regarding the beautiful, well-dressed woman with slack-jawed amazement.

"Yes, Mr. Stubbs." Odalie spoke impatiently. "Can you help me or not? I can pay."

At the mention of money, Stubbs's rheumy eyes narrowed. "Well, now, let me think a bit, let me think. Yes, I might be able to come up with a sturdier animal, but it will be a hardship, such short notice, don't ye know?" He moved toward her. "How much are you willing to pay?"

Odalie felt a red burst of panic. Her ladies' pistol was in her bag, hanging from her arm. Could she hold these three men at bay with it? Would she even be able to get it out before this brute jumped her? She took a step backward.

"Well, miss?" Stubbs smiled and came closer. "How much?"

To Odalie's great relief the door opened with a bang, and the ticket agent walked in. "I'm sorry, miss, I was delayed." He looked from her to Stubbs, then back again. "Is everything all right here?"

Odalie flew to his side and took his arm. "No, I don't think it is."

"Stubbs?" the agent said angrily. "Have you done something to frighten this woman?"

"Hell no, Rob. No." Stubbs shifted from one foot to the other. "Me, I was only tryin' to help her out, rent her a horse. We was

341

just negotiatin' my fee. No need to get riled up."

Odalie laughed derisively. "He was preparing to rob me."

"No, Rob, I wasn't." Stubbs forced a smile. "That ain't how it was, was it, boys?" He appealed to the two gray men who stood silently by. "Tell him, boys. Tell Rob how it was."

"Never mind, Stubbs. Your services won't be needed after all." He picked up Odalie's bags. "Come with me, miss. I believe I've found an answer for your problem." Together they walked from the dark livery stable into the sunlight, where Odalie drew a deep, sweet breath of relief.

"What a horrible man! However can I thank you, Mr. . . . ?"

"Hardy. Robert Hardy. Call me Rob. I should've warned you about Stubbs, but you were in a hurry. Stubbs used to be all right, but he took to the bottle when his wife died. Anyhow, I shut down the offices and came fast as I could. But I meant what I said, I think I can get you to Buffalo, if you really mean to go."

"I mean to go."

"All right then. My sister, Anna, has a buggy and a strong pair of horses. I believe she'll give me use of them. I think you're right about the telegraph lines. I haven't had any traffic from the north for hours. That's not normal."

Odalie put her hand to her head. "Yes, I was afraid of that. I pray we're not too late!"

Hardy put his hands on her waist and lifted her easily onto his horse, then Hardy mounted behind her. They rode to his sister's ranch, a tidy, well-tended place two miles west of town. A widow, Anna was five years older than her brother and harder. She refused to lend her buggy and team and did not soften, even when Rob told her lives were at stake.

"What do I care?" she said. "Those people up north don't mean nothing to me." With disapproving eyes, she took in Odalie's tailored traveling suit and veiled, narrow-brimmed hat. "And you neither. Why should we put ourselves out for the likes of them? They wouldn't do for us."

"Anna, we can't let innocent people be slaughtered. The lines are down, and there's no way to warn them."

Anna would not budge until Odalie said, "I'll give you two hundred dollars." She reached into her purse and pulled out four fifty-dollar gold certificates, each bearing the sour likeness of Silas Wright. "Take the money," she said, offering Anna the limp currency. "This is all I have with me."

The woman's faded eyes gleamed. "Well, all right then. I guess you can use them." She took the bills in her calloused hands and stuffed them in her waist pocket. "But Robbie, you see to it I get those horses back in good shape. If they ain't . . ." she turned to Odalie and patted her pocket, "I'll be needing more of this."

Within minutes, Rob and Odalie were settled in the buggy, a sturdy rig previously used by Anna's late husband, a drummer, and on their way north to Buffalo.

Dixon had moved Nate's body from the floor to his operating stand. He had been dead for hours and rigor mortis had begun, his neck and jaw stiffening in unnatural positions. Nate had died from a crushing blow to the back of his head. The killing instrument, an iron doorstop, had been found beside him on the floor, with bits of hair and brain matter adhering to its surface. Dixon struggled to make sense of it. Who had done this? And where was Cal?

An examination of his son's room showed Cal had left with packed bags. Dixon stood by his son's unmade bed and surveyed the room's contents: a table with a stack of books, including some of his father's medical texts, a sketchbook with a charcoal drawing of Lorna on the top page, a deck of well-handled playing cards. Under the bed he found a cigar box containing a dusty doll with a head of painted bone and limbs of twisted leather. Though he had not seen it for years, Dixon recognized the thing. Biwi made it for the children when they were very small. Why had Cal saved it, and why was it hidden? Dixon took the doll from the box and examined it more closely. It wore a garment of faded fabric cut from one of Rose's dresses. The sight of that fabric, a pattern of tiny yellow flowers against a blue background, kindled such powerful memories Dixon's hand shook.

"What does it mean, Pa?" Lorna's voice startled him. He had been so lost in the past he had not heard her enter. "Did Cal do that to Nate?" she said.

Dixon shook his head, unable to speak. His world had gone sideways, he could make no sense of Nate's death and Cal's disappearance. Lorna stepped close and put her hand on his arm, a gesture of tenderness her father did not expect from her.

"I don't know what's happening, Pa," she said, "but I'm sorry for it. I'm sorry for you, me, Cal, Billy — all of us. I'm scared."

Moved, Dixon covered her hand with his. Perhaps there was a heart under his daughter's shrewish exterior after all. "Is there anything you can tell me, Lorna?" he said. "Anything at all?"

She shook her head. "Cal hardly talks to

me anymore. I never know what he's thinking; I don't know what's important to him." She looked at the doll in her father's hand. "I haven't seen that in years. Where did you find it?"

Dixon pointed to the cigar box on the table. "In that box, under the bed."

"Whatever made him dig that old thing out?" Even as she spoke, Lorna thought she knew the answer. Cal was saying good-bye to the things of his youth, the things he used to love. She turned and hurried from his room to hers, knowing what she would find there. On her bed was a letter. She tore it open.

April 6, 1892

Dearest Sister — I am sorry you are learning things this way. It's not what I intended, but nothing in my life has turned out as I intended. The only thing that's been constant is you.

Some time ago, Lord Richard Faucett offered me five thousand dollars to kill Pa. I took the money. It would give me a clean start and he would find someone else if I said no. Mrs. MacGill found Faucett's letter and threatened to tell Pa so I smothered her with a pillow. It was the night of your party. I told myself she was dying anyway, but I hate myself for what I did. I can't stop thinking about it.

When the time came I didn't go through with killing Pa, I don't think I ever really intended to, but I went for Nate instead. His name was on the list — you'll hear more about Lord Faucett's list — and I hope it might do me some good, but it could be I'm dead, too. I'll know soon enough. To tell you the truth, I don't much care anymore.

You will want to know why I've done these things, and I don't have a good answer. I wanted the money and I wanted to get away, but, even more, I wanted to matter. I was always invisible to everyone but you and Biwi. She saw my future and suspected what I would come to be. She tried to change me but she couldn't. Biwi knew me best of all, and she loved me anyway.

Good-bye, dear sister. I hope you will be able to remember some good about me. Cal

The letter trembled in Lorna's hand. Cal took Faucett's money to kill their father? Yes, she and Cal had drifted apart, but could it really be possible she knew her own brother so little? He was the person with whom she had shared her childhood and, before that, their mother's womb. She sank to her bed, sick with grief. How could a life that held so much joy and promise at its onset come to so little? She mourned her poor lost brother, but at the same time, even as she wept, she was grateful to him. Her father still lived. And so did Billy Sun.

Billy Sun

"Get up, Nestor." Billy nudged the sleeping man on the floor with his foot. How could a man who'd been stone-cold sober the night before sleep so heavily? "Dammit, Nestor, get up and get your gun." Billy returned to the window and peered out, carefully keeping to one side and holding his rifle close to his body. They were in the stand of trees down by the creek. Billy couldn't make them out, but he saw one flash and then another as the rising sun reflected off an object, a gun barrel maybe or a pair of eyeglasses.

"What is it?" Lopez was fully awake now, sitting in his blankets. "What's going on?"

"Pat's shot." Billy spoke without turning from the window. "Kinch went to the creek and he ain't come back. Somebody's down there by the water; I can't make them out."

Lopez jumped up and grabbed his rifle, joining Billy on the other side of the window.

His eyes bulged at the sight of Pat's body, lying faceup on the bloody snow. "Poor Pat," he said. "*Probrecito.* He was just a kid."

"He didn't deserve to die that way." ·

Lopez shook his head. "He wasn't smart but he was *un hombre, sabes?* A good one to ride with. Should we go for his gun?" Pat's rifle lay beside him in the snow.

Billy shook his head. "Don't try it. Whoever's down there has a good eye."

They waited in the bright early morning sun, eyes trained on the dark stand of cottonwoods. They were quiet until Lopez audibly broke wind. "Jesus, Nestor," Billy said, "if you're —"

A bullet crashed through the window, hitting Lopez in the jaw and showering both men with glass and bits of shattered teeth. Lopez screamed and fell to the floor, twisting in pain while Billy flattened himself against the wall next to the broken window. At first, he saw nothing. Then a man he did not recognize stepped from the trees, holding a rifle. Lopez's shrieks were loud enough for all to hear.

"Billy Sun!" the man called. "Come out now before anyone else gets hurt. You've already lost two men; you don't want anything to happen to old man Kinch here, do you?"

Billy raised his rifle to his shoulder and positioned the barrel so the stranger was squarely in his sights. His shot went wide, hitting a tree to the man's left. He turned and dived back into the woods.

"Nestor?" Billy left the window and kneeled by his friend. Lopez held his right hand to his jaw while bright red blood dripped from his fingers and onto the floor. Lopez's frightened eyes told Billy all he needed to know.

"I'm sorry, Nestor, but can you still handle a gun?" Billy said. "Can you shoot if they come through that door?"

Lopez managed an animal sound. Billy picked up the fallen man's rifle and put it in his hands. "Do what you can," he said, and Lopez nodded.

Billy returned to the window. The day would be a warm one. Already the snow was beginning to melt. Billy's eyes were in constant motion, moving from the barn to the creek and the scrubby hill behind it. He needed to know how many men were concealed in the trees and if there were others in another location. The barn troubled him. Billy knew that's where he would hide if he were stalking the house. After about twenty minutes his vigilance was rewarded. The barn door opened slightly to allow a yellow arc of urine.

"Damn, Nestor, they're in the barn, too." When he got no response he turned to find his friend dead on the floor. Nestor's hand had fallen to reveal his ruined face, with its shattered jawbone and broken, blood-covered teeth. Billy turned away. Russ and the boys were his only hope. According to Kinch, they were expected on Friday, still more than a day away. Could he hold out that long?

ODALIE

If she lived to be as old as Methuselah, Odalie knew she would never forget the misery of that long ride to Buffalo. The snow that had melted during the day froze again at night, making the road icy and treacherous. Several times the horses lost their footing and nearly fell, once the buggy slid sideways and almost went down a steep hill, taking horses, buggy and passengers with it. But bad as that was, the cold was worse. In addition to two coats, Odalie wrapped a thick woolen horse blanket around her legs and another over her head and shoulders like an Indian squaw, but even so the cold penetrated to take root deep in her stomach and in her bones. Never in all her years had Odalie known such cold. She marveled at the strength and fortitude of her intrepid escort. Rob Hardy drove all night without complaint, only stopping to rest and nourish the horses.

"I am so grateful to you, Rob," she said. "Whatever would I have done had I not met you? My God, what would have happened to me at the hands of that horrible Stubbs?" She shuddered. "It takes all the fly out of me just to think of it."

"I would've blamed myself," he said. "After all, I sent you there. Like I said, Stubbs has taken a hard turn, but then plenty of folks around here have done that. The winter of eighty-six changed things, including people."

"Yes. That's when things started to go wrong."

Hardy gave her a sideways glance. "Wrong? For people like you? For the rich and mighty Lord Richard Faucett and his wife? Forgive me if I find that hard to believe."

Odalie felt a prick of alarm. "How do you know me? I didn't sign the telegram. I don't believe I gave you my name."

"No?"

"No. Have we met before? I think I would have remembered."

"Yes, we did meet once but very briefly." He spoke without looking at her. "I recognized you at once, but I wouldn't expect you to remember me. It was years ago, and I was just one of your husband's cowpunchers when Anna's husband died. I had to go back to Olympus, to take care of her and her family." He turned to Odalie and smiled, his teeth white in the darkness. "But I remember you quite well, Lady Faucett." His smile faded. "And your husband, too."

Odalie heard the change in his voice. "Did Richard mistreat you in some way?"

"No, I wouldn't say that. To tell you the truth, I don't think he ever noticed me. I was just one of his riders. I had more truck with the skunk, Jolly. He cheated us every chance he got, even refused to pay me for two weeks I was due. No, I have no love for that man."

"That makes two of us," Odalie said. "I'm curious, what does your husband have planned exactly? What is Frank Canton's involvement?"

Odalie hesitated, turning her face to the craggy mountains showing black against the starry sky. How much should she say? She wanted to save Daniel and Billy, but beyond that she had no plan. Vile though he was, did she really want to consign Richard to the black maw of frontier justice? Even if the law did not prosecute him — as seemed likely, given Sheriff Angus's timidity and Richard's connections — would he be safe from the mob? Again, she glanced at her

356

escort. Richard had misused him. Did Rob represent the mob? No, he was unlike the average unwashed, unschooled sodbuster, a creature she believed fully as capable as Richard of savagery. And Odalie had to think of herself. Without Richard, and his money, where would she be? She trusted Rob, but she had to tread carefully.

"I'm not sure exactly," she said. "I overheard bits of Richard's conversations. I know he was assembling an army; they planned to storm the courthouse and seize the weapons there, but after that, I don't know. I'm afraid they mean to harm good people, people who are my friends. I can't let that happen."

Rob kept his eyes on the snowy road. He was quiet for a long time, and Odalie thought he meant to let the matter drop. Then he said, "I think your husband and Frank Canton and the WSGA stockmen plan to do a lot of killing, and there's no one in Johnson County who can stop them."

Odalie shivered and burrowed deeper in her blankets. Rob was right, but she did not want to say so. She did not want to admit that a man she had given so many years of her life to, the best years, she feared, was a murderous animal. Unbidden, a memory of her girlhood home in New Orleans came to her, so strongly she felt a lump form in her throat. *Oh, what I wouldn't give to be sitting in the warm, sweet-smelling kitchen, sipping a hot mug of chicory coffee with milk and sugar, and eating from a plate of fresh, powdered-sugar beignets. How sad that young people take their moments of happiness and security for granted. If only I could have known how rare and precious they were at the time!*

Rob shook her from her reverie. "We've got company." He pointed to a solitary rider on the road, approaching from the north. "Who'd be out in this cold, at this time of night?"

"He may well be thinking the same of us," Odalie said.

The horseman stopped, and she saw the moonlight reflect off the field glasses he raised to his eyes. After a pause, he urged his horse forward. She recognized something about the way he sat a saddle, tall and straight as a rifle barrel. "I believe I know this man," she said in a low voice, pulling the blanket up over her head and shoulders. "Please, Rob, do not reveal my identity."

They met in the road. Rob reined in his team.

"Hello, friends," the rider said with a broad smile. "What brings you out on this cold night?"

"My wife is ill," Rob said. "She needs a doctor. I'm taking her to Buffalo."

"Buffalo? What's wrong with her?" The rider moved closer, guiding his horse toward Odalie's side of the buggy.

"Female trouble," Rob said. "She's in a family way."

Odalie turned her head from the rider's curious gaze. She could almost feel the heat of his black eyes on her, trying to penetrate the woolen blanket.

The horseman laughed. "Why, if I didn't know better I'd think this fine lady was none other than Lady Odalie Faucett. But, now, that couldn't be, could it, friend? I mean, you just said she was your wife."

Odalie threw off her hood and raised her head. "Hello, Mr. Horn."

Tom Horn's smile widened. "Well, I'll be. So it *is* you after all. Now, why would this young fellow lie to me? Did you tell him to do that?"

"What do you want?" she said.

He shook his head in exaggerated puzzlement. "Why, I just don't understand. I mean, ain't you supposed to be in Denver? Sir Richard says you are. He told me himself. He said his man, Jolly, took you to the station."

Odalie's heart was thudding like a bat in a

barrel. "Once again, Mr. Horn. What do you want?"

"Well, ma'am, your friend here says you're going to Buffalo. If that's so, I believe I best come along to make sure you get there all right. I'm sure this fellow is fine, but I wouldn't want you to meet up with any troublemakers."

Odalie withdrew a pistol, a Merwin and Hulbert five-shot, double-action revolver with a birds-head grip, from the folds of her blankets and pointed it at Horn. Her hand, she was pleased to notice, was steady. "The only troublemaker here is you," she said. "Rob, get down and take Mr. Horn's long gun."

Horn's smile faded. Even in the darkness, she could sense him coiling, like a snake preparing to strike. "You can't do much damage with that little lady gun," he said.

"Are you sure of that, Mr. Horn?" Odalie said. "I won't miss at this range, and I've got five opportunities. I wouldn't risk it if I were you." As she spoke Rob pulled Horn's rifle from its scabbard and pointed it at him.

"Throw down your pistol, Mr. Horn," she said. "Throw it to the ground or I will shoot you."

"You wouldn't."

She smiled brightly. "I've never liked you,

Mr. Horn, or your great friend Frank Canton, either. You are sycophants and vermin, the pair of you, and I would enjoy shooting you. Canton, too, if it comes to that."

Rob stepped forward, holding the rifle only feet away from Horn's belly. After a brief hesitation, Horn unholstered his revolver and tossed it to the ground where Rob recovered it.

"Now, climb down off your horse," Odalie said.

"Wait just a minute," Horn said. For the first time Odalie heard fear in his voice. "You can't mean to leave me out here without my horse. I'll freeze."

"I said get down."

"I won't." Horn folded his long arms across his chest. "Go ahead and shoot me, lady. Shoot an unarmed man. I will not surrender my horse."

Odalie fired her pistol, sending a bullet whistling past Horn's ear. He quickly dismounted, handing the ribbons to Rob who tied them to a ring-bolt on the back of the buggy. Horn watched with narrowed eyes as Rob climbed back onto the bench and took up the reins, slapping them on the horses' backs. Throughout all this, Odalie never took her eyes, or her gun, off Horn.

"Lady, you are the devil," he said as the horses lunged forward. "I knew it. I saw what you were all along. You'll be sorry you didn't kill me!"

And that, Odalie thought as Horn grew small in the dark and distance, may be the one true thing Tom Horn said tonight.

BILLY SUN

There was no water in the cabin, other than the warm, stale fluid in Billy's canteen. He took it sparingly as he waited and watched by the window. *How many men am I up against, and when will they make their move?*

He got his answer at noon. A man he well knew, a small man with a long, thin face and white-blond hair, stepped out of the tree line with his arms raised above his head.

"Billy!" he yelled, "Billy, don't shoot! It's me, Cal."

Billy was stunned. Was Cal a captive, like Kinch, or was it something else? "State your business," Billy shouted, careful not to show himself in the open window.

"These men are keeping me prisoner," Cal said. "They want me to deliver a message. Can I come up?"

Billy did not respond, trying to make sense of what was going on. A nagging thought stirred in the depths of his mind.

What was it? A warning? A memory? He tried to bring it forward.

"Billy, they'll kill me if you say no. They got no use for me otherwise." Cal looked over his shoulder toward the trees where two or three men were barely visible. One was the stranger Billy had shot at earlier; the others he could not make out.

"Don't let them kill me, Billy!" Cal's voice broke.

"All right," Billy shouted. "Come on, but come unarmed."

Cal's body sagged with relief as he lowered his arms and started climbing the hill. The melting snow made the slope slippery, and twice he fell. Billy kept his eyes moving from Cal to the barn. He hadn't seen any motion from that direction since the urine stream, but that didn't mean someone wasn't there.

Cal was within fifty feet of the cabin when Kinch burst out of the tree line, running full out and yelling at the top of his lungs. "No, Billy, no! He's with them — he's got —" Shots rang out and Kinch fell like a stone, facedown in the snow. At the same moment, Cal dropped to a crouch and struggled to pull a six-shooter from his belt. Billy fired a shot at his feet and Cal froze.

"Put the gun down, Cal," Billy said. Cal did as he was told.

"Who are those men? What's this about?"

An ugly smile, one Billy had not seen before, twisted Cal's features. "You know who they are," he said. "Faucett's men. He means to kill you, you and all the range trash you ride with. Nate's dead, by the way. I finished him off myself, after my father was done with him."

Poor Nate. Billy could only imagine the shock he must have felt when Cal attacked him. "And you're with Faucett?" he yelled. "Why? What's in it for you?"

"Money, that's in it for me. Money buys freedom from my father, from Wyoming, from this godforsaken, punishing country. This was never the life I wanted, but no one ever asked me. No one ever gave a damn about what I wanted!"

The barn door swung open and Frank Canton jumped out into the bright sunlight, his carbine at his shoulder, and fired. His shot was wide, striking the side of the cabin. As Billy returned Canton's fire, Cal dove for his gun, raising it and shooting in one motion. He was not a practiced gunman, and his bullet hit the window frame above Billy's head, driving a sliver of wood into the skin just below Billy's left eye. Still, he got a shot off. Cal clutched his stomach, dropped to his knees in the snow, and pitched over onto his side, doubled in pain. He rolled, moaning, on the ground between Canton, who had retreated to the cover of the barn, and Billy. He raised his head in Billy's direction. "Finish me, Billy," he said. "Please!"

Neither Billy nor Canton responded. Cal continued to whimper and cry, twisting on the wet, muddy ground. He called out again. "Billy, please. Just do it!"

No matter what he had become, Cal had once been a small, lonely boy with a shy smile. Billy had taught Cal how to ride and groom a horse, how to make coffee over an open fire, how to skin a rabbit. In many ways, Billy thought, Cal had never had a chance. From the womb, his sister had dominated every aspect of his life. If his mother had lived, maybe he would have known some love and tenderness, but as it was he had been denied that.

He would expose himself to Canton's fire, but Billy owed Cal at least this. He took a deep breath, then moved to the window and aimed carefully at Cal's head. His Winchester barked once, and the boy's misery was over.

Canton and the others opened up on the cabin, pouring lead through the window and splintering the walls and the door. One bullet took Billy's hat off, but otherwise he was lucky. He fired back from alternating positions around the cabin, hoping to delude his attackers into thinking they were fighting more than one man, though he knew there was little chance of that. Kinch would have told them how many were in the cabin.

During lulls in the shooting, Billy sat on the floor by the cold fireplace, writing in his notebook.

Boys,

It's about three o'clock and I'm the only one left. Faucett's men and Frank Canton have done for Hi Kinch, Nestor Lopez, and Pat Comstock, and they'll probably put me through before the day is out.

They are splitting wood down by the creek and I see smoke. Probably they aim to fire the house tonight and I will have a job of stopping them. They can come at me from the back as the wall is blind with no window. If they burn me out I'll have to run for it. My only hope is that Russell Burnell and the boys get here first.

He wet the lead of his pencil on his tongue, then continued.

Doc Dixon's boy Cal was with Faucett's men and he is dead. He killed Nate back at Doc's house. Why I don't know. Cal took that to the grave with him.

Billy stared at the cold ashes. More than anything else, he wanted to write of his love for Odalie and to tell her good-bye; he wanted to tell the world she was a woman of heart and courage and not what they thought she was, for he knew the people of Johnson County did not hold her in high regard. But he could not speak of these things because the love of an Indian would not lift her in their eyes.

Well, good-bye, boys. If I never see you again, I hope you will remember Billy Sun as your friend. There was a woman I loved from the first time I saw her and I love her still. She might someday see letter, and if she does, she will know.

He tore the sheet from the notebook, folded it, and put it in his shirt pocket.

The hours passed and it grew dark. Billy ate a piece of elk jerky and washed it down with the last of his water. He stood by the window, watching the fire burning by the creek. They would come soon. He patted the paper in his shirt pocket and sent a prayer to his protector in the spirit world behind this one. *Please let her see it.*

Billy heard a dull thud as something landed on the wood-shingled roof. It was starting. At first there were just a few tongues of flame, but they grew quickly, licking upward. Soon the entire roof was engulfed, and the fire spread fast, descending the walls. The heat and smoke were suffocating. Billy crouched on the floor, catching gulps of clean air where and when he could. Occasionally the thick smoke would part and he could glimpse his attackers, creeping up the hill with their long guns before them.

The killers expected him to make his run through the door, but Billy had other plans. The north wall, opposite the door, had burned first and most fully; it was partially collapsed. The roof would fall in any second. Billy's only chance, though a skeletally thin one, was to dash through the diminishing sheet of fire, like a finger through a candle flame, and make for the dry ravine north of the cabin.

The heat was becoming unbearable, and the smoke was choking him. He had to make his move. Billy raised his .45 and fired a single shot. *Let them think I've killed myself rather than burn alive.*

Billy took his Winchester in one hand and his revolver in the other and ran for his life, flying through the dying wall of flame and glowing embers of the north wall. Smoke rolled off him as he raced across the flat plain that lay between the cabin and the ravine.

"There he goes!" a man yelled, and the bullets began to fly, whizzing by his head or striking the ground around him, sending up fan-shaped sprays of dirt and rock. Billy had only fifty yards to go until he reached the ravine. There he could take shelter. There he would find a chance, his only chance, to hold them off.

Only twenty yards left. His lungs burned with effort and the effects of the smoke but he did not slow. Despite the pain, his heart soared. He was going to make it! At the same time, Even so, a question formed in his throbbing brain. Where was Frank Canton? Had he seen him with the others? He wasn't sure; he couldn't be certain . . .

Five yards to go! Billy jumped into the dark of the ravine, his Winchester over his head, feeling pure joy as his feet felt the ground. *I've made it! I have a chance!*

He landed on the soft, sandy soil and crept forward toward the V bend where he could see both means of approach. There he would make his stand. He heard the Texans yelling and cursing as they ran toward him. Soon Billy would be in a good place to take care of them once and for all. He smiled as he reached the bend.

Frank Canton was down on one knee, his carbine at his shoulder. Billy tried to raise his Winchester, tried to get a hip shot off, but he was too late. Canton fired, hitting Billy square in the chest. He felt it like the kick of a mule, and fell back onto his back. There was no pain. He lay still, unable to move any part of his body except his eyes. He fixed them on the evening sky and waited, hearing Canton walk toward him. Billy Sun's last view of this world was the face of Frank Canton, gazing down on him above the barrel of his carbine.

"Good-bye, chief," Canton said as he pulled the trigger.

ODALIE

Hardy stopped to rest the horses when they were within ten miles of Dixon's ranch. Odalie complained but he insisted. "We've done thirty miles in eight hours," he said. "I don't want to kill them."

Odalie made a sound of impatience and jumped down from the buggy, pacing on the frozen ground. The eastern sky was beginning to lighten. What if Richard and his army of assassins had beat them? What if Daniel and Billy were already dead? If that had happened, if Daniel was killed, Odalie thought she would take up a gun and shoot Richard herself, and to hell with the consequences.

They were stopped by a creek that widened to a frozen pool. Hardy broke the ice and led the horses to drink. After they had taken their fill, he gave each a nosebag of grain. When they were done eating he checked their feet. Rob was kind to animals,

Odalie noticed, in this he reminded her of Billy Sun. Both men were so very different from Richard, who could not manage his mounts without the whip and the spur. She pictured her husband with his self-satisfied smile and well-tailored suits of Scottish tweed, and she hated him.

After an hour they were underway again. The horses moved with a new energy, and Odalie knew Rob had been right to rest them.

"These people mean a lot to you, don't they?" he said.

"Yes, I suppose they do. More than I realized."

They traveled in silence until at last the Dixon ranch came into view, tranquil in the blue morning light. Odalie sighed with relief, for she had feared they would find a smoking ruin. A light burned in the kitchen of the white, two-story frame house and the rest of the outbuildings — barn and attached corral, a small wooden shed, a windmill, a pump house, and, some distance from the house, a privy tucked away in the sagebrush — appeared undisturbed. To her eyes, the modest Dixon property was more inviting by far than her own stone castle.

Hardy drove the buggy up to the front door and Lorna opened it even before

Odalie could climb down. Though partially concealed in her skirts, Odalie could see a pistol in Lorna's right hand.

"Odalie!" she said, eyes widening in surprise.

"I must see your father at once."

Even as she spoke she heard the barn door slide open. She turned to see Dixon walking toward them, cradling a rifle in his arms. Odalie realized she had never seen him with a gun before.

"Lady Faucett," he said. "I would say I'm surprised to see you, but nothing surprises me anymore." His eyes cut to Hardy. "Who's your friend?"

"Daniel, this is Rob Hardy, the ticket agent and telegrapher at Olympus. He's just brought me from there, we've been traveling all night. You can trust him. We've come to warn you of — oh, I hardly know how to explain it — Richard and the WSGA, including Frank Canton, they've assembled a kind of army, that's the only word for it, and they say they're going to kill all the so-called rustlers in Powder River country. You and Billy are on their list. It's true, I heard them planning it."

When he showed no reaction, she looked pointedly at the gun in his arms. "But maybe I'm telling you something you already know? Has something happened?"

He came forward and took her by the arm. "Odalie, I could use coffee and I'm sure, if you and Mr. Hardy have been traveling all night, you could, too. Mr. Hardy, take your horses to the barn, give them whatever they need, then join us in the house. Keep your eyes and ears open and come for me at once if you see anyone coming."

The kitchen was warm and well-lit, and for the first time Odalie could see how exhausted Dixon was. He was unshaven and his eyes were sunken. Even Lorna's lovely face was pale and drawn with fatigue.

"What is it, Daniel? What's happened?" Odalie said again.

Dixon sank down in a chair and ran a hand through his hair, making it stick out at all angles. Odalie felt a great wave of tenderness for him. She wished she take him in her arms and hold him, give him some peace and comfort. It seemed to her he had had precious little of that. He was a kind man who deserved a better hand than Lady Fortune had dealt him.

"I'm aware of Lord Faucett's expeditionary force," he said, "and his plans for me and my family, but, unfortunately for your husband and his associates, they misjudged

375

the good citizens of Johnson County. The people are mobilizing against them — oh, a few of the businessmen may support him, but the average man, the homesteader, the small ranchers and farmers, are coalescing in a way Richard and the WSGA did not anticipate. They'll be in for a big surprise when they reach Buffalo, if they make it that far."

"I'm very glad to hear it," Odalie said, sitting across the table from him. Perhaps her telegram from Olympus had been received after all.

Dixon continued. "The hell of it is my son Cal. Somehow your husband reeled him in, offered him money, five thousand dollars, if he would kill me."

Odalie gasped. This was unspeakably vile, even for Richard.

Dixon continued. "Cal took his money, but then I guess he couldn't go through with it. He killed Nate Coday, though. Poor Nate, he'd been shot and was weak as a kitten. He couldn't possibly have defended himself." Dixon shook his head and rubbed a hand across his eyes. "Cal, I don't know where he is now and frankly, I don't give a damn. I don't care what happens to him."

Odalie reached across the table to take his hand when Rob Hardy threw open the door and ran into the room, flooding the kitchen with cold air and sunlight.

"Riders are coming!" he said, pointing to the north.

Dixon jumped to the window, pushing aside the curtains. Odalie followed; three wagons and a handful of riders were gathered on a hilltop about a mile distant.

"It's them." Dixon turned back to Odalie and said, "Can you handle a gun, Lady Faucett?"

"I can. Quite well, as a matter of fact."

Dixon smiled for the first time since they arrived. "I suspected as much. I'll take the front room, Lorna, you stay here in the kitchen. Mr. Hardy, if you'll cover the south side, that leaves the upstairs bedroom only. Odalie, will you take that window?"

She nodded.

"When they get in range, I'll give a signal and we'll open up. We'll let them know we're here and we won't go down without a fight."

RICHARD FAUCETT

He sat on his tall black Thoroughbred, smoking his pipe and squinting in the noonday sun. Despite his regal appearance, Faucett was frustrated. For almost thirty-six hours he'd been staring at a harmless-looking white frame house that had turned out to be an impregnable, miniature fortress with a gunman at every door and window. They should have burned it down a day ago; instead, here they sat, paralyzed. Each time they tried to advance on the house, defenders drove them back with well-aimed shots. Two of his men, Texans, had been hit, and one was seriously injured. Faucett was angry, hungry, and cold. Despite the sun, a sharp April wind penetrated his overcoat of fine Irish frieze like whey through cheesecloth. Again, the Englishman was reminded that no amount of money or the fine goods it purchased could guarantee comfort in this harsh land.

"What shall we do, sir?" Jolly said. "How much longer shall we wait?"

"Shut up, man. I'm trying to think."

Tom Horn, seemingly impervious to cold, lay on his back in the sun with his hat covering his face. The hat concealed a smile. Horn did not like Faucett and enjoyed watching the fat Limey twist. This expedition had turned out to be a disaster of the first water, just like he, Horn, had tried to tell Faucett it would be, but the great lord wouldn't listen. The thing had been wrong from the get-go, starting with Faucett's decision to break his army up into separate "raiding parties." It only diminished the force's impact and left the men confused and fragmented. Who knew what was happening and where? Had Canton's group taken Billy Sun and the Lazy L and B boys? No one knew. Also, as Horn had cautioned, the people of Buffalo had not welcomed Faucett's invaders as saviors, neither had they retreated to their homes like scared animals taking to their holes. No, the citizens were massing in the streets and mounting a stout defense. Even the miserly Tom Raylan had thrown open the doors of his mercantile, offering guns, ammunition, blankets, and bacon to any man willing to fight the WSGA invaders.

Not only that, but folks they were counting on, men who'd promised to lend manpower and muscle, had shown the white feather at the last minute and backed out. Could be they'd even thrown in with the rustlers. Horn wouldn't be surprised. Yes, he'd tried to warn him, but Faucett knew better, so let him stew in it for a while. Next time, he'll know Tom Horn was a man worth listening to.

"Uh, Lord Faucett?" Albertus Ringo said.

"What do you want, Ringo?"

"We could build a go-devil. Thataway we could get at 'em without getting shot up ourselves."

"A what?" Faucett said.

"Go-devil. We could cut down them trees, use the lumber and a couple hay bales to build up one of the Studebakers, then shelter behind it when we roll it toward the house. An ark of safety."

Faucett made a sound of disdain. "That's ridiculous."

"Not so fast," Horn said, rising from the ground. "It might work, and it's sure worth a try. We're not getting anywhere like it is."

Faucett looked from the house to the Studebaker, then back to the house. "Oh, hell, go ahead and build your ark-devil or whatever you call it. Just get me close enough to do what I came for. If I can't get Billy Sun, at least I can watch Daniel Dixon die."

From the house, Dixon and the others watched Faucett's men chop, hammer, and wire logs to the gears of a wagon until the sides were six feet high. Platforms fixed to the wagon's sides held hay bales for extra coverage. Within twenty-four hours they had built a sort of moveable breastworks that was big enough to provide cover for all twenty of Faucett's men. At noon, as the men were finishing, Frank Canton and the two Texans rode up on lathered horses. The Texans dismounted and made for the chow tent while Canton went directly to Faucett, drowsing on a camp chair before a warm fire.

"Well?" Faucett rousing as Canton dismounted. "What happened? Did you bring me that damn half-breed?"

Canton upended and drained his canteen. He'd give twenty dollars for four fingers of whiskey. "I had to finish him. He might have got away otherwise. Bill Sun, he was a brave man. In the end, it seemed a shame to kill him."

"Please, spare me your recriminations, Canton. He was a renegade and a thief of the first water. He got what he deserved."

"Cal Dixon is dead, too," Canton said. "Sun took him out."

Faucett shrugged his narrow shoulders. "If he'd done what I paid him to do, we could have avoided this nonsense." He waved his hand toward the white house. "I shouldn't have used him. He was weak, and I knew it."

Canton turned his head to spit. His mouth tasted of bile and dirt and his clothes smelled of smoke. "Yeah, that was a mistake. I don't know many men who could kill their own father. I don't think I'd want to know a man like that."

Ringo approached to say the go-devil was finished. After a brief inspection, Faucett ordered it forward. The men put their shoulders to it, and it began to move, inching slowly over the bumpy ground.

Faucett looked on with a smile. "By God, this just might work. In an hour or so we'll be in range."

"What's your plan?" Canton said.

Faucett walked to a tarpaulin-covered box, away from the fire. He threw back the canvas and pulled out a stick of dynamite.

"Dynamite?" Canton shook his head. "Faucett, you don't want to do that. Hell, there's probably women in that house. That daughter of Dixon's, Lorna, she's probably in there. You'll blow her to bits."

"I don't care about that, Mr. Canton. Anyone in that house is an associate of Dixon's, and therefore my enemy. Yours, too, I should think."

Canton raised his hands, palms out. "I signed on for killing rustlers and thieves, not women." Canton wasn't sure Dixon deserved this, and he'd been thinking of the three men caught in the line shack with Bill Sun — Kinch and the kid, Comstock, and the Mexican — he wasn't convinced they deserved to die, either. Their only crime was to be in the wrong place at the wrong time with the wrong company.

"No, I'm not for it," Canton said. "This ain't right."

"Sheriff, these things are never simple. I should think you knew that." Carefully, Faucett returned the stick of dynamite to the box and mounted his horse. "But cheer up, soon you'll have your money. Perhaps that will soothe your conscience." Faucett turned his horse and kicked him into a trot. Tom Horn joined Canton, and together they watched Faucett ascend the hill to monitor the devil's progress.

"You know, Horn, I'm sorry I got us into

this," Canton said. "There's no honor in it."

"Yeah, things haven't turned out so good," Horn said, "and now I think Lord Richard's in for a nasty little surprise himself. Lady Odalie's in that house. I saw her myself at the upstairs window, and you know what?" He grinned at Canton. "She's a damn fine shot."

DIXON

Dixon sat at the front window, watching the contraption roll toward them. It was coming slowly, but it was coming and there was no way to stop it. A knot of fear tightened in his stomach. He trained his field glasses on the lone horseman on top of the hill. Faucett. Dixon wished he hadn't sold the needle gun a buffalo hunter had given him years ago as payment for setting a broken arm. With that weapon's great power and range, he could easily pick Faucett out of his saddle, even at this distance.

Odalie came down the stairs, still wearing the blue traveling suit she had worn for days, even though it was stained with road dirt and perspiration. As the day warmed, she had unbuttoned the top buttons of her jacket and kept it so, revealing the lace of her chemise.

Dixon heard her enter the room but he could not look at her. He did not want to see the exhaustion on her face, or the emotion he knew he would also find there. Bad things happened to women who loved him. First, his wife, Laura, and their infant daughter. Then Rose. Now, he feared the same fate was about to befall his daughter, Lorna, and this woman, Odalie. He vowed to save them, no matter the cost.

"Daniel," she said, placing her hand on his shoulder. "Let me talk to Richard. He doesn't know I'm here. Let me go out there and talk to him."

"No," he said. "It's out of the question. Those men are killers. They don't care who gets hurt." Days before Dixon had asked Sigge Alquist to deliver a letter to Colonel Smith at Fort McKinney, informing him of the threat to the people of Johnson County and Buffalo asking him to send troops. He had no way of knowing if the message had been received, or how the colonel would respond if it were.

"Daniel," Odalie said. "Look at me."

At last he complied. He had never seen her in a dirty dress, and her hair was half down, but she was beautiful. Again, he noticed the silvery skin below her eyes that so reminded him of Rose. He found it difficult to speak.

"If I appeal to Richard, if I promise to go

with him, I think he'll leave you and Lorna alone. It will give him an out, a chance to save face in front of his men. He doesn't want this, not really. Let me try."

"Odalie, I don't believe that, but suppose you're right," Dixon said. "What happens then? Do you really think you and Faucett can return to The Manor and carry on as before? After everything that's happened?"

Odalie took his hands. "I don't know. I can't think that far ahead. I'm just thinking about right now, about how to stop him!"

Dixon had never admired her more than he did at that moment. She was a brave woman, and far from stupid. She had to know Lord Richard Faucett would have special plans indeed for the woman who had betrayed and made a fool of him. He was not about to let her sacrifice herself for him.

"Odalie," he said, "whatever Richard was when you married him, he's something different now. He's a killer — I even question his sanity. You must have the same fears. For whatever reason, the only thing he wants now is to destroy me. Your presence here won't dissuade him. It'll only make him angrier."

Odalie turned back to the window, pushing aside the curtain. "How many men are behind that thing, do you think?"

"Fifteen or twenty," Dixon said, "and things will start happening soon. There's a root cellar off the kitchen; it's big enough for you and Lorna, and it's not directly below the house. If they intend to burn us out, you'll be safe in there. Come, I'll show you." He moved to take her hand, but Odalie backed away.

"I'm not leaving you," Odalie said.

"Neither am I," Lorna said. She and Hardy stood together in the doorway. "We won't hide in some hole — we'll stay and help you fight them."

"Dixon," Hardy said. "Do you really believe they mean to harm the women? Don't you think —" Before he could finish Odalie darted across the room and flung open the door. Dixon ran after her, but she was already off the porch and running into the yard. "Richard!" she yelled. "Richard, don't do this. Leave these people alone!"

The devil came to a halt as the men waited to see what Faucett would do. After a brief hesitation, he applied the spurs and charged down the hill, flying by the devil and his men. When he reached his wife he jumped to the ground and came to her in two long strides, his riding crop in his hand. His red face was contorted with rage.

"What the hell are you doing here?" he

said. "I thought you were in Denver."

"You must not harm these people — they've done nothing to you. It isn't right!"

In a flash, Faucett lashed out with his crop, striking his wife across the face. She fell to the ground, covering her head with her arm. "Whore!" he screamed. "You filthy cheating whore! I should have left you in that New Orleans hovel where I found you!" He raised his arm, but Dixon was on him before he could hit her again, striking Faucett in his soft, fleshy mouth. The Englishman fell to the ground and grabbed for his sidearm. Too late, he realized he was not wearing his pistols and his rifle was still in its scabbard on the saddle. Dixon ran to the Thoroughbred and pulled the rifle from its sheath, training it on Faucett who remained on the ground.

"Canton!" Faucett screamed as Dixon helped Odalie to her feet. Her face bled profusely from a laceration on her left cheek. "Shoot this man!" Faucett yelled. "For God's sake, what are you waiting for?"

Frank Canton stepped from behind the go-devil, his six-gun in his hand. He came toward them, keeping his eyes on Dixon. "Do it!" Faucett cried, bloody spittle flying from his mouth. "Do it now!" He clambered to his feet.

Canton kept coming forward until he and Dixon were only feet apart. Faucett looked from Canton to Dixon. "Damn you to hell, Canton — if you won't do it, I will!" He ran to his horse and the pistols concealed in his saddlebags. Coolly and without a word, Canton turned from Dixon and fired, hitting Faucett squarely between the shoulder blades. The running man took three more steps, then pitched forward onto his face.

"Anyone else?" Canton said, looking at the startled faces of the men who'd been watching from the cover of the go-devil. "If not, get on your horses and go home. This thing is over. It should never have started."

Slowly, in some cases reluctantly, the would-be invaders melted away, leaving Faucett's body facedown in the dirt. Only Tom Horn and Canton remained. They did not interfere when Dixon lifted Odalie in his arms and carried her into the house.

She sat on the examination table. The wound on her face continued to bleed, saturating the front of her suit jacket. She covered it with her hand.

"Let me see," Dixon said.

"No," Odalie said, turning her head. "Don't look at me."

"I can help," he said softly. "Let me see."

She dropped her hand and Dixon saw the cut was deep, clear to the bone. He would suture it carefully, using the smallest stitches he was capable of, but even so she would be badly scarred.

"My face is ruined," she said. "It's all I have, all I've ever had, and now that's gone, too."

BILLY SUN

The day of the funerals was the warmest of the young spring. Buffalo's cemetery was filled to overflowing with the families of Hi Kinch, Nestor Lopez, and Pat Comstock, but most of the people had come to honor Billy Sun. Cowboys from the Lazy L and B, every member of the Northern Wyoming Farmers' and Stockgrowers' Association, and men who rode with him in roundups came in their Sunday clothes to pay their respects.

Dixon stood between Odalie, her face still bandaged, and Lorna. Though he had not known Billy Sun, Rob Hardy came from Olympus for the service. He was never far from Lorna's side, and when she wept, he offered his handkerchief.

The bodies were in pine boxes beside the empty graves. Brother James White delivered the sermon, reading from a Bible whose pages blew in the warm April wind. After, he spoke in a soaring voice.

"These men gave their lives for you, the people of Buffalo and Johnson County. They sacrificed themselves so that you, the humble and hardworking homesteaders of this great land, could build your houses and raise your children and graze your livestock and cultivate your fields in freedom, without fear of a feudal oppressor. Now the world knows that this land belongs to all of us, not just a wealthy and privileged few. These four men died to hold back the tyrants who would take it from you."

Some in the crowd turned angry eyes on Odalie, who pretended not to notice. Dixon held her hand.

"Had these men not fought as bravely as they did, who knows how many of us might have been massacred before our president dispatched the United States Army to put the invaders in jail, where they remain to this day awaiting justice? How many of you women would be widows, how many of your children fatherless? We will never know the answers to these questions, but we do know this: each and everyone of us owes Hi Kinch, Nestor Lopez, and young Pat Comstock, who had not yet seen his twentieth year, a high debt of gratitude.

"But now I want to talk about Billy Sun,

a man who had one foot in the world of the red Indian and one foot in the white man's world and a solid place in neither. His Indian kinsmen are gone, and the white people never fully accepted him. Oh, yes, you're here today, but before your congratulate yourself, admit you sometimes looked down on him, considered him less than yourself, because of his aboriginal blood. Would you have welcomed Billy Sun as a suitor for your daughter, or a business partner for your son? I think not."

White's voice grew louder.

"Yes, you hired him to break your green horses, but would you have welcomed Billy Sun into your home for Sunday dinner? No! You would not, but he gave his life for you anyway, not asking for reward or recognition or a place at your table. He did this because he was a brave man, an honest man, and a man worthy of your deepest respect."

White nodded and the gravediggers silently lowered the bodies into the ground. White threw a handful of red soil onto each coffin, with the words "dust to dust, ashes to ashes."

"Now, as we stand at these graves I ask each one of you to look into your own heart. Are you honest? Are you kind and respectful to those who love you? Are you brave enough to risk ruin, pain, and, yes, even death, to defend what you believe in, as these men did? Look into your heart and ask yourself, Am I as good a man as Billy Sun?" White bowed his head.

"Let us pray."

After the service, as the mourners melted away, Dixon and Odalie stood alone at his grave. Dixon reached into his coat pocket and pulled out Billy's bear claw necklace and a folded piece of paper, stained with blood. "Sheriff Angus gave these to me because the letter mentions Cal. Billy wrote it in the line shack. I think he'd want you to have it, and the necklace, too."

Odalie read the blockish printed letters, written in pencil. *There was a woman I loved from the first time I saw her and I love her still. She might someday see letter, and if she does, she will know.* Her eyes burned with tears as she refolded the letter and put it, along with the necklace, in her bag. *He was too good for me.* After a few minutes of silence, she cleared her throat. "What's happening with Canton and the others?" she said. "Will they truly face justice?"

Dixon laughed bitterly. "No. The president called out the army mostly to protect them from us, the good people of Johnson

County. I suppose there will be some kind of trial, but it will be only for show. They won't face any real punishment."

"What about Tom Horn? Was he taken with the others?"

"No. No one seems to know where he is, but he'll turn up again. Men like him always do. But what about you, Odalie? Where will you go?"

She shrugged. "I don't know, back to New Orleans maybe. I still have some family there. The Manor I'll leave to the county. Perhaps they can find a good use for it."

They started walking to the wagon, where Lorna and Hardy were waiting. "Those two have grown close," Dixon said. "I'd be happy to welcome Rob to the family if it comes to that, and I wouldn't be surprised."

"He is a fine man."

"There's someone else I'd like to welcome to the family, if she'll have me."

Odalie's heart quickened. "And who would that be?" she said.

Dixon put his hands on her shoulders and turned her to him. "I think you know."

She touched the bandage on her face. "You pity me. I will be ugly and disfigured and you feel responsible for some reason. Well, you needn't. I'll get Richard's money, or some of it. I'll be fine. You don't have to worry."

"I love you, Odalie," he said. "I have for some time. Would you be happy as a physician's wife? We'll never be rich, but we can do good things together. Maybe we can be the kind of people Billy Sun thought we were."

Only then did the tears come. They ran down Odalie's face, wetting the bandage on her cheek and burning the healing wound below it. Dixon tasted their saltiness on her lips when he kissed her.

"What do you think?" he said. "Can we do it?"

She smiled up at him. "We can try."